SHADOWED BY MOONLIGHT

SHADOWED BY MOONLIGHT

KRYSSA STEVENSON

TOFAGALEI
PUBLISHING

Cover Art, Typeface, and Chapter Headings by Tawsh Lav

Logo Design by Folo Tafua

Interior Illustrations by XaTi Draws

ISBN: 979-8-9867860-0-1

First Edition: November 2022

Printed in the United States of America

For my grandparents: Saovale & Tofaga Stevenson and
Tufi & Luse Magalei.
Thank you for being my first and favorite storytellers. I love you.
~Kryssa~

Dedicated to the memory of our son and brother, JeShan "Jay".
May your legacy continue.
~Shawn, Rena, Preston, & Saraven~

"O le i'o i mata o le tama o le teine."
"The apple of a brother's eye is his sister."
~Samoan Proverb~

Character Guide

Light

High Chief Alai

High Chief of the Light Village. Father of Toaolelā and Masina. Husband of the late High Chiefess Ta'ifetū. Believed to be the greatest warrior in the history of the Light Village

High Chiefess Ta'ifetū

The late mother of Toaolelā and Masina, and wife of High Chief Alai. In life, she was an excellent diplomat who increased economic prosperity in all the villages. However, her greatest joy came from being a wife and mother.

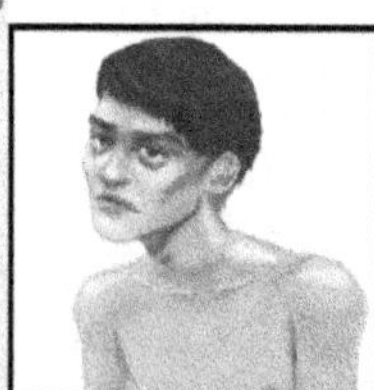

Toaolelā

Age: 15

The eldest child of High Chief Alai and High Chiefess Ta'ifetū. Not much is known about him due to the fact he has no outstanding talents.

Masina

Age: 10

The youngest child of High Chief Alai and High Chiefess Ta'ifetū. Gifted in everything from fighting to lei-making, Masina is the golden child of the Light Village.

Wind

High Chiefess Manaia

High Chiefess of the Wind Village. A very practical woman who takes pride in maintaining law and order. Her intimidation tactics have been proven to work on her enemies as well as misbehaving children.

Tawhiri

Age: 14

The firstborn of High Chiefess Manaia. Unlike his mother, Tāwhiri is openly forgiving and compassionate. More often than not he ends up being the peacemaker for any group he's in.

High Chief Senidra

High Chief of the War Village and father of Alani. Also a close friend of High Chief Alai. Upbeat and optimistic, many have wondered how he can be so happy despite the bloodshed he's seen.

Alani

Age: 13

The eldest child of High Chief Senidra. Like her father, Alani is a formidable warrior. Specializing in close-range combat, Alani relies on her quick-thinking to win against larger opponents.

High Chief Moe

High Chief of the Navigator Village and father of Ori. True to his title, High Chief Moe is a master wayfinder well-versed in non-instrument navigation. He also has a reputation for making incredible seafood.

Ori

Age: 17

The second son of High Chief Moe. While not the firstborn, Ori took on the family title because his older brother was unable to. Under his father's tutelage, Ori has mastered basic navigation.

High Chiefess Mailelauli‘i

High Chiefess of the Earth Village and mother of Puana. In addition to being a gifted lei-maker and botanist, High Chiefess Mailelauli'i uses her knowledge to train aspiring healers from all of the villages.

Puana

Age: 13

The firstborn of High Chiefess Mailelauli'i. Puana is an excellent healer, having studied medicinal plants under her mother. When asked what role she would have if she couldn't be a high chiefess, Puana said she would like to be a surgeon or an orator.

Contents

Chapter 1   1

Reference: Buli, Tuiga, & Lei Poʻo   14

Chapter 2   15

Reference: Plants   29

Chapter 3   30

Chapter 4   46

Reference: Weaponry   55

Chapter 5   56

Chapter 6   72

Chapter 7   76

Chapter 8   80

Chapter 9   88

Chapter 10   98

Chapter 11   105

Interlude   108

Chapter 12   112

Interlude   125

Chapter 13	130
Chapter 14	144
Chapter 15	150
Chapter 16	154
Chapter 17	164
Chapter 18	172
Chapter 19	181
Chapter 20	186
Chapter 21	201
Chapter 22	212
Chapter 23	219
Interlude	231
Reference: The Inati	233
Chapter 24	234
Chapter 25	241
Chapter 26	257
Chapter 27	265
Interlude	272
Chapter 28	284
Chapter 29	290
Chapter 30	306

Chapter 31   314

Chapter 32   322

Reference: The Tuiga   327

Epilogue   328

Acknowledgements   332

Chapter 1

Masina really was the perfect child. She was only in her tenth year, but she had always been the best at everything. Whenever she went diving with the fishermen, Masina speared the most fish. When she joined the hunting parties, Masina came back with the biggest pig on her shoulders.

Tall and athletic, Masina was like our father; she was a natural leader. And while she had the strength and speed of a man twice her size, she was by no means masculine in appearance. With her earthy skin, big brown eyes, and long hair the color of cooled lava, Masina's beauty went unchallenged among the village girls. I might be the firstborn and bear the title of future chief, but if the villagers could have it their way, there's no doubt in my mind they would rather have Masina lead them instead of me.

I wondered if everyone would still love her if they knew how she had become so strong.

I woke up to the smell of flowers and the sound of Masina humming. Yawning, I stretched on my mat, staring up at the thatched roof of my hut. Sunlight peeked through the coconut fronds covering the open walls, telling me I had slept in. Grunting, I rolled to my feet. If I was late to the last protocol meeting, it would not look good.

I tied a sulu around my waist as Masina knocked on my hut.

"Good morning, brother!" she sang. "Are you up?"

"What do you want, Masina?" I growled, running my fingers through my hair.

Masina pulled up the coconut frond curtains in front of her, flooding that part of the hut with sunlight. She wore a light-brown dress that sat under her shoulders and cut off at the knee. Aside from the tapa cloth tied around the middle, the fabric was unadorned. Her hair was in its usual bun and she wore her favorite bone necklace carved to look like boar tusks with a wooden kaulima on each tricep. She carried a tray covered with a burlap cloth.

She smiled. "Hi, Lā!"

"Didn't Father tell you it's rude to barge into a man's hut?" I said. "That sort of thing will get people talking."

Masina's grin widened. "Technically you're not a man yet. And even if you were, you're my brother. That doesn't count."

Masina was five years younger than me, but she was already as tall as I was. Sometimes even I forgot she was my little sister instead of my twin. Seeing her standing there, hair brushed and bracelets highlighting the contour of her arms, I was reminded of just how small I was in comparison.

Where Masina was strong and beautiful, I was thin and homely. I was so skinny I often heard how my face resembled the dead more than the living, or how one gust of wind could blow me off the island. Adding insult to injury my parents had named me Toaolelā, *the sun warrior*. Masina was named for the moon. If people weren't reminding me how scrawny I was, they were commenting on how "the moon outshines the sun" in our family.

But all of that ended today. Masina might be the darling of the Light Village, but she would never be High Chief. That was the one thing she could never take from me.

"Are you ready to start your chief training?" she asked, rocking on her toes.

I ignored her and reached for the water bowl left by the servants. I waited for Masina to leave, but she just sat down with her tray, making me uncomfortable with the way she stared. I started washing my face, annoyed that she couldn't take a hint.

"Don't you have another village to plunder?" I said.

Masina laughed. "I don't do that, silly."

"Then what do you want?"

"I have something for you. I thought about giving it to you after protocol, but I'll be practicing for the ceremony by then, and I want you to have it."

I glanced sideways at her. Masina had never tried to hurt me. Yet. A part of me always worried she might, though. She certainly could if she wanted to. I watched her finger the cloth covering her tray as she bit her lip.

"Is it alright if I show you?" she asked.

I nodded. Masina let out a squeal as she pulled off the cloth, revealing the best kahoa lei I had ever seen. A neck adornment worn only for special occasions, the lei had braided ti leaves with multicolored flowers sewn on top in intricate half-moon patterns.

I held it up by the ends, admiring its beauty. Where did she get this? I knew all the women who sewed lei in the village, and none had ever made one this fine.

Masina beamed. "I made it myself!"

I groaned inwardly. *Of course you did.*

I'd never seen Masina pick up a needle or braid ti leaves before—but since she's Masina of course this is what her first lei would look like. She probably grew the flowers overnight and lured in honeybees for a rush pollination. Everything was easy for Masina.

"I made one for Dad, too, so that you could be matching." Masina added. "I stayed up late to finish them, so they might look rushed, but do you like it?"

She tied the lei behind my neck and let it drape around my shoulders. The fragrance was intoxicating. Masina had picked flowers that were bright reds and yellows. The petals were sewn in a way that looked like the rising sun. She really had thought of me while she was making this.

"It's...really nice." I said. "Thank you."

She grinned. "I love you, Lā!"

I nodded my thanks. Then, remembering how late I was, I took off running for the orator's house.

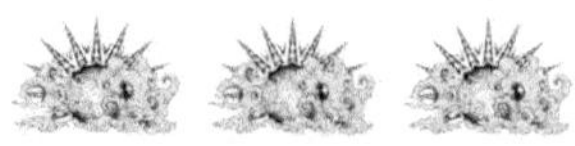

I skidded in front of the line as the village orator stepped out of his hut. Alani of the War Village sniggered behind me.

"There's our little sunspot," she muttered. "About time you showed up."

I clenched my teeth, ignoring her. Orator Ra'i let out a grunt before stepping aside, allowing us to enter. I bowed low, excusing myself as I walked in front of him. The hurried whispers behind me told me the eight other future chiefs were doing the same.

Nine masts held up Orator Ra'i's circular hut, each one carved to represent the nine villages. Sitting cross-legged in the center were the High Chiefs, each one aligned with the mast representing their village.

My father was easiest to spot, the multicolored lei strung across his chest making him stand out from the rest of the council. As I stood in my place over his left shoulder, I noticed Masina had used the same stitching on his lei as she had on mine. His was bigger to match his larger stature, but still. I had to admit she did a great job. Standing behind Father like this, I could almost pass for a future chief.

I waited as everyone else filed in, taking their places around the circle. Alani stood behind her father, the war chief. Next to them was Tāwhiri, who wore a woven cloak that matched his mother's, the high chiefess of the Wind Village. Beside them were High Chief Moe and his son Ori from the Navigator Village.

Once Puana of the Earth Village was in place, Orator Ra'i stepped away from the entrance. Outside I heard four blows of the pū shell, signaling to the rest of our village that this hut was not to be disturbed until the pū sounded again.

As the song of the pū faded, Orator Ra'i beat his staff against the ground. "We begin our meeting by giving thanks to the ancestors," he said, his elderly voice little more than a rasp.

I knelt down and turned with all of the future chiefs. Our parents behind us did the same, each paying their respects to the ancestors.

I looked up at the carved image of the light god Havaiki. He was our ancestor and the patron god of our village. As the next high chief, I was expected to exemplify his leadership ideals and be a shining example to others. According to legend, if I did this right I would find favor with him and be granted a portion of his power.

They say this was true for all of the villages. Those who brought pride and glory to their patron god were rewarded, and their village thrived. This was how the people from the Navigator Village found their way home after crossing uncharted waters, and how the War Village fought off foreign invaders even though they were outnumbered four to one.

Orator Ra'i claimed my father had earned a place in Havaiki's good graces. After imprisoning the demon Mā, he was promised an heir with the strength of a thousand suns.

To this day I wondered if my father felt cheated once he saw the heir the gods had actually given him.

I bowed low to the wooden image and tried not to think about it.

"Praise to the ancestors," I murmured. Then I turned and bowed to my father, acknowledging him as the head of the village and the standing representative of Havaiki.

Orator Ra'i thumped his staff, and I waited for my father to face the middle before pushing myself up. I swung my feet around and sat cross-legged, awaiting Orator Ra'i's instructions. With today being my last day of protocol, it was time for me to complete the exit exam, which was required to begin one-on-one chief training with my father.

"To be a high chief is a sacred responsibility from the gods," Orator Ra'i began. "It is both a privilege and a burden. For the day you children become high chiefs is the day you no longer live for yourselves."

Alani shifted uncomfortably. She wasn't the only one; many of the future chiefs looked the same. It was a scary thing; knowing that someday the entire village would be looking to us to solve their problems. Personally, I didn't fear the responsibility; I worried more that the village wouldn't think I could handle it.

"Today marks the final protocol meeting for one of you," Orator Ra'i said, his cataract eyes focusing on me. The other high chiefs and their children looked, too. I kept my chin up and my gaze forward, pretending not to notice.

Orator Ra'i nodded at my father. "High Chief Alai."

Father stood, I bowed my head as he guided me to the middle. He rested his fingertips against my bony shoulders, careful not to ruffle the flowers on my lei.

"I present to the council my firstborn son." he said, his voice deep like the rolling tides. "Tomorrow, he completes his fifteenth year and will be presented to Havaiki as the next High Chief of the Light Village. He has completed the necessary protocol lessons and is well-versed in our lineage. I find him to be worthy of the position and the timing to be right. Is this agreeable?"

Everyone nodded in unison. "Agreeable."

I exhaled in relief. I had a feeling not everyone truly agreed with the what they had said, but it didn't matter. The important thing was they didn't say no. I still had years before I would officially become the high chief. Surely that was more than enough time to prove myself.

"Young Toa," Orator Ra'i said, "have you anything you'd like to say to the council?"

Father took his seat in the circle. He had a tight-lipped smile, eyes pleading for me not to make a fool of myself. I cleared my throat.

"I give thanks to our ancestor Havaiki and to all the great chiefs who came before me." I started, doing my best to follow the speech Father and I had practiced yesterday, "To be a high chief is an opportunity to serve my people to the fullest. I will labor with you in the fields. I will walk with you through the mountains. And in times of trouble, I will—"

A shriek thundered outside of the hut, cutting me off. The High Chiefs and their heirs sprang to their feet—startled, yet alert. Alani pulled out her bone daggers, Tāwhiri grabbed his quarterstaff.

Alani's father, the High Chief of the War Village, brandished his club as he rushed out of the hut, the rest of the council behind him. Cursing, I rushed to follow them.

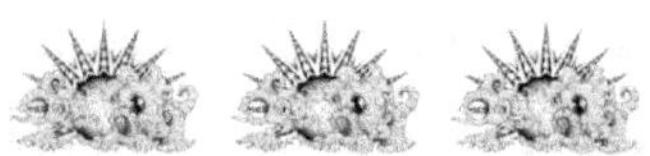

I blinked, not sure if I believed what I was seeing.

Running amok in the village were at least a dozen demons big enough to swallow me whole. They were black as tar, with mottled wings protruding from their arms and an eel-like tail instead of legs. Their heads and torsos were vaguely human, but the similarities stopped there. With bulbous eyes and beaked mouths, their upper halves were a mashup of man, bird, and squid.

Everywhere villagers ran, screaming in panic. Some looked stunned, turning to the high chiefs for direction.

The high chiefs looked equally baffled, but they wasted no time. All nine of them fell into action. Alani's father jumped into the fray, smashing demons with his spiked club. Alani darted in circles behind him, sinking her daggers into one demon's back, then pulling them out to slash at another's wings.

Father had the villagers form a barrier for the children and the elders fleeing the area. He took a spear from a nearby hut and joined the battle, stabbing at the demons that snaked his way.

I should be helping. I needed to be helping. What kind of chief would I be if I froze up when there was trouble?

Fight, you coward, I screamed at myself. *FIGHT!*

Ori of the Navigator Village batted one of the smaller demons up with his oar. Alani slashed it down with her knives. Tāwhiri and his mother stood back to back, quarterstaffs whirling in the air as they struck down oncoming demons. Splotches of black feathers rained down and eel tails flopped to the ground. The battle was almost over, and I hadn't moved a muscle.

Coward.

Suddenly, there was another shriek, this one louder and much, much closer. The sound of it shook the trees and made my teeth rattle. High Chiefs and villagers alike closed together, exchanging looks of uncertainty.

"Form a line!" Father yelled. "Form a line! No matter what comes, we must protect the villagers!"

The high chiefs and their successors obeyed, regrouping for another attack. They looked to the skies, searching for the new threat.

Seconds later, another demon erupted into view—this one bigger and more terrifying than all the others combined. Its winged arms were muscled, and instead of a beak it flashed a mouth full of rowed teeth. Spit flew from its fanged mouth as it snaked through the air, taloned hands aimed at me.

Panic gripped my heart as I watched my impending doom come closer and closer.

I should run.

I should hide.

I should do something, *anything*. If I couldn't save myself now, how could I hope to be chief someday?

"Move, son!" roared my father. He barreled into me, and I went flying. I watched in a daze as my father braced himself, his spear ready. The demon stretched its mottled hands, mouth open in a garbled shriek.

But before the creature or my father could attack, a blur zipped out of a coconut tree and struck the demon on the side of the head. The demon shrieked, halting midair. The brown blur wound around its body, and the demon started to writhe. It flopped down, then jerked up. It clawed at its head as it flew higher and higher, arcing in a backward loop before spiraling out of sight. The earth shook beneath me when it crashed. Then it was silent.

I felt my body relax as I regained control of my arms and legs. Fear now replaced by curiosity, I ran to see where the monster had crashed.

As I got closer, I saw familiar faces in the crowd. Alani winked as she cleaned her knives off on the grass. Tāwhiri acknowledged me with a nod as he rested his quarterstaff against his shoulder.

Up ahead, I saw the creature on its back, writhing against a war club clamped to its throat. Two arms wrapped around the ends of it, and I realized someone was down there, underneath the demon. Whoever it was, they were using the club to choke it out. I listened to their high-pitched grunts of effort as the demon tried and failed to pry the club off its neck.

I stood next to Father, his eyes wide in amazement. I was, too. This was the biggest of all the demons, and one of the high chiefs was grappling with it on the ground. I couldn't see their face, but anyone who had that kind of courage had my respect.

With a final grunt from the fighter, the demon's body went limp. Its winged arms fell to the sides, and its snakelike body became still.

Father and the other high chiefs rushed forward to help the victor. I looked around, trying to identify which high chief was missing. Which of them had been so daring as to conquer this monster alone?

"Stand back, please." called a voice, a voice that made me stop mid-step.

No, I thought. *No way.*

The hands gripping the war club clenched tighter. There was another grunt as the demon was flipped onto its stomach. Clinging to the back of its neck was the last person I wanted to see. Her low bun had come out in the fight the front of her dress was filthy.

She gritted her teeth as she pried her war club from under the demon's neck. She rested it against her legs as she tilted her head back, eyes closed as she tried to catch her breath.

"Masina!" my father cried, running towards her.

Masina stirred, opening her eyes to look at him.

"Hi, Dad," she said as Father scooped her up. Big as she was, Masina still looked like a small child when our father held her. She didn't object as he lifted her off the ground, one hand cradled against the back of her head as he squeezed her.

"Are you alright?" he asked.

She nodded, beaming up at him. "Nobody got hurt." Then, her eyes growing wide she pushed away from him, looking around frantically. "Where's Lā? Is he okay?"

Father pointed me out and she broke into another smile, her shoulders relaxing.

"Hi Lā!" she called. "How was your last day of protocol? Oh no, it looks like your lei got messed up in the battle. Don't worry; I'll make a new one for you."

The village erupted into cheers. Ori and Tāwhiri lifted Masina onto their shoulders, ignoring her protests as they paraded her through the crowd. Realizing they wouldn't put her down any time soon, Masina waved shyly to her admirers. She looked back as the procession took her further away from me.

"I'll see you at home, Lā!" she called. "I'll try find some new flowers for you, too. I love you!"

I waved, plastering a smile on my face. On the inside, however, I was fuming. Why did Masina always feel the need to outshine me in the most humiliating ways possible?

"She'll do great things, that one." said Alani's father behind me.

"She has the grace of her mother and the strength of her father," said Tāwhiri's mother. "Combined with her inherent goodness, she would excel in a leadership position."

"It's a pity the gods couldn't send her first."

They strode past me as they spoke, not once looking in my direction. I wanted to cry out, but what good would that do? After all, they were right. Masina was the better child. She shone brighter than the sun and I stood invisible in her shadow. I listened as the villagers sang praises to Masina, daughter of High Chief Alai and the hero of the Light Village. She was perfection personified—everything I needed to be and everything I wasn't.

And I hated her.

Buli

A white or golden cowrie shell worn as a choker around the neck. The buli is used by both men and women.

Tuiga

A ceremonial headdress worn only by chiefs, the tuiga is a symbol of status meant to humble leaders due to the fact that it's made from things that belonged to the ancestors.

Lei Po'o

A short lei worn around the head, lei po'o could be made with all greens, all flowers, or a mixture of both.

Chapter 2

After Masina's parade had ended, the high chiefs paired up with our doctors and architects to see where they could provide the most assistance. We were fortunate that no one had died in the attack, but the village was in shambles and many were injured.

Puana and her mother administered medicinal herbs, Ori and his father repaired the meetinghouse. Alani's father led a search party to see where the demons had come from and whether any more were on their way. Those not helping with repairs took charge of the feast that would be held tonight in Masina's honor.

Of the fifteen demons that attacked the village, Masina had only beaten one. And she didn't even kill it. But apparently, I was the only one who noticed that.

Unsure of where else to put me, my father asked Alani and I to walk through the village, helping others when needed. He would join the search parties, and said he needed me more in the village.

He didn't say it out loud, but I knew he really meant I would get in the way if I tried to help him.

Alani smiled politely and bowed to my father. The moment he was gone, however, she threw a kick to my shin.

"Ouch!" I yelped, the blow nearly knocking me over. What was really pathetic was I could tell Alani hadn't meant for that to hurt.

She cocked an eyebrow and folded her arms. "Why do I always get stuck with you?"

"Believe me, I'm not crazy about it, either."

My leg smarted, and I knew it would bruise later. Still, I forced myself to stand up straight, shooting her a dirty look.

Alani was two years younger than me. She didn't have Masina's size or strength, but that didn't make her any less deadly. Her body slender and lithe, Alani moved with a deftness that reminded me of a spider. Bone knives were her weapon of choice, but she was skilled with a patu, throwing clubs, and other close-range weapons. She held her buli in her hands and cocked her eyebrow again as she tied it around her neck.

"Well?" she said. "Lead the way, sunspot."

I gave her another withering look, but said nothing. That was the annoying thing about Alani. She wasn't as strong or as fast as Masina, but she knew she could beat me in hand-to-hand combat. And unlike Masina, Alani didn't let me forget it.

We went first to the healer's hut. Puana's mother, High Chiefess Mailelauli'i, was massaging Orator Ra'i's knee. The orator insisted he was fine, yet grimaced every time the high chiefess pressed into his kneecap.

Puana knelt behind Uncle Logo, the master carver in our village. He was on his stomach, teeth bared as Puana squeezed saina juice into the wounds on his back. Her fingers were green from the fistful of leaves she held, and she rubbed Uncle Logo's shoulder with her free hand.

"Sorry, uncle. I know, it hurts," she said, dabbing with a clean cloth. "But this will keep it from getting infected."

Uncle Logo gave a throaty laugh. "Of course. My muscles can't get infected if your devil juice burns them all away, eh?"

Puana smiled as she squeezed the pulp harder, dripping more juice into Uncle Logo's open wounds, making him scream.

"Uncle if I did that, who would build my wedding canoe when I come of age?" she teased.

Puana looked just like her mother. She had the same round face, button nose, and eyes like two round pearls. Her flowing hair was held back by a lei po'o of plumeria flowers. She smiled when she saw us.

Alani greeted her with a kiss on the cheek as she knelt beside her. I bowed to Uncle Logo and sat across from them.

"How are they?" Alani asked, looking out at the men and women being attended to.

"Surprisingly, not as bad as I thought they would be." Puana replied. "A few shallow wounds, some sprains and bruises. The only one we're worried about is Koa over there."

She pointed with her chin. Koa, the son of the high chief in the Fire Village, was on his back in the far corner of the hut. Three of the healers huddled around him. His eyes were closed, but his body twitched as though he were having a nightmare. Sweat peppered his brow and his breathing came in labored gasps.

Alani looked disturbed. "What's wrong with him?"

Puana grimaced. "It looks like one of those things bit him."

I shuddered. Demon bites were lethal. If left untreated, the victim would die overnight. And the scariest part about them was the bite marks never appeared until the victim was already dead. It wasn't as common now, but I had heard many tales of men and women dying because the healers wasted the night treating a fever and chills. Never realizing the danger until it was too late.

Only one plant on the island could cure demon bites—a blood-red leaf that grew in the shape of a heart up in the mountains. When heated and applied to the wound, the teeth marks became visible, and symptoms disappeared within minutes.

"He'll need the red-heart leaf," I said, jumping to my feet. "I'll head inland. I think there's a bush by—"

"Toa, it's okay." Puana interrupted. She motioned for me to sit down. "Masina grabbed some for us. Look, they're heating them up now."

She pointed. Outside of the healer's hut, two of her mother's handmaidens warmed the maroon red-heart leaves over a fire. Weighed down by a stone next to them were several more bushels just like it.

"Oh," I said, my face hot. I felt every eye in the healer's hut staring at me, and cleared my throat. "That's—that's good. I'm...glad."

Puana nodded. "We're lucky Masina came here first. Even if you went now, there's no telling how sick Koa would be by the time you came back."

My jaw stiffened. "Yes. Lucky Masina."

Puana started binding Uncle Logo's wounds, not noticing the impact her words had on me. Alani, however, did. She tilted her head, brow furrowed. She looked like she wanted to say something. Whatever it was, I didn't want to hear it.

"Stay with Puana," I said. "I'll check on the rest of the village."

I waited for Alani to make a face or give a snarky remark. Instead, she bowed to me as she stood.

"As you wish, future chief Toa," she muttered.

For some reason, that irritated me more than when she called me a walking stick or a dying sunspot. I wouldn't be surprised if that was one of her war tactics; using false humility to psyche out an opponent. As she left to wash her hands, I stalked out in the opposite direction.

Tāwhiri didn't need any help.

He worked with the plantation farmers, clearing away the demon carcasses and restoring the landscape as much as possible. His mother, High Chiefess Manaia, supervised them.

"We really could've used you a few minutes ago," Tāwhiri said. "You know how hard it is to move a bird, man-eel thing? A lot harder than it looks."

"What did you do with the bodies?" I asked, cursing my luck at being too late again.

Tāwhiri pointed up the mountain. "My mum sent a team inland to make a pyre. We wanted to dump them in the ocean, but Mum reminded us that whatever the fish ate would come back to us."

I wrinkled my nose, grateful for the high chiefess and her wisdom. Still, a part of me couldn't believe they'd gotten rid of the demons so quickly. There had been so many, and not much time had passed.

"Are you sure you got rid of all of them?" I tried again. "What about the spot where—where that big demon landed?"

Tāwhiri looked confused. "You mean that one your sister choked out? It's already gone. She said she felt bad about the mess and took care of it herself. You should've seen her—dragging that beast up the mountain. Even came back to take another one."

"That's...convenient."

"I know, right?" Tāwhiri laughed. "That's some sister you've got, Toa. I wish mine were more like her."

He clapped me on the back. Then, seeing that I wasn't laughing, his smile faded.

"Toa? You okay?"

I shook my head, biting back rage as I forced a smile. "It's nothing. Thank you, I'm glad everything worked out."

"Yeah...."

Tāwhiri still looked troubled. But like Alani, he decided that whatever he wanted to say wasn't worth the effort. He nodded, then went back to work.

Everywhere I went it was the same. Masina patched up the broken roof. Masina straightened the support masts. Masina scaled up the meeting house with a roll of twine and fixed the lashings none of the men could reach with their big hands. I knew Masina was fast, and strong, and perfect, but at times like this it seriously felt like she was rubbing it in.

Look what I can do, brother, she seemed to be taunting. *Try and beat that.*

"I don't know what you're so mad about," Ori said, shaking me from my reverie as he swung down from the rafters in the meetinghouse. He landed light on his feet. I hated how a group of girls giggled as they passed by, all of them staring as Ori stood up.

Ori was two years older than me. Before he came of age, protocol meetings had been held in the Navigator Village. Now that he had officially begun his chiefly training, he only came to protocol on special occasions to represent his village. I tried not to stand next to him because, like Masina, he exaggerated my flaws without even trying. With his cool demeanor and the toned physique of an experienced wayfinder, Ori made all the women swoon. Chiseled features, piercing eyes, and hair the same dull yellow as a ginger root—apparently, that made him the complete package.

I scowled. "I never said I was mad."

Ori shrugged as he picked up a roll of twine. "Maybe not with your mouth, but your eyes? Different story there."

I wrinkled my nose and looked away. Ori always talked like that—like he was a seer, or a future orator rather than a future chief. It was as if looks wasn't enough for him; he had to prove he had a brain, too.

"I'm not sure what story you're listening to," I said. "But whatever it is, I'm not the one telling it."

Ori raised an eyebrow, the twine working in his fingers. I knew if I stayed he would launch one of his philosophical debates, and I was not in the mood for that. I turned to go.

"She really cares about you, you know."

I looked back at him. Ori was leaning against one of the masts holding up the meetinghouse. He wound the twine absentmindedly, his gaze unfocused.

I frowned. "What?"

"Your sister," Ori said. He started looping the twine into slipknots and pulling them loose. "She looks up to you a lot."

Anger flared inside of me. That was easy for Ori to say; Masina wasn't his sister. Ori wasn't walking around the village with the constant, unspoken knowledge that everyone wished he could've been born just a minute after Masina.

"You don't know her like I do," I said.

I thought about my day in the village, about how everything I was supposed to do, Masina had already done. No matter what I did, she was always one step ahead of me. Nobody needed me in the healer's hut, nobody needed me to clean up the demons. Nobody...nobody needed me.

Ori shook his head, his face impassive. "You're too hard on her. She's your little sister. She needs you. You shame yourself with your jealousy."

He left to join his father, who had taken the rest of his party to drop nets for tonight. The high chief of the Navigator Village was known for making the best seafood, and it looked like he was prepared to live up to his reputation. I imagined High Chief Moe leading his group back from the sea, nets sagging with fish ready to be wrapped and cooked.

I stalked back through the village and up the hills behind our family's encampment, Ori's words ringing in my ears. He must've had too much kava at the last ceremony. Masina didn't need me. The feeling was mutual; I didn't need her, either. Life would be much simpler if she were some other high chief's daughter and left things the way they had been before she was born.

Thick plumes of smoke rose from the cooking huts as the village prepared for the feast. Every month we dined with the high chiefs and their heirs after protocol, but this was the first time we would eat with the entire village. Everyone was thrilled by the honor. Teenagers skinned the fa'i and husked the coconuts. Fathers stoked the rocks in the 'umu and mothers sent their little ones out to pick kalo leaves from the plantations. All the while voices chattered excitedly about the feast.

I passed them all, for once not bothered that nobody noticed me. As the high chief's son, people should clear the way for me, bowing in respect like they did for my father and Masina.

But me? Nobody looked twice as I walked through our encampment and up the trail towards my mother.

Every high chief and chiefess was entitled to be buried in the way that best suited them. The high chiefs of the Navigator Village were buried at sea. In the Earth Village, the high chiefs were buried in the ground with stones piled on top to mark their graves.

My mother, High Chiefess Ta'ifetū, loved flowers. She was the most gifted lei-maker in the Light Village, her skill rivaling that of High Chiefess Mailelauli'i. At the time of her death, my father decided she would be buried in a garden. He cleared away the bush himself and planted every flower she loved to soothe her spirit into the afterlife. As a young boy all I could do was help him with the ti leaf saplings, but now I tended to the garden myself.

Ten years of careful tending had helped Mother's garden to blossom. My eyes were greeted with an explosion of color and my nose tickled by the comforting aromas that reminded me of her. The elders say that our ancestors are sometimes reborn into plant or animal form. I hadn't seen or heard from my mother since she passed, but I liked to think a part of her lived on in her garden.

The pink, white, and yellow plumerias were thriving. So were the rows of teuila and bird of paradise flowers lining the grove. The four hala trees planted in the corners stood like sentinels, their spiny leaves poking out like spears in the tropical blossoms.

The orchid bushes were in full bloom, their petals a deep shade of purple. Next to them were the pua kenikeni trees. The golden, trumpet-like flowers rose from their leaves like birds announcing the sunrise.

The ti leaf trees surrounding Mother's grave had grown into solid walls of greenery. Grass covered the dirt where she laid, and a small opening was at the foot of her grave. That had been unconventional, but Orator Ra'i allowed it, as it gave us a way to talk to her.

As I completed my routine checkup of the garden, I could almost imagine her walking beside me.

"See those plumerias, little Lā?" she would've said. *"They'll make a beautiful lei po'o for Alani's birthday. Won't you pick some for me? And the maile shrubs are starting to grow wild. We should trim them back and use the leaves for Lupe's wedding. I think he'd like that."*

My mother was like that, always giving. Her philosophy was that material things were meant to be given away. To honor that we donated all her flowers to anyone that needed them. Sometimes we had to turn people away when a certain flower wasn't in season or if we were on the edge of overpicking—but as much as possible we made sure that nothing went to waste.

A grin tugged at my lips as I remembered how stubborn she had been. People blushed at the way the high chiefess refused to live a life of luxury. Fine clothes, expensive jewelry, enough food to feed our family ten times over, she became flustered whenever anyone encouraged her to get or use more of it.

"And what would I do with all those things?" she'd tell them. "You lot plan to smother me with riches? Don't you dare try to bury me with any of it; I'll not have the ancestors think I spent my days hoarding goods instead of being useful."

I ripped off the dead leaves dangling from the ti leaf trees, my heart aching. Ten years, ten long years my mother had been gone and I still pined for her. Father said my sorrow was honorable, that it paid tribute to the great woman our mother had been. But as I tossed the dead leaves into the compost heap, I thought about how I didn't want to pay tribute to my mother. I wanted her back.

Mother had a way of bringing out the best in me. I didn't have to prove myself to her, and she never looked at me like I was a sad, watered-down version of Masina. When she kissed my forehead or pulled me into her arms, she made me believe I could become the sun warrior she named me to be.

All of that changed when Masina was born. Halfway through her pregnancy, my mother became ill. And when it was time to deliver Masina, birthing complications arose. Combined with a body weakened from months of illness, it was too much. High Chiefess Ta'ifetū joined the ancestors moments after Masina was born.

I stabbed the dry ti leaves with my shovel, chopping them in half. It shouldn't matter. It shouldn't matter that my mother was gone; she'd been gone for years. No power on earth or in all the heavens could change that. And if she were here, she would want me to do the right thing. She would want me to look after Masina.

Still, as I ground up the dead leaves, I couldn't help thinking how much easier it would be to mourn a sister I never knew than to grieve for the person I loved most. And if Masina hadn't been born....

I pressed my forehead against the tip of my shovel. *I shouldn't be thinking this*, I scolded myself.

Ashamed of my thoughts, I knelt at the foot of Mother's grave and rested my fingertips in front of the ti leaf trees.

"I miss you," I murmured.

I looked up to the head of her grave. Tied to the thick ti leaf stems was a kahoa lei. Instead of bright reds and yellows, this one had orchids, tuberose, and pikake blossoms. Annoyed as I was, I couldn't help but smile. Masina had been here.

Taking one last look to make sure nothing was out of place, I stood up to leave, grateful that I could at least help somewhere in the village today. I walked backwards, my eyes not leaving the sight of mother's final resting place. As the ti leaf trees marking the entrance entered my peripherals, I turned to go.

"Isn't that sweet?" said a voice.

I spun on my heel, alarmed to know someone had been watching me. I choked on a scream and stumbled back.

The woman's mouth split into a wild smile. "Hello, little warrior." she said, "It's been a while."

A thousand thoughts raced through my mind, none of them coming out as concrete words. Standing behind the entrance to Mother's garden was a woman who had to be at least ten years older than me. Light brown hair fell down her back and the frayed gown she wore barely kept her decent. Her skin was sallow and she tilted her chin up as she looked down at me, as though I were somehow unworthy of her attention.

"You're smaller than I thought you'd be," she said, amused at my discomfort. "Did I frighten you?"

"No." I blurted, my voice cracking.

She covered a laugh, and I felt my cheeks grow hot.

"What are you doing here?" I demanded. "This place is for the high chief of the Light Village and his family. No one else is allowed."

Her lower lip stuck out in a pout. Reaching an arm past the ti leaves between us, she ran her fingers down the left side of my face. Her touch both chilled and excited me.

"Must it be forbidden, little warrior?" she sulked, tracing my right cheek with her hand. "Think of how much greater you could be if you simply let me in."

She locked eyes with me, there was something hypnotic in the way she stared. My skin prickled as she continued to stroke my face.

"It could be you that everyone celebrated in the Light Village." she said. "You could be the Toaoleā your mother wanted you to be."

Hearing my name shocked me back to reality. I slapped her arm away and stepped back, suddenly on guard.

"How do you know my name?" I asked.

She laughed, as though that was the silliest question in the world. "Of course I know your name, Toaoleā. I know a lot of things about you. I was there the day you were born. I've always been close by, just waiting for the right day."

Something about her tone rattled me, and I felt my stomach turn.

"I need to go," I said, rushing past her. She grabbed my wrist but I shook her off. "Do not contact me again," I said. "I'm warning you."

She giggled. "'I'm warning you,'" she mimicked, her mockery making my insides boil. I whirled around. She held her hands up.

"Very well, little sun warrior," she said. "I won't come to you. I'll wait for you to come to me."

Now I laughed. "That will never happen."

She winked. "You'll see."

I shook my head and stalked away, reminding myself to tell my father and the other high chiefs about her. I didn't want her coming near me or anyone else.

"I'll be waiting." she called. "Do give my regards to your sister for me."

The poisoned sweetness in her voice snapped something inside me, and I felt my insides swell with a rage I didn't understand.

"You are no match for Masina," I spat.

I don't remember turning around, but before I knew it, I was facing the garden entrance again, my fist pulled back to strike.

But it was too late. The trees were quiet, and once again I was alone.

Pua Kenikeni

Found on trees or bushes that can grow up to 40 feet tall, the puakenikeni is well-known for its bright colors and intoxicating smell.

Ti Leaf

Across the islands ti leaves are used for healing and warding off evil. It's not uncommon to find ti leaf leis garnishing an entryway to the home or planted outside of sacred spaces.

Pikake

With its tender blossoms no bigger than a human fingernail, the pikake is known for its gentle scent and pale white flowers.

Teuila

A fiery ginger plant ranging from 3-9 feet in height, teuila flowers symbolize love, passion, and pride.

Hala

The leaves of the hala tree (often called 'lauhala') are ideal for weaving. Lei can also be made from hala flowers, but should be gifted with caution as they also symbolize death.

Chapter 3

That night the Light Village held the feast of a lifetime. The elders and the high chiefs sat in a long oval at the center of the meetinghouse, the food displayed before them down the middle. Three fat pigs lined the center, with mountains of food on either side.

Everything that made my mouth water was laid out on banana leaves and lauhala mats to protect it from the ground. Pork lau lau, roti curry, palusami and fresh lu sipi, all of it was there. So was the fish High Chief Moe had prepared after a successful huki in the bay. There were piles of fruit, fresh kalo, and lots of ulu and fa'i to balance the richness of the main course dishes.

I sat at my father's right side. Masina clung to his left arm. She stared up at the crowd's appraising looks. We gave thanks to the ancestors, the musicians started playing, and the feast began. Laughter filled the air as everyone helped themselves to as much food as they could cram into their bellies. Father went for the pork and lu sipi, Masina unwrapped her lau lau. I savored the taste of warm fe'e, loving the creamy sensation that ran down my throat. Even as the High Chief's son I almost never ate like this. Given the way we were feasting, one might've thought the light god himself was attending.

Several hours later conversations lulled as people started to slow down. The feast wasn't over; we simply needed to rest before attacking the food again with renewed gusto. This in-between time was usually when we heard from the orators or listened to speeches prepared by visitors.

Orator Ra'i raised a hand. All conversation quieted as everyone turned to him.

He raised his cup, "Today we celebrate a great victory in the Light Village. Glory to the gods and to our ancestors that we did not fall prey to the demons."

He paused as the villagers called out words of approval. When it was silent again, he continued, lifting his cup to the high chiefs. The high chiefs, in turn, raised their cups to him.

"We are indebted to you, most noble leaders of our sister villages. We honor you today for your courage and your sacrifice. Were it not for your intervention, our village would have suffered much greater losses."

The villagers echoed their approval again; the nine high chiefs drained their cups with Orator Ra'i. Setting their empty coconut shells aside, Orator Ra'i gave the time to the high chiefs. They weren't obligated to speak, but out of respect, they were always given the opportunity.

High Chief Senidra nodded to Alani. She cleared her throat. "On behalf of the War Village, we wish to express our gratitude to High Chief Alai and to the Light Village for your hospitality. We also would like to commend your brave warrior, Masina, whom we honor here tonight."

She winked at Masina, who grinned shyly.

"We would like to add our praise on behalf of the Wind Village." said Tāwhiri, holding up a closed fist, "The high chief's daughter fought valiantly, demonstrating a strength and will that belie her age. My mother also wishes to add how impressed she was by Masina's work ethic in the aftermath."

The well-wishing continued around the circle. Every village heir expressing their gratitude to the Light Village, and then describing what they admired about Masina. Ori thought she was selfless, Puana praised her intelligence. On and on it went.

When the speech-making was at an end, Orator Ra'i gave the time to Masina. She looked at our father. He nodded, and she sat up on her knees, bowing low before sitting up tall. Her hands rested in her lap, and when she spoke her voice rang out over the masses.

"I give thanks to the gods and to our ancestors for blessing us with this day," she said, her tone regal. Gone was her timidity and her childish antics. Masina looked back at Orator Ra'i, who motioned for her to keep going.

She cleared her throat. "I am both humbled and honored to receive the accolades of the high chiefs. I will do my best to always serve in a way that is worthy of your approval."

She bowed to the chiefs, who acknowledged her with a nod. Pride brimmed in their eyes, as though they wished Masina could be their daughter. As she sat up, Orator Ra'i addressed her.

"Young Masina." he said, his gaze reflecting the pride mirrored by the high chiefs. "Tonight's feast is held in your honor, but if you so desire you may dedicate it to another."

Masina bobbed a nod, her royal air slipping. "Ooh, I do! I mean, I would like to. If—if that's all right."

A few of the elders smiled at her eagerness. My father gave a throaty laugh. Masina took a deep breath, composing herself.

"I want to dedicate this feast to our ancestral god Havaiki, and to my parents who gave me life. I am who I am because of my father, and while I never knew my mother, I like to think I could be like her, too."

My heart skipped a beat at the mention of our mother. Masina never spoke of her. I glanced around, noting how the women dabbed at their eyes at the mention of their beloved high chiefess.

"And lastly, I want to dedicate this to the other person who has always been there for me." Masina said. "The one who is my quiet strength, and makes me want to be better every day, my brother."

Several people gasped. I nearly dropped the cup in my hands. Had Masina just dedicated her victory feast to me? I stared past our father at her, not sure what she was playing at.

She smiled, lifting her cup to me. "To the next high chief of the Light Village!"

Silence.

If I thought I was shocked by her words, it was nothing compared to the rest of the village. Nobody moved. For a painfully long time all I could hear was the sound of my heart thumping in my ears.

High Chief Loa of the Song Village was the one to break it. He chuckled as he rested his hands on his folded knees, a playful smile on his face. Then he dipped his cup into the wooden bowl in front of him and raised it in amusement.

"To the next high chief of the Light Village." he echoed, grinning at Masina.

Not wanting to shame the high chief, the rest of the village joined the toast. But from the cutting glares that came my way, I knew what they really thought. My face grew hot. Once again, Masina had humiliated me in public.

Whispers rippled through the crowd. I caught a few murmurs of, "Such a merciful sister," and "She gives him more credit than he deserves."

"I should hope no one in our village would speak so poorly of my son." Father rumbled, his eyes roving over the families seated in the outer circles.

There were hurried looks of shame, and all chatter about me ceased immediately.

When the feast ended, the council retired to my father's hut. According to Alani they were about to have another meeting. That was strange, since they had already met before the feast, but not unexpected. This was the first time demons had openly attacked a village in generations; surely that worried the chiefs as much as it did the villagers.

I wanted to join them—so did the rest of the heirs. But our parents reminded us we had clean-up duty. It was one of the many responsibilities we had to prepare us for our calling as future chiefs.

As I helped Ori pile up the meat scraps, I watched Penina, a village girl in her fifth year, shimmy her way up a nearby tree. Her curly brown hair cascaded down her back and she held a stick in her teeth. When she was four feet off the ground, she hugged the tree with one hand and waved her stick in the air.

"Look, Tulo!" she called to her brother. "I'm Masina!"

Tulo laughed. "Oh, no! Does that make me the demon?"

"Yup. And I'm coming to get you!"

She leapt off the tree. Tulo caught her in his arms, spinning her in a circle before lying down so Penina could pretend-stab him with her stick.

"Die! Die! Die!"

Tulo feigned expressions of pain as he tried to ward her off. Then when Penina aimed both hands to his heart, he flopped to the side and let his tongue loll out.

Penina threw her hands up. "Victory for the Light Village!"

"Oh my goodness, look at these children over here doing nothing!" their mother scolded.

Tulo sprang back to life and Penina tossed away her stick. They scooped up the empty dishes and sprinted away. Their mother was right behind them, a broom in her hands.

Alani laughed. "Remember when that used to be us?"

"Used to be?" Puana asked. "I feel like your mom still scolds us like that every time we go to the War Village."

Tāwhiri nodded. "It's true. Never mind your rank or how many wars you've fought in. When Aunty Levani's mad, there is no hope for you."

He filled up his basket with the fruit rinds and ulu skins that would go to the compost heap. Koa, who had been doing the same, set down his basket next to Tāwhiri's. Alani started sweeping out the meetinghouse as Puana cleared the lauhala mats.

"Eh, and how's about you?" Tāwhiri teased, flicking his wrist at Koa. "When we need help burning dead demons you're too sick. But when it's time to eat you're all better."

Koa made a face. "Pssh! And how good would you stay standing if you got bit by one of those? I swear I saw my ancestors today."

"Oh yeah? Did they tell you to get off your lazy bum and help Tāwhiri?"

"No, but my dad did when I woke up."

All jokes aside, everyone was relieved Koa was okay. The red-heart leaf had worked wonders for him. Just minutes after applying the leaves, bite marks appeared on his left arm. Not long after that he was walking again. Puana's mother wrapped the wound in the leaves and covered it with a thin cloth. Koa would have to change his leaves three times a day and drink the juice of the red-heart leaves morning and night until the symptoms went away. He still looked pale, but he would live.

Tāwhiri switched jobs with me, giving me his small basket so that he could help Ori carry the heavy bones and inedible meat scraps. I held up a torch as I went with Koa to the plantations. We emptied our baskets on the compost and quickly made our way back, not bothering to turn the pile. With demons on the loose, neither one of us wanted to be out of the village at night.

As we walked I thought about the demon attack. It really didn't make sense. Demons loved to torture humans; that was nothing new. But that always happened in the dead of night, usually to unlucky individuals who slept too close to an open door or wandered into forbidden lands. To go after an entire village in broad daylight was unheard of; it was like declaring war against the gods themselves. Those demons must've either had a very clever plan, or they were incredibly stupid.

When Alani finished sweeping and everything was back in its place, I walked the future chiefs up to our family encampment. Since protocol had been cancelled, we would have to re-do my exit exam tomorrow. Because of that the high chiefs and their heirs would spend the night with us. Extra sleeping mats were laid out in my hut for all the boys. The same thing had been done in Masina's hut for the girls. She was sitting on the ground in front of the encampment, and sprang to her feet when she saw us coming.

"Hi, Lā!" she said, running up to me.

"Hi." I muttered, cringing as she threw her arms around me. I shrugged her off to Ori. "Is Father still in his meeting?"

Ori shot me a disapproving look. But Masina looked content as he knelt down to hug her.

"Dad hasn't come out yet." she said, her smile growing wider as Puana took off her lei po'o and put it on her head. She then went to Tāwhiri, who pressed his nose to hers first before embracing her.

"How's our favorite little demon slayer?" he said, lifting the lei po'o so he could ruffle her hair. "Did you enjoy the feast tonight?"

Masina giggled as she rubbed her tummy. "I ate too much. Everything was so good!"

Alani tiptoed up to kiss Masina's forehead. Masina beamed at her. That was always odd for me to see; Alani was smaller than Masina, but Masina deferred to her because Alani was older.

Once everyone had their turn fussing over Masina we parted ways; she took the girls to her quarters and I went with the boys to mine. Coconut shells filled with kukui nut oil burned inside my hut, the candlelight revealing four mats that were laid out for us. I waited as Ori, Koa, and Tāwhiri decided who was going to sleep where. I didn't mind which mat I ended up with, and as their host it would've been rude for me to even consider that.

"Toa, do you have any extra blankets?" Tāwhiri asked. "I think the one they gave Ori is too short."

I fought the urge to laugh as I looked at Ori. The woven mat he had was long enough for his tall frame, but the blanket was pathetically small. Ori, always the serious one, stared forlornly at the ceiling while his bare shins stuck out from under the fabric.

"This is good." Ori mused in a faraway voice. "To explore the unfamiliar is to connect with the divine."

"Which is Ori talk for 'I'm gonna freeze tonight.'" Tāwhiri laughed.

Ori insisted he didn't mind, but I was more inclined to believe Tāwhiri. I left to ask Aunty Tua for another blanket. Her hut was closest to ours, and her husband was around Ori's height.

She laughed when I explained my dilemma and gave me two extra blankets.

"In case the Navigator boy gives you any more trouble, eh?" she said with a wink.

The night was quiet as I went back to my hut. One by one, candles burning in the huts were blown out, leaving only the twinkling light in the heavens. Stars glittered and a full moon painted the village in blue and silver hues. I tilted my head up, appreciating the heavens in all their beauty.

"Lovely night out, isn't it?"

I clenched my fists, not needing to see her to know she was the woman outside of Mother's garden. Out of the corner of my eye

I saw she still had that raggedy dress from earlier, and she was still just as unnerving.

I kept walking, not looking as I entered the encampment. Her footsteps trailed behind me.

"Ignoring me will not serve you." she said, her voice uncomfortably close. Her hand brushed against mine and I yanked away.

"What do you want?" I grumbled, hugging the blankets to my side with a death grip.

"A better attitude would be a good start."

When I didn't respond she danced into view, squaring off with me. She had a haughty, teasing look in the way she leered at me, like she knew something I didn't. I didn't care. I stared back at her, growing more annoyed every second.

"Now that's better." she said, her lip curling. "You almost look like you could be chief."

"I am going to be chief." I snarled. "The high chief." There were very few things I was certain about in life, but my right to claim the title was one of them. It was my one hope that things could get better, that I could someday prove I was more than this.

The woman sighed. "I'm sure you would've made a decent one. But I'd look for alternatives if I were you."

She glanced at my father's hut. The candles were still burning inside, and I could make out the shadows of the high chiefs sitting around it. They discussed in low whispers, sounding urgent.

I narrowed my eyes at the hut, then at the woman. "What do you want from me?"

She pressed a finger to her chin, thinking. "In the future, a favor would be nice. But for now, I'll settle for a warning. Run fast, little sun warrior. You're about to be shadowed by moonlight."

My eyes darted back to the hut, panic flaring in my chest. I looked back at the woman, but once again she was gone.

I turned to the hut and started to run.

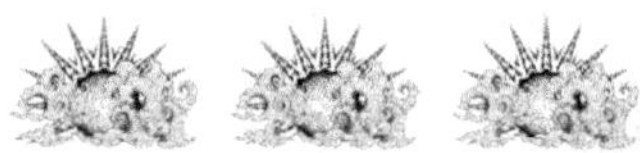

I knelt behind the hut and threw a hand over my mouth, stifling my own labored breathing. I crouched where my shadow wouldn't be seen and listened.

"I worry about that boy of yours, Alai." High Chief Moe was saying. "He seems to lack the competence to do...well, anything."

"He's young." my father said. "He'll have years of training before he takes over. By then he'll be ready."

"That may be, but shouldn't he at least show some potential?" asked High Chiefess Manaia. "All due respect, Alai, what has your son done to prove he is worthy of his title?"

"He...."

I squatted there, holding my breath. None of the chiefs were saying anything now. I waited for one of them to speak up, to defend my right to rule. At the very least, I knew my father would say something.

Go on, Father, I thought. *Tell them. Tell them why I deserve to be chief.*

But a weighted silence was my only reply.

High Chief Senidra spoke up. "I cannot speak for his leadership, as I've never seen him govern, but his combat skills leave much to be desired. Were he to lead an army, the Light Village would perish."

"I saw his so-called leadership today," said Tāwhiri's mom. "Believe me, it was pathetic. He spent more time looking for places Masina hadn't been than he did trying to help his people."

Her words came as a slap. That's not what happened! I *was* trying to help. It wasn't my fault that Masina was always ahead of me.

Come on, Dad, I pleaded. *Tell them.*

"He's quite knowledgeable about plants," said Puana's mother. "He seemed confident in the healer's hut today."

"But then why didn't he stay and let Alani finish the walk-through?" another high chief objected. "A good leader should know when it's time to delegate."

Grudgingly, I had to admit that was true. Why didn't I ask Alani to finish? That would have made more sense since she knew what to look for in the aftermath of a battle.

"I heard he was angry Masina picked the red-heart leaves before him." High Chief Manoa growled. "Rather than be happy my son would live, he wallowed in self-pity because he hadn't been the one to save him. Apparently he would've preferred Koa suffered a little longer, came closer to death to make the rescue even more dramatic."

The complaints started rolling out after that, each one crushing me like the surf at high tide.

"He didn't even fight when the demons came."

"Did you see his face when Masina dedicated her night to him?"

"Ungrateful brat."

"The boy is useless."

On and on it went. Toa was hopeless. Toa couldn't do anything. Toa brought shame to his family name. But what hurt most of all was my father not saying anything. He couldn't disagree with them because he thought they were right.

"Enough." he said finally. He wasn't loud, but the effects were immediate. The words stopped as though they'd been sliced in half.

I could hardly breathe. A lump welled in my throat and I felt the shame burning in my eyes. I always knew nobody thought I could be chief; nobody thought that I *should* be chief. And while I always suspected my father was the same, hearing the confirmation rattled me. No one, not even my father, thought I could do this.

"What would you have me do?" I heard him ask. "Toa is not perfect, but he is my son. The one true heir to the Light Village. It is his birthright."

His voice was heavy with resignation. He wasn't angry, or protective like he'd been at the feast. This time he sounded tired, almost defeated. The only reason he tolerated me was because tradition mandated it.

"He's not the only child you have, Lai," murmured High Chief Loa. "You do have another candidate."

"A better one, I might add," said High Chiefess Manaia.

"She is a great warrior," chimed in Alani's father. "One that is beloved by her people."

Conversation buzzed as they discussed the possibilities. With Masina as high chief, the Light Village would be lifted up. They would have a warrior to lead them in battle and a skilled healer to help the sick and injured. Masina would be perfect. Masina was the one they needed.

Outside the hut, I felt the wind rush out of me. My chest exploded in pain. All my life—*all* my life I had known that Masina was better at everything. She was stronger, faster, better looking. The one thing I had that she couldn't was my title. My right to rule over her as the high chief. And now....

"Masina is not my firstborn," Father said. "She already has a title as my eldest daughter. That isn't the same as being the next chief."

"But it could be," High Chief Moe insisted. "Look at Seni, or Maile. Having a daughter simply means she'll be a high chief with two titles instead of one."

"She is too young," my father objected. "She's had none of the training Toa has already completed."

"Be honest, Alai, do you not think Masina could both retain and execute the trainings better than that boy ever could?"

The others murmured in agreement. I felt my heart sink deeper when Father didn't object.

"If it's age that concerns you, why not call for chief trials?" High Chief Loa suggested.

Chief trials. No one had done them for generations. It was a way for younger siblings to challenge the eldest for the family title. If they won, the oldest would forfeit their position, and the younger sibling would become the high chief.

Father didn't like that idea. "Chief trials are only conducted because of treason, or because the rightful chief is incapable of leading."

"It's no question that boy is incapable," remarked the high chief of the Heart Village. "He can't do it physically, mentally, or in any capacity whatsoever."

"You would do well to remember whose house you are in." Father growled.

There was another pause, then he let out a weary sigh.

"I appreciate the council's concerns on the matter," he said. "But the decision rests with me. And I cannot in good conscience pit my children against each other. Toa is a young man and a fool, but I will stand behind him. I won't let the village fall."

Hearing my own father call me a fool is what did it for me. I pushed off the ground, knees wobbling as I stood up. One foot trudged in front of the other until I was standing in front of the open wall of the hut. The nine high chiefs, all sitting in a circle, turned to me in a stupor. None of them believed anyone, let alone me, would have the audacity to interrupt their meeting. I got down on my knees.

Father, who was sitting directly in front of the door, looked startled as he met my eyes.

"Son—"

"I accept," I said. The words rushed out of me before I could stop them.

More surprised faces. Some were confused. High Chiefess Manaia pursed her lips as she examined me. She lifted her chin.

"You accept what?" she challenged.

I lowered my head, but kept my posture firm. "I accept the council's motion to call for chief trials. I wish to prove that I am the rightful heir to the Light Village."

High Chief Loa laughed. Alani's father looked impressed. Their expressions of minor amusement were reflected by everyone except for my father. He looked angry.

"This doesn't just affect you, son," he warned. "Masina's life will change because of it."

Will change. Not *could* change. In his mind, Father thought I had all but forfeited my title. He, like the rest of the council, had already picked out a winner.

"If Masina wins the trials she can have my birthright," I said stubbornly. "I would rather die in combat than lead a village full of people feeling sorry for me."

High Chiefess Manaia rolled her eyes. "She won't kill you, idiot boy. But when she wins you will become subject to her. You understand this?"

"I understand," I said, a lump rising in my throat.

The high chiefess nodded and turned to my father. "The boy has accepted the terms. High Chief Alai, what say you?"

Father looked at me long and hard. He ground his teeth, then steepled his fingers under his nose. Finally, he closed his eyes and gave a nod.

"Very well," he said. "So be it."

Chapter 4

The next morning I jerked awake when Masina fell on me. She flapped my shoulders like a frightened chicken.

"Lā!" she hissed. "Lā, wake up!"

"I'm up." I grunted, straining to push her away. Masina wasn't fat, but for a girl her size she was *heavy.* "Get off me!"

She scrambled aside. I waited for her to leave, but she didn't. Annoyed, I made a shooing motion with my hands.

"Do you mind?" I said, pinching the corner of my blanket. "I'm not even dressed."

Masina blushed. "Oh. Oh, sorry."

She turned away and clamped her hands over her eyes. Realizing that was all the privacy I would get from her, I sighed and snatched a clean sulu. I tied it around my waist and ran my fingers through my hair.

"Okay, I'm ready." I said. "You can look now."

Masina turned, clutching at her hair and chewing her lip.

I frowned. "What's wrong with you?"

Masina rocked back and forth, searching for the right words. "I...I heard from the council this morning." she said. "They said we're going to do chief trials. Lā, they said they want me to *fight* you."

I shrugged. "I know."

"You do?" Masina paled. "But Lā, they want us to fight like, like a *real* fight. And whoever wins will—"

"Will be the next high chief," I finished. "Yeah."

I rolled up my mat and went for the bowl of water outside of my hut. I splashed my face, remembering my talk with the council. This was real. This was happening. If I won the trials, no one would ever question my right to rule ever again.

"They're not really going to make us do it, are they?" Masina said. She leaned on my shoulder, and I shoved her away.

"We're doing it," I said. "It's time we settle this once and for all."

"Settle this?" Masina inched forward, trying to look me in the eye. "But Lā, this is crazy. I don't want to fight you."

She sounded so sincere, almost scared. I wrinkled my nose at her, confused. Masina couldn't be scared. If word about the trials was out, then the whole village already thought she would be the next high chief. What did she have to be scared about?

Unless, of course, she was really scared for me.

I growled, squeezing the cloth in my hands. "I don't need your pity. We're doing the trials. Win or lose, I'll have the village know I defended my title with honor."

And with that, I left for the god pool.

The village buzzed with the news as streams of people made their way inland. I cringed at their enthusiasm for the "new chief," but kept my head high. If I was going to be branded a failure, I would do it on my own terms.

At the base of the tallest mountain rested the god pool of Havaiki. Every village in our union had one—each for one of the patron gods. They were a meeting place between gods and men, and sacred places of refuge.

The god pool for our village was a lagoon at the base of a waterfall. The surrounding hills could seat hundreds, but the pool itself was only fifteen feet wide. The god pools were designed that way on purpose, as only the high chiefs could use them. Anyone else would die if they touched the water. And even then, the high chiefs only dipped in the pools when they were inducting a new heir, or if they wanted to cleanse themselves before communing with the gods. It was vital that the purity and sacred nature of the god pools were maintained.

This was where my father had been when the gods promised him a mighty warrior for a son. He earned that right after many victories in battle, the most famous of which was when he bound the great demon Mā. After liberating the village, my father came here, where the forerunner of Havaiki descended. She pronounced that from the line of High Chief Alai would descend the greatest rulers of the Light Village. The first of whom would have the strength of a thousand suns.

Looking at the crowd gathered around the god pool, I almost laughed.

Some great ruler I turned out to be.

Escorted by Ori and Tāwhiri, the villagers parted to both sides as I came through. Most had the decency to hush their voices. Others mocked me with open scorn. I bit the inside of my cheek and swallowed my pride, moving to where my father and Orator Ra'i stood by the god pool. The rest of the council stood behind them in a line.

Moments later Puana and Alani arrived with Masina. Her hair was still down. She wore her kaulima on her arms and an ula nifo around her neck.

Orator Ra'i raised his staff, and the village fell silent.

"It is the will of the council, and of the current heir of the Light Village that we hold chief trials today," he declared, his voice barely audible above the waterfall. He looked down at Masina and I. "The two of you will please come forward."

We obeyed. At Orator Ra'i's command, we knelt in front of him. He had a hollowed gourd in one hand, which he passed to my father. Father dipped it into the god pool. He gave it back to the orator, who lifted it up for the entire village could see.

"With the sacred water of Havaiki, I strip both Toa and Masina of their titles, declaring before the gods that they are equals until the trials are over." He lowered the gourd, looking first at me, then at Masina. "Whoever emerges triumphant will bathe in the pool as the next high chief."

He brought the gourd to my head, spilling some of its contents onto me. I shivered as the water trickled down my face and the back of my neck. When Orator Ra'i did the same to Masina, the water running down her face almost looked like tears. She blinked it out of her eyes, staring up at him.

Orator Raʻi gave the gourd back to my father. His expression was sour, and he wouldn't look at me as the orator continued.

"The trials are divided into three tasks. Each will test the high chief's mind, heart, and strength. No man can fully serve his people without those three things." he cleared his throat. "The test of strength will be a battle between our contestants. But the other two will only test the hearts and minds of the royal siblings. Whoever wins the most tasks, will be our next high chief."

I felt my heart skip a beat. Only *one* of the trials was an actual fight. Even if Masina could beat me at that, I could still win!

The orator gripped his staff. "Do you both find this agreeable?"

"Agreeable." I said immediately.

Masina furrowed her brow, her response hesitant. "Agreeable."

The orator nodded, thumping his staff on the ground. "So be it. We begin with the trial of the mind."

The orator sat on a nearby rock as High Chiefess Manaia rose to her feet. She was accompanied by High Chiefess Mailelauliʻi. High Chiefess Manaia jerked her chin at me, while Puana's mom smiled at Masina.

"The trial of the mind is to test the intelligence of the next high chief." said High Chiefess Manaia. "No man or woman worth respecting would want to be led by an idiot."

"It will also be the longest task you go through today." High Chiefess Mailelauliʻi added. "Long, but simple; conducted in question and answer format. We have people to track your scores, but by the end it should be obvious who deserves to win this trial."

Masina and I were allowed to make ourselves comfortable as the trial began. The high chiefesses covered everything from agriculture to combat strategies. Masina answered the questions about battle tactics and navigation, but that was really all she knew. She didn't know anything about planting or harvesting seasons. Nor had she ever learned the political relationship our village had with other tribes in the union. All of that had been covered in the protocol lessons.

With every question I answered correctly I felt my confidence soar. By the time Orator Ra'i called for the trial to end, the sun was nearing its midday peak. The water he had poured on us had long since evaporated, and my skin felt hot from the prolonged exposure, but my head was in the clouds. The scorekeepers didn't even need to compare the numbers.

I turned to my father, a broad grin on my face. In that moment I almost forgot about my run-in with the council, and my humiliation at the feast. For once, I had done something right—I had won!

But when I saw my father, he wasn't smiling. His face was hardened and he wouldn't look at me. Glancing around the village, my happiness evaporated when I realized I was the only one celebrating.

Orator Ra'i held a hand over my head. "The winner of the first trial is young Toa! Should he win this next trial he will maintain his status as the future chief of the Light Village."

The villagers murmured behind me, and I felt my face grow hot. Out of the corner of my eye I could still see my father, silently stewing behind the rest of the council. Anger flared inside me. If Mother had been here, she would've been happy for me.

Right?

Orator Ra'i raised his staff for silence. "We will proceed to the second trial."

He took his seat again as High Chief Moe stood. He crouched low so that he was almost eye level with us without sitting down.

"The trial of the heart will be the shortest trial of the day." he said. "But that does not make it any less important. A high chief without a good heart is nothing more than a tyrant."

There was a weight in his words that made me fidget. This trial, like the one before it, didn't require physical strength. That should've given me the advantage. But I had no idea what to expect. How did you prove to someone that you had a good heart?

High Chief Moe had a twinkle in his eye as he looked at Masina. "Since the true nature of someone's heart can hardly be revealed in a day, the council met early this morning to discuss the admirable traits in both contestants. I feel it only fair to warn you that we all reached the same conclusion; we believe we already know which of you has the better heart."

I felt my insides shrivel. They already picked a winner? But how could that possibly be fair? It was like they were trying to rig this for Masina!

Sensing my rage, High Chief Moe held up a finger. "But, in the interest of the trials, we have selected a question that could change our minds. If answered correctly, either contestant could tip the scales in their favor."

I clenched my fists, determined to get this right. What would the question be about? Ethics? Morality? I knew enough of our people's customs to answer for either of those.

High Chief Moe met my gaze, his head tilted. "Who do you admire most in the entire world?"

"Who do I...?"

The question came as a shock. Who did I admire? How did that prove I had a pure heart?

"Young Toa?" High Chief Moe asked. "Who is it? Whom do you admire?"

My first thought was my father, the great hero of the Light Village. I felt the words forming in my mouth, but in a flash I remembered what he'd said last night.

Toa is a young man and a fool.

I swallowed. "The person I admire most is my ancestor, the light god Havaiki."

Whispers rippled through the crowd behind me. High Chief Moe silenced them with a wave. He turned back to me, an inquisitive look on his face.

"That's not what I was expecting," he said. "Why did you choose your patron god?"

"He...he was a great leader and a powerful man," I invented. "One who earned his place in the pantheon of the gods."

High Chief Moe nodded slowly. "I see. And it's important for you to become a great and powerful man?"

"Yes," I said. "Men with power can keep people from hurting them. They've earned their place in the world."

The high chief rubbed his chin, considering this. He shifted his gaze to Masina.

"And how about you, little one?" he asked. "Whom do you admire most in the entire world?"

She stole a sideways glance at me, then turned back to Ori's father. Timidly, she inched forward and whispered something in his ear. High Chief Moe's eyebrows went up.

"Also unexpected," he said, eyes flicking towards me. Then he laughed. "Although, not so hard to believe. Tell me, Masina, why is he the person you admire most?"

"Because he always does his best no matter what," Masina said. "People don't give him the attention he deserves, but that doesn't bother him and he keeps going, anyway. He doesn't look it, but he's kind, and compassionate, and everything I hope to be someday. No matter what I'm going through, I know he's gonna be there for me."

The high chief smiled. "Those people do make our lives worth living. How does this person inspire you to be different?"

Masina brushed her hair out of her face, looking determined. "Because if he can be that kind of person after everything he's been through, then I have no excuse. I want to be someone who chooses to do good, even when it's not easy; I don't just want to be a warrior, I want to be a good friend that people can count on."

My stomach flipped at the way her words seemed to melt all the high chiefs like pork fat in the 'umu. I bit the inside of my cheek; they weren't seriously eating this up, were they?

But as High Chief Moe looked back at the council, I knew that was exactly what was happening. Nods of approval all around, all except for my father, who looked somber.

High Chief Moe rested a hand on Masina's head before pulling her to her feet. He took her hand in his and raised it up high.

"Masina wins the second trial!"

Everyone in the village cheered.

Culacula

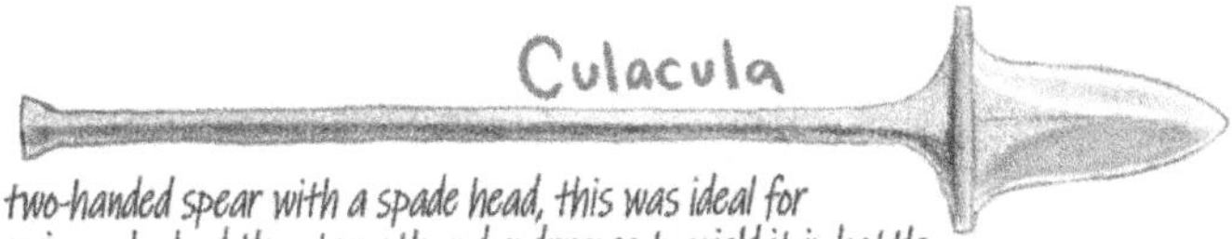

A two-handed spear with a spade head, this was ideal for warriors who had the strength and endurance to wield it in battle.

Bulibuli

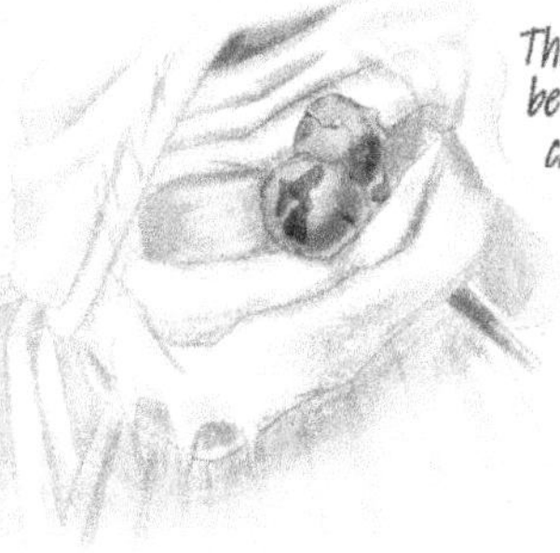

Throwing clubs that can easily be concealed in clothing, bulibuli can crack an opponent's skull when thrown with enough force and accuracy.

Nifo Oti

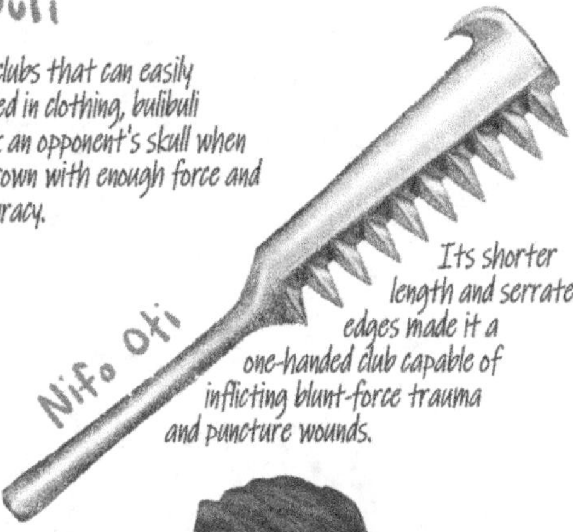

Its shorter length and serrated edges made it a one-handed club capable of inflicting blunt-force trauma and puncture wounds.

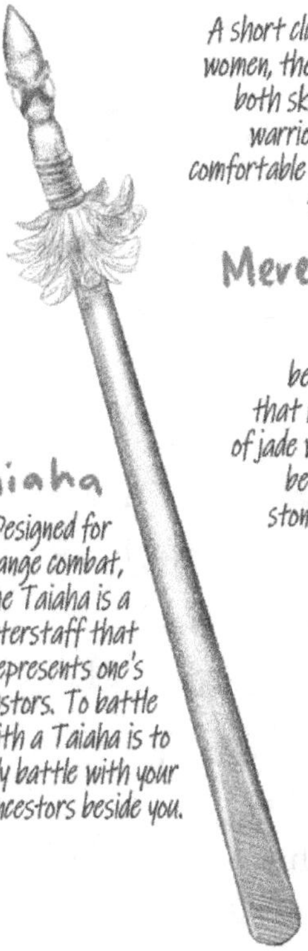

A short club used by both men and women, the mere and patu required both skill and confidence since warriors would have to be comfortable closing the distance with their enemies.

Mere|Patu

The difference between the two is that mere are made of jade while patu can be carved with stone, wood, or bone.

Taiaha

Designed for -range combat, the Taiaha is a arterstaff that represents one's cestors. To battle with a Taiaha is to ally battle with your ancestors beside you.

Talavalu

Literally interpreted as "eight spikes", the talavalu has eight ridges on each side. Some have pointed spikes like the nifo oti while others have rounded edges.

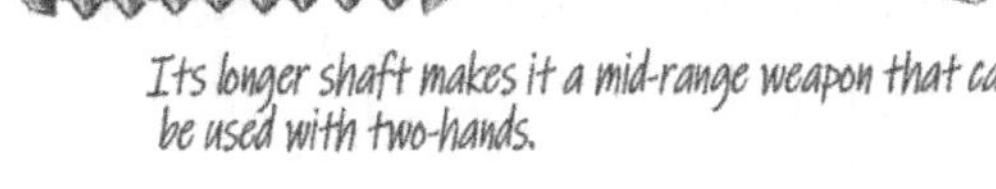

Its longer shaft makes it a mid-range weapon that can be used with two-hands.

Chapter 5

The third and final trial would be at sunset outside the meetinghouse. Masina and I had until then to prepare for it. Puana and Alani took Masina to our family encampment, while I went with Ori and Tāwhiri to the village armory.

"What about this one?" Tāwhiri asked.

I looked up as he tossed a thick, flat-bladed club at me. It was made of wood so dark it almost looked black, and the spaded head was wider than its cylindrical shaft. I yelped as I caught it with both arms, staggering under its weight. This was the kind of weapon Alani's father used. When wielded properly, it could split someone's skull. The problem was, I couldn't even get it off the ground. I strained with effort before Ori relieved me of it.

"Too heavy," he said, tossing it back to Tāwhiri. "He needs something his skeleton body can handle."

I flinched at his words. I knew Ori wasn't trying to be mean, but sometimes I wished he could be as vague in criticism as he was when I asked about the weather. Still, he was right. All the weapons Tāwhiri brought were meant for bigger, stronger warriors.

Tāwhiri rubbed his chin as he considered the arsenal lining the walls. There were spears, staffs, battle axes, and clubs of all shapes and sizes. He picked up a jade mere and started twirling it by the cord.

"The problem with these smaller weapons is Toa doesn't know how to use them," he said, tossing the mere up and catching it. "Sure, he could hold one, but I don't think he has the confidence to let Masina get close to him."

"At least he wouldn't be unarmed," Ori took a bone patu and handed it to me. "Here, try."

I wrapped the cord around my wrist and gripped the handle. The patu was short and flat, about the length of my hands if I were to stack one on top of the other. While it was lighter than other clubs we had tried, I could see what Tāwhiri was saying. With a weapon like this, I'd have to be comfortable with letting Masina get close enough for me to hit her with it, which meant she in turn could use the distance to her advantage.

Ori grabbed a spear took his stance. He nodded at me. I raised the patu overhead as I ran at him, screaming. I swung; Ori sidestepped with ease. He swept my right leg with the shaft of his spear and I flew backward, landing hard on my back. Moaning, I felt Ori rest his spear tip against my throat, a hint of a smile on his lips.

"Maybe not that one," he chuckled.

I swatted his spear tip aside, irritated. "Were you even aiming for the patu?"

We tried every weapon I had the strength to carry. Each attempt ended with varying degrees of humiliation. Tāwhiri twisted my wrist to disarm me. Ori caught my throwing club and bopped me on the head with it. And when I tried the slingshot, I punched a hole in the weapon master's roof that Ori promised to patch up later. No matter what the object was, it seemed that if it was meant for war, it wasn't meant for me.

"Maybe if you're lucky, she'll take it easy on you?" Tāwhiri said, racking the spear I had clumsily wielded.

I shook my head. "It can't end like this. There has to be *something* we can do."

Ori frowned. "I still don't understand why this is so important to you. What's so bad about Masina being the next high chief?"

I glared at him. "How would you like it if one of your sisters took your title?"

"If she was more worthy of it, I would give it to her."

"And you think Masina deserves it more than I do?"

Ori didn't answer. He looked at Tāwhiri. They kept their mouths shut, but I heard the message loud and clear.

I plodded out of the armory and stalked into the jungle, looking down at my bony hands. Could I really blame the village for not wanting me? People like me didn't stand at the head of a village. Those people looked more like Masina.

The smell of teuila flowers tickled my nose, and I looked up to see the entrance to Mother's garden. I hadn't planned on coming here, but now that I was I felt relieved. Even in death, Mother still had a way of making me feel better. As I reached for the wiry ti leaf trees, I heard something rustle behind me.

I whipped around. No one there. Heart thudding, I turned to enter the garden, when I heard it again. This time it was accompanied by a shadow flickering at the edge of my peripherals. I crossed my arms.

"Show yourself," I said, suspecting that I already knew who was there.

Like an eel slithering from its hole, she emerged from the clustered vines of the jungle. I wondered if I was imagining it, but she seemed smaller than before. The veins on her arms and legs more pronounced than they had been last night.

"About time you showed up," she said. "I was beginning to think I'd been forgotten."

I glowered at her. "I wasn't looking for you."

She laughed and took a step towards me. I stepped back, both feet planted in the garden. Seeing the ti leaf trees in between us her puffed-up attitude deflated a little.

"Still hiding behind mommy, are we?"

I clenched my teeth. "What do you want?"

She turned her palms up. "My apologies, chiefling. I should've known better than to insult your mother. As to why I am here, well, I think that's obvious."

She closed the distance between us with two long strides, her face uncomfortably close to mine. I stumbled back, thrown off by her boldness.

Her hands gripped the ti leaf trees like bars on a prison door. "You want your title," she hissed. "I can get it for you. You wish to defeat your sister, so do I. With my help, no one will question you ever again."

I was stunned. The thought of defeating Masina, and the idea that I could be the one to make it happen.... It felt too good to be true.

I shook my head. "This has to be a trick. What do you really want?"

"Just that," the woman said, a hand over her heart. "I promise. I am highly invested in making sure you are the next chief of the Light Village, that's all."

She held a hand out to me. My fingers twitched to reach for it. My stomach churned. Something about this wasn't right; things couldn't be that simple. Could they? She had to have another motive.

But if she really could help me win against Masina....

It was tempting. I hated myself for thinking it, but it really was tempting. Would it really be so bad to hear her out? It's not like I had to do anything she said, and I couldn't deny my curiosity was almost as overwhelming as the offer itself.

"What's in it for you?" I asked.

"Let's just say your sister complicates things for me." She flicked the ti leaves in annoyance. "Besides, don't you want to show what the rightful heir can do?"

I thought of all the hatred I had endured over the years. All the taunting, the ridicule. The pitying looks and whispers that followed me everywhere I went. I thought of my father and the high chief's council, and how none of them, not even my father, wanted me to be chief.

In that moment I knew that more than anything, I wanted power. I wanted to be strong, to be the kind of man that could shut them all up. I wanted, no—I *needed* to prove I wasn't the worthless whelp they thought I was.

"How—how would this work?" I asked. "You helping me, that is."

A glint of pleasure flashed through her eyes. "It's quite simple, really." she began, her hand reaching out. "All I need is for you to say the right words and give me a little bit of your blood."

"My blood?" I stepped back, alarms going off in my head.

She smiled reassuringly. "Just a drop, nothing more. I have powers that you won't find in a typical village girl, and to unlock them I require the blood of a high chief. Which, conveniently, you happen to have."

"Okay." I reached for her with trembling fingers. Her hands felt cool against my skin and made me shiver.

"Out of there, of course," she chided, pulling me out of the garden and into the jungle.

I followed her numbly, the alarms in my brain fading as I watched her. She pulled a sharp rock out of her dress and ran it across her palm, hissing with pain. She passed the rock to me, watching me expectantly.

I imitated her, biting my tongue as I sliced a gash in my hand. I looked down at the blood and felt the sting as the wind blew over it.

In the back of my mind, I knew I shouldn't be here. I needed to stop. I needed to run away. But I was in too deep to turn back now; I had to see this through.

The woman held her hand over mine, staring at our wounded palms hungrily. "Now repeat after me," she whispered. "Say the words, 'Hana of the starless night, I grant you permission to enter.'"

"Hana of the starless night," I began, then paused. Something about her name awoke a part of me, but what or why that was I didn't understand. "Your—your name is Hana?"

"Yes!" she hissed. "Now, hurry! The spell must be completed before the blood dries."

"Oh, um." I cleared my throat. "Hana of the starless night, I—I grant you permission to enter."

Hana's bloodied hand clamped down over my own. Chicken skin erupted down my neck as her blood mixing with mine. And when I looked up at her face, everything inside me went cold.

Hana's smiling teeth became pointed and her delicate eyes turned malevolent. She threw back her head and started to laugh. And it wasn't the silly, shallow laugh I'd heard before, but hard and cruel. The kind of sound that came from someone who enjoyed causing pain.

I tried to let go; I pried at her fingers with my free hand, but it was like our blood had sealed us together; I couldn't get her off.

Then her body split into a billion clouds of darkness. Each one burning midair like black-flamed candles. I stood there in shock, fear rooting me to the spot. The black burning masses rushed at me, and I scrambled to get away.

I ran for the garden, but the black flames engulfed me before I could make it inside. I twisted as they tore at my skin and dug into my ears. Then forced themselves down my throat and up my nose. Pain exploded inside of me; freezing and burning my body at the same time. I crumpled to the ground, unable to control my body as it spasmed near the roots of a banyan tree.

Just when I thought the darkness would overwhelm me, it stopped. For the longest time all I could do was lay there, sprawled with my back against the earth, arms and legs out to the sides. Everything hurt. I stared up at the jungle canopy, wondering if I was about to join the ancestors.

Rise, my brave warrior, came a voice. *Rise and stand with me.*

The voice sounded like Hana's. My blood boiled and I clenched my fists. "What did you do to me?" I growled, my voice sounding lower than it normally did.

See for yourself, I heard her say. *You may be some of my finest work yet.*

Grumbling, I rolled onto my side and stretched my left hand out to push myself up. But when I saw my hand, and the arm attached to it, I froze. That hand didn't look like mine. My body was skin and bones, with the knobby knuckles of an elderly man.

This hand looked nothing like that. What had once been flimsy and pathetic now belonged to a set of strong arms. I flexed, watching with wonder as muscles bulged under my skin. The same was true for my legs. I felt strong enough to uproot a tree with my bare hands. I was taller and wider, and there was no softness in me. My entire body was a wall of solid muscle.

I reached my new hands up to my face. Curiosity getting the better of me, I took off running for the nearest river. The ease and power of it excited me; I always got winded easily, but now I felt nothing as I bounded up to a stream.

Peeking inside, I saw a face I didn't deserve to wear. Staring up at me was a man who could steal all of Ori's admirers. With chiseled features and deep set eyes, I wondered if this is what it would've been like had I grown up with Masina's strength.

Like it?

"I love it," I said. "Thank you."

See? You've already got the makings of a chief inside of you, she said. *You just needed me to bring them out.*

I laughed. She was right. What had I been so afraid of? I could've felt this way a lot sooner! Then, looking around, I realized something.

"Where are you?" I asked.

I'm right here.

My hand started to come up to the side of my head. Alarmed, I threw it back down. But, as though it had a will of its own, it flew back up and thumped my right temple. I thought I might be sick.

"Are—are you *inside* me?!"

My head nodded. All my joy evaporated. I fell to my knees, clutching at the sides of my head.

"Get out!" I shrieked. "Get out of my head!"

Hana quieted my fear and willed my legs to stand. "Calm yourself," she said with my voice. "This is just for the third trial."

I cringed, hating how her words were coming out of my mouth. Suddenly I felt like a prisoner inside my own body.

"This isn't right," I said. "I don't want to win like this."

"Would you rather not win at all?"

I opened my mouth to say yes, but the word stuck in my throat. I did want to win, I wanted it more than I've ever wanted anything. But this....

"It feels like cheating," I blurted.

Hana's voice cackled in my head. *Think of it more as leveling the playing field. Masina had the upper hand because she was born that way. Now you can fight as equals.*

I wasn't convinced. "I don't know...."

I may be steering the canoe, but this is still your canoe, little warrior, she countered. *Besides, I can't leave your body until after the trial. Once that's over, I'll be done with you.*

I still didn't like it, but what choice did I have? I couldn't stop her, and without her I'd be a human twig again. And if she couldn't leave until the trial was over, what was the harm in letting her help until then?

"Just until after the trial?"

Satisfaction bloomed in my chest, an emotion I knew belonged to Hana.

Good boy. Now, let's go win a title.

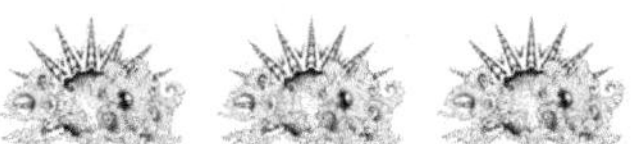

The council sat at the edge of the meetinghouse. Their eyes bulged in unison when they saw me. My father, High Chief Senidra, and High Chiefess Manaia rose to their feet, weapons at the ready.

"I don't know how they do things in your village." said High Chief Senidra. "But here it's not polite to walk in unannounced."

"I know how things are run in my village." I said, twirling my club with one hand. It was the spaded one I couldn't lift in the armory; now it felt like nothing. "A high chief's son should at least know that much, eh, Father?"

My father's hands tightened around his spear. "Who are you?"

I put my hand over my chest, feigning a look of surprise. "Why Father, it's me. Your firstborn. Don't you recognize me?"

I swelled with satisfaction as his wariness turned to shock. He lowered his spear and stepped forward, searching my face.

"Son?"

I grinned back. "Hello, Father. Now, shall we get this third trial over with?"

Those last words felt more like Hana's than my own; a part of me shrank knowing she was still inside me.

Father looked horrified. "Son, what have you done? What kind of magic is this?"

"Who said magic had anything to do with it?" I asked. "I am simply a boy ready to assume a man's role. There was no rule that I wasn't allowed to hit a growth spurt before the third trial."

High Chiefess Manaia scoffed. "A growth spurt that only took a couple of hours? Good gods, boy. Not even the wildest weeds in the forest could grow this fast."

"I sense foul play, as well," said High Chief Senidra. "This hardly seems fair for Masina."

I bristled. "If Masina is the great warrior you all think she is, she'll be fine."

High Chiefess Manaia raised her patu. "Mind your words, boy. You still answer to the chiefs."

"Peace, Manaia," my father ordered. He rested his spear on the ground, still looking at me. "Are you sure you want to do this, son?"

I nodded. "More sure than I've ever been of anything."

"And what do you hope to find if you win?"

"I—" my words caught in my throat. What did I hope to win? That should've been obvious. I wanted all the power and attention he refused to give me. I wanted to smear his face into my victory and show him that—

"Lā?"

I whirled around. Masina gawked at me. It was amazing how small she was now; she barely reached my stomach. She had a wide-eyed look of curiosity as she studied me.

"Is that really you?" she brushed her hand against my arm. I pulled away, and she looked down at her outstretched fingers. Her smile faltered.

"Yeah, it's you," she said. "Why are you like this now?"

"It's for the trial," I huffed, annoyed at how unthreatened she was.

Masina bit her lip, looking past me to the high chiefs.

"I wanted to talk to you about that," she said, lowering her voice. "I'm gonna forfeit the trial. I don't want to be high chief, and I know how much it means to you."

Resentment flickered inside me. "We're doing it," I said flatly. "It's not up for debate."

She bowed her head. "Okay."

She looked up again. Our eyes met for a moment, then she dropped her chin to her chest and scuttled away.

Moments later Masina returned, dressed and ready for battle. She wore a one-shoulder gown that cut diagonally across her collarbone and hemmed above her knees. She wore her kaulima and ula nifo, hair hanging in a long side braid. Alani ran red paint along her cheeks in the war patterns before giving Masina her club.

It wasn't the serrated one she normally had. This one had a longer shaft, and instead of sharp teeth it had smooth bumps on the end. It was still deadly, but I bristled to know what she was doing. Smaller weapons showed off skill and bravery; Masina could've easily brought one of those. By using this, she was sending a silent message that she wanted to maintain the distance between us.

Either that, or she was still trying to go easy on me.

Her club hung loose in her left hand as she stood at the far end of our makeshift arena. I gripped my flat-headed club, arms open in a challenge. Between us Orator Ra'i raised his staff. Usually he did it to call attention, but everyone in the village was already watching with bated breath.

"The third and final trial is about to begin," he announced. "When one of the contenders yields or is no longer able to battle, the trial will be over." He paused. "Whoever wins will become the next high chief of the Light Village."

His words faltered, and he shot me another inquisitive look. I ignored him, too focused on the coming battle. My legs twitched to run at Masina, every part of me eager to strike her down. Orator Ra'i retreated out of the circle, standing next to the high chiefs in the meetinghouse. Then he banged his staff and the trial began.

I rushed at Masina, legs bounding effortlessly as I closed the distance between us. She wavered as she waited for me. I raised my club to strike, but as I swung down Masina ducked out of the way. My club sank into the ground. I pried it out of the earth, whipping around to counter her offensive move, but she just stood there—club still dangling at her side and her brow furrowed.

"Lā..."

I bellowed in rage, cutting her off. In my mind Hana nudged me to strike at her legs.

She's heavy on her feet, she said. *Use that against her.*

I obeyed, swiping down at Masina's ankles. Masina stumbled, but righted herself and leapt out of the way. She tucked into a ball, sprang back to her feet, then side-stepped as I swung at her again. Following Hana's next orders, I calculated where Masina would evade my next hit, and threw a counter strike with my free hand. My fist connected with the side of her head and I roared as her body flung up under my arm. She spun in a full circle, landing hard on her back.

I moved for the finishing blow, but Masina recovered. She dropped her club to grab my hand with both of hers and pulled. Using my momentum against me, she flipped me onto my back and threw a kick into my throat. My windpipe pinched closed under her foot. Masina twisted my arm and forced me down as I struggled to get up. Then, pushing off with her legs, she spun around and locked my arm with her legs, throwing herself down in an arm bar. I cried out in pain.

Masina's fingers loosened. Her hips dropped and I felt the pain ease in my arm.

You've got more weight than her now, Hana hissed. *Roll into the lock. She can't pin you down for very long.*

From the force she had put on me earlier, a part of me thought she could do just that. But I did as commanded and rolled into the arm lock, then pushed up onto my feet. Masina hung there for a moment, then let go as I raised my other arm to strike her. She rolled away, picking up her club and landing in a crouch.

"What's the matter, Masina?" I taunted, speaking the words Hana put in my mouth. "Don't tell me this is the best you can do."

She ran her fingers along the smooth ridges of her club. "I do not wish to fight you, brother," she said. "I love you."

"Oh, but I do want to fight you," I sneered, now voicing my own thoughts instead Hana's. "Come at me, why don't you? *Devil child who killed our mother!*"

Masina screamed. She ran at me and I rushed to meet her. I swung my flat club over my shoulder, Hana barking orders inside my head. She foresaw each of Masina's moves and helped me dodge them with ease. I jabbed, swung, rolled, and parried. My weapon thudded into Masina's over and over again. Adrenaline coursed through my veins as it hit me that I was fighting Masina. I was fighting Masina, and I wasn't losing. With Hana's power, I couldn't lose.

Hana called for me to duck left as Masina swung up with her club. I obeyed, but then Masina dropped the club and threw a knee with her opposite leg. I doubled over as she hit me in the stomach, her hands coming up over my head to force me deeper into the blow. She kneed me twice, then a third time. She followed up with an elbow strike to the chin and I spat out blood.

Masina snatched her club and struck at my legs. Her arms like a blur, she hit the side of my knee, then my hip, my stomach, and another jab under my chin. I staggered forward and she scrambled up my back. She clamped her club across my neck and pulled, forcing both of us to topple backward. I bucked my hips and twisted my body, prying at her fingers. But she didn't budge. Masina was choking me.

Panic rose inside me as it became harder and harder to breathe. I reached behind me to grab at her hair, her shoulders, anything to ease the rising terror that I would suffocate at my sister's hand.

"Ma...sina..." I gasped.

I heard her let out a yelp. Her grip slackened, and she kicked out from under me.

Hana roared with excitement. *The girl has been emotionally rattled! Now is the time to strike!*

No, I thought. But Hana was already using my hands to reach for my club. I tried to stop her, but my will crumbled under hers as she forced me to my feet, forced me to run toward my sister. My sister who had a bloody nose and tears streaming down her face. Hana raised my club overhead.

Someone struck us down from behind. Hana's blood boiled as we fell, but I was relieved. We rolled over, and standing there was my father. Rage burned in his eyes as he pointed the spear at us.

"We're not finished, old man," Hana spat. Her words flew out of my mouth like poison.

Father's scowl deepened. "This battle is over."

He lifted his spear to Masina. She sat on her knees, hands in her lap and her head bowed. In front of her was her weapon, laid horizontally in a position of surrender. She was crying.

Behind me Orator Ra'i banged his staff against the ground as he stood. "Masina has forfeited the third trial. Toa will maintain his title as the next high chief."

Chapter 6

High Chief Alai was not pleased as he watched his firstborn descend to the god pool. He had always known Toa was jealous, but this was something else. The inklings of remorse he had shown at the end of the third trial were gone now, and Alai feared for his children because of it. Toa's greed had taken him to new lows, to the point that he was willing to hurt his own sister to get what he wanted.

And Masina... Alai loved her dearly, but she cared too much about what her brother thought of her. Had he not intervened, Alai had no doubt Masina would've allowed herself to be pummeled unconscious. All for the sake of making her brother happy.

Seeing the way his son swaggered to the sacred pool, Alai doubted his son felt happy. He looked vindictive, arrogant—probably drunk on his newfound powers. It really was a pity. Toa had admirable traits of his own; he was just so focused on Masina's that he never cultivated them. The fact that he had used an enchantment for help all but proved that.

For Toa's coronation bath, Alai sat with the high chiefs on a cliff overlooking the pool. The sun had set behind the mountains, and torches were placed to increase visibility. Villagers gathered below, sitting with their families as they had done earlier that day. Alai thought of how excited they had been then—all their chatter about getting a "new" chief. It disgusted him; how could anyone find joy in his children fighting each other?

He looked down at Masina, who was closer to the pool. She stood with Alani and High Chief Moe's boy. Alani squeezed her in a side hug, and Ori rested his hands on her shoulders protectively.

How Alai wished his own son would treat his daughter like that.

Masina looked up at him, giving a watery smile. Alai's heart broke for her, and he loved her all the more for her vulnerability. Masina was utterly devoted to someone who did not deserve her affections, yet she insisted there was more to him. She was unshakable in her belief that Toa could become the hero she believed him to be.

Orator Ra'i gave the traditional speech, reciting the history of the god pools and how they were vital to a high chief's training. At first, Masina listened with the others. But as Orator Ra'i neared the end, Alai saw her stiffen. She squinted at the pool, then turned wide-eyed to the people around her. She nudged Alani and pointed, but the war chief's daughter looked confused. Masina looked up at him for help, nodding at the sacred waters. Alai frowned, not sure what she was seeing.

Masina rocked on her toes, then twisted away from Ori and Alani. She broke into a run, heading straight for Toa.

Trusting his daughter's instinct, Alai sprinted away from the council, ignoring their calls as he ran towards his firstborn.

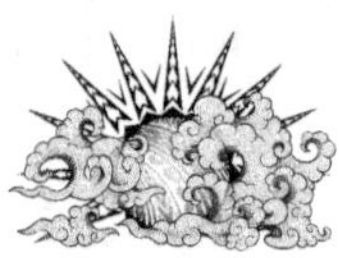

I took a deep breath, waiting for Orator Ra'i to wrap up the histories. I knew it was important to go over them, part of keeping our people's traditions alive and everything, but they were so *boring*. I wished he would hurry up and be done with it already.

Patience, hummed Hana. But even she sounded eager. I could feel her excitement pulsing inside me. So much so that it was hard for me to tell where her emotions stopped and mine began.

Our partnership had turned out to be mutually beneficial, after all. Hana got what she came for, and I retained my title as future chief. Everything worked out for the best.

When at long last Orator Ra'i was done, he stepped aside and motioned to the pool with his staff.

"High Chief Toa," he said. "Your calling awaits."

Excitement fluttered inside me as I stepped forward. The pebbled rocks grew damp under my feet as I drew closer.

Then, suddenly, a blur zipped out of the corner of my eye as someone raced towards me. Startled, I turned to see Masina—hair flying behind her as she waved for me to stop.

"Lā!" she screamed. "Watch out!"

I wanted to shove her aside, but she crashed into me. I staggered back. If Masina had done that this morning, she would've knocked me over. Now, however, it only took a few steps for me to right myself. Masina was the one who stumbled. She tottered unsteadily, shaky feet taking her towards the god pool.

Grab her! Hana shrieked. *GRAB HER!!*

I reached out, but as Masina's body touched the water, black mist erupted underneath her. It coiled around her body. Her fingers brushed against mine as her mouth opened to scream. My hands closed on empty air as she was pulled away from me, her face a mask of sheer terror.

"Lā, help me!" she cried.

But the cloud of mist encased her. It hoisted her in the air, then slammed itself against the god pool. The mist dissolved, and Masina was nowhere to be seen.

Chapter 7

I stood there, mouth dry, unable to wrap my head around what had just happened. I was going to bathe in the god pool. Masina stopped me. Masina touched the god pool. Masina was now gone. Her last words echoed in my head like a nightmare.

"Lā, help me!"

Why didn't I help her? Why had I been so slow to grab her? She was right there. And I just... I just...

Behind me, my father broke through the crowd.

"Masina!" he cried out. *"Masina!"*

Standing at the edge of the god pool, he turned to me. I shook my head. He grunted, then ran to the water and dove in. The entire village waited in silence, praying that he would find her. But when my father came up, he looked panicked.

"Search everywhere!" he yelled, swimming back. "Divide into groups. Leave no stone unturned until she is found!"

"Yes, High Chief!"

Ecstasy boiled up inside me as Hana's emotions took over. She forced me to double over, laughing as she gripped my sides with glee.

All around me the villagers froze, their faces a mix of disgust and horror. They must've thought I was glad Masina was gone, that her disappearance was somehow hilarious. I tried to tell them it wasn't me, but Hana's will was too strong. She cackled as my father glared down at us. His eyes narrowed.

"Are you not my son?" he said through clenched teeth.

Hana pulled my lips into a smile. "Oh, you are a fool, Alai. A fool!"

She pushed me down onto all fours. My body exploded in pain again. And this time, instead of the horrible sensation of Hana forcing her way in, I felt myself shrivel as her essence spewed out of me. My hands started to wither, so did my legs and feet. The muscled physique was evaporating, leaving a skeletal shell in its wake. When I knew she was gone, I looked up at my father.

But he wasn't looking at me. He stared at the blackness hovering over the god pool. It bubbled and contorted, twisting itself until it solidified into Hana's corporal form.

I gasped. If I hadn't known Hana before, I never would've guessed it was her. Her brown hair was sleek where it had been scraggly. Her skin glowed like polished wood. Instead of rags for clothing, she wore a flaxen gown that cascaded from her shoulders to her waist—a waist that melded into the slender tail of an eel where there should've been legs. She grinned, fanged teeth glinting against the torchlight as she hovered in the air, black wings beating methodically.

"It can't be," my father murmured. He snatched a spear from one of the villagers and threw it at Hana. She dodged easily.

"You've gotten slower, old man," she taunted.

My blood ran cold. Hana was none other than the demon Mā, the one my father had imprisoned years ago. The one who had wreaked havoc on the village long before I was born.

"How did you break free?" my father yelled, his voice dripping with anger.

"You can thank your offspring for that." Mā jeered. "Who knew that his jealousy was all I needed to break you troublesome curse?"

"You're—you're lying."

Mā winked. "Am I?"

Father rounded on me. "Son, tell me you didn't do this."

"I swear, I didn't know—" I started.

"Of course he knew." Mā laughed. "How could he not? Oh, how I hoped he would kill the girl and damn himself by entering these waters unworthily, but this works just as well."

"Go back to the hell where you came from." Father spat.

Mā lifted an eyebrow, clearly amused. "Oh, I'm leaving. And I'm taking a part of you with me, Alai. Actually, she should be there now."

Father's face went slack. "No..."

"Oh yes." Mā broke into another wicked grin. "Your daughter is mine now. Her spirit shall rot with me in the deadlands. That leaves you, High Chief Alai, with *that* for your legacy." her face twisted as she pointed at me, "And that will be your line. Not one of chiefs, not one of great warriors, but an eternal line of weaklings and cowards."

Black mist swirled around her. Thunder boomed, and the demon Mā vanished.

Chapter 8

No one moved. No one breathed. All of us stared dumbly at the spot where she had been. A million thoughts raced through my mind, none of them good. Hana had been a demon this entire time. Her plan was to kill off our bloodline. And I had, I had...

Someone yanked my hair from behind and threw me to the ground. There were cries of outrage as I tried to ward off the men pinning me down. Uncle Logo's eyes bored into me. Aunty Tua's husband gripped my shoulders and High Chief Manoa threw a kick into my side.

"Well, boy?" he demanded. "Is it true? Are you the reason your sister's dead?"

"I—"

The words wouldn't come, but my face said it all. Uncle Logo roared as he struck the side of my head. My eardrum popped, and I thought I would vomit.

"Release him."

Swallowing grunts of disapproval, the three men backed away. Standing where they had been was my father. He didn't look angry, or upset. There was a somber kind of knowing in his gaze, as though this was what he had expected all along.

Somehow, that hurt more than any physical beating ever could.

"Son, why?" he asked. "Why did you do this? *How* could you do this?"

I didn't know what to say. All the rage and hurt I experienced at their hands was nothing compared to what had happened. No matter what was said or done to me, it couldn't justify what I did to Masina.

"I—I didn't mean to," I managed.

"He didn't mean to?" sneered High Chiefess Manaia. "So the demon held a knife to your throat and forced you to free her?"

"No, I—"

"Then it must've been blackmail," said High Chief Moe. "She said she would kill your entire village if you didn't do it."

"Not exactly, I—"

High Chief Senidra cut me off with a sigh. "Boy, you don't have a good reason for what you did, do you?"

Again, I let my silence speak for me. I had no words for them. Even if I did, I doubted they would do any good. Once again, I was keenly aware of how much the village and the council hated me. Only this time, I knew I deserved it.

Light flashed over the god pool, startling everyone into silence. The light pulsed again, and the people surrounding me cowered back, making the image on the water more visible.

Striding toward us was a man dressed in white. He looked eighteen or nineteen, yet something about him seemed ancient. His white sulu cut above his calves, and he had a kīhei tied over his shoulder. Ti leaves adorned his head, and his body radiated light. It clung to him like dew drops on morning grass. The surface of the god pool rippled as he walked, but his feet didn't touch the water. He trod the air inches above it, not touching anything until his feet stepped onto solid ground.

Recognizing his divinity, the crowds fell to their knees, bowing in respect to the heavenly messenger. His poised, regal face regarded them with compassion. He wasn't the light god himself; his clothing marked him as an emissary, or the forerunner.

"My lord Havaiki sends his greetings," the man said to my father. "As well as his condolences for your suffering."

My father, who was on one knee, dropped a fist to the earth. "Is there nothing that can be done?"

"Actually, there is." The forerunner touched my father's shoulder, prompting him to stand. "Arise, my good chief. Your daughter yet lives. It is the will of my lord that I help to bring her back."

Father let out a strangled cry of relief, one that was echoed by the villagers. He gripped the forerunner's shoulder, unsure how to express gratitude to a demigod. "What must we do?"

"I need to counsel with the high chiefs and their heirs," the forerunner said. He glanced at the surrounding villagers. "In private."

The god pool was vacated quickly. The forerunner stood before us as we sat on the rocks, eager to hear his message. He clasped his hands behind his back.

"By way of introduction, I am Marama," he said, "the first forerunner of Havaiki. He wishes for me to emphasize his sorrow that such a time has come to pass for his people. But he is eager to help restore the balance."

"We are forever indebted to your lord and ours," said Orator Ra'i, bowing low. "It is by his grace that our village has thrived. His extended kindness is a mercy we do not deserve."

"My thanks, dear orator," said the forerunner. "Your work to keep our history alive does not go unnoticed in the heavens. Many are indebted to you." Then, turning his attention to the council at large, he continued. "Forgive me for cutting the formalities. It is my understanding that our high chief is eager to see his daughter."

Father nodded. "Where is she?"

The forerunner grimaced. "Her body was indeed taken to the underworld. But she is not dead. Because she was innocent, the great demon had no claim to her spirit. The same could not have been said for you."

He glanced at me. I swallowed as the others stared daggers before turning back to him.

"Does that mean we can rescue her?" Alani asked hopefully.

"It does," the forerunner confirmed. "But we need to hurry. Masina is not dead now, but she will be if her body is left in the underworld too long. We must set sail at once. At most, we have maybe a month."

High Chief Senidra frowned. "And at the least?"

"Ten days. Two weeks if we're lucky."

My mouth fell open. Two weeks? I'd seen my father spend that much time *planning* for a voyage.

"How far away is the underworld?" High Chief Loa asked.

"If conditions are good, we could get there in five to seven days," he answered. "It'll take a skilled crew to navigate there."

"I can do it," High Chief Moe said immediately. "I've brought some of my men. Ori can come with us."

"That's very kind of you, my good chief," the forerunner said, "but this was caused by the follies of a future chief. So it must be a future chief that sets it right."

"Not a problem," High Chiefess Manaia assured. "Tāwhiri will go. Moe, your boy can navigate."

"An excellent idea," said Alani's father. "Please allow me to send my daughter, as well. Of the rising chiefs, her skill in combat goes unchallenged."

"Thank you, my friends." Father bowed to them before turning back to the forerunner. "They are young, but they are ready. They've been preparing their whole lives for this. If Ori could be allowed to have a small crew to help him, they should be able to make it in time."

A part of me felt insulted that my father had so easily brushed over me for the rescue. The thought was quickly replaced by the reminder that this was all my fault. Was I really surprised they didn't want me tagging along?

The forerunner nodded. "I do not doubt their strength nor their character. However, I believe there is one future chief you are forgetting."

Seeing their confused faces, the forerunner pointed at me with his whole hand. "If you wish to have my lord's blessing, this boy must accompany them."

High Chiefess Manaia bit back a protest. Alani glared at me.

"With all due respect, my lord," High Chief Loa started, "he'll only get in the way."

"He doesn't deserve to go with them," echoed the high chief of the Song Village.

"It's his fault Masina was sent there in the first place!"

The forerunner held up a hand for silence. "I appreciate your concerns, but my lord's will is final," he said. "I will accompany young Toa to the underworld. So long as he is actively participating, the rescue party will go with the grace of the light god himself."

No one dared to grumble against him, but several people—chiefs and heirs alike—shot dirty looks my way, like they couldn't believe I had the gall to be alive for something like this.

"Toa's position is non-negotiable," the forerunner continued, "but anyone else who would like to accompany him is more than welcome. No more than two, or three people at most."

"I'll go," Ori said.

"Me too," added Tāwhiri.

High Chief Senidra nudged his daughter. "What about you? Will you go?"

Alani nodded. "Masina is our best friend, and a sister to all of us. Of course I'll go."

"We have our four champions, then," the forerunner nodded in satisfaction. "I need to speak with High Chief Moe and his son with regards to our transportation, but this concludes our meeting. Sleep well, chieflings. We leave in the morning."

I walked back with Alani, Puana, and Tāwhiri. Puana inhaled sharply as we stepped into the encampment. Alani and Tāwhiri looked somber, too. All three of them likely remembering how, just last night, Masina had been here to greet us. She hadn't even been gone for an hour, and already everyone was missing her.

Tāwhiri lit the kukui nut candles as I lowered the coconut-frond curtains around my hut. My foot bumped against something hard and I looked down in surprise at a wooden tray covered in burlap. I bent over and uncovered it.

Sitting on top of the tray was another kahoa lei. It was even more beautiful and colorful than the one I had yesterday. I ran my fingers against the sewn petals, marveling at Masina's handiwork. The smells of our mother's garden rose from it, breathing comfort into me as I inhaled.

"She was up all night making that."

I spun around. Alani was there. She had brought extra blankets for Ori and Koa. She set them down and looked at the lei as she spoke.

"That was why she didn't go with you to the first trial," she said. "When you left before she could give it to you, she assumed it was because something was wrong with it. So she ran back to your mother's garden to sew an extra layer of pikake over the red blocks." She sighed, her eyes going misty. "It was your birthday present."

Alani left, leaving me to feel as though I'd been slapped. My birthday, my own fifteenth birthday. Nobody in the village said anything about it; everyone, including me, had forgotten.

Masina, however, had not.

Chapter 9

That night I dreamt of Masina.

It wasn't a good dream. Her face appeared over and over again, bringing me nothing but pain even though she was always smiling. I saw Masina lifting the curtains to my hut. Masina holding up her kahoa lei. Masina raising her cup to me at the feast.

Masina crying after the third trial....

In between every image of Masina was the image of her face as she was sucked into the underworld. For as long as I lived, I would never forget the panic in her eyes as she reached out to me. I wondered if she was in pain, wherever she was in the underworld. Even worse, I wondered if she blamed me for it.

I woke up when I heard dry leaves rustling. It sounded like someone was coming inside my hut. Yawing, I rolled over to see if it was Koa, or Ori. But the person crouched in front of me was too small to be either of them.

It wasn't even a man.

I wanted to scream, but Alani pinned me down and pressed a damp cloth over my nose and mouth. I breathed in an overpowering smell that made my eyes water. Every muscle in my body went limp, and I was out cold.

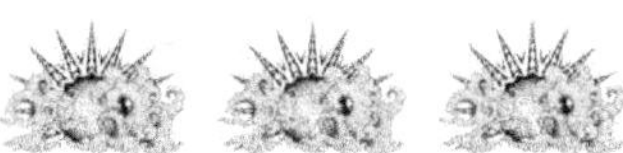

Something hard slapped my face.

I stirred, and tried to turn away from it. When I couldn't do it, I realized I was tied up. Someone, most likely Alani, had bound and gagged me to a tree. Coconut fiber ropes bit into my arms and made my hands itch. I scrunched up my face and shook my head, trying to wiggle out of the gag on my mouth, but it wouldn't budge.

A shorthand torch staked in the ground burned a few feet away from me. Poised next to it was Alani. She held a patu in one hand and Tāwhiri's quarterstaff in the other. Her hands were wrapped like she was about to go in a boxing match. Given the distance, I'd say the quarterstaff was what she used to hit me.

Behind her I saw the shadowed outline of a double hull canoe. I recognized it as the one Ori and his father used. Waves lapped against the shore, and I realized we were in the landing bay. As my eyes adjusted I saw the other canoes the high chiefs had sailed in on.

I blinked away the grogginess of the sedative, wondering why Alani had brought me here. She looked like she wanted to fight me, but if that were the case she wouldn't have tied me up. To my right,

I saw a pit with a mound of earth sitting next to it. For a moment, I wondered if she was going to bury me.

"Are you up yet, you little weakling?" Alani spat. She raised her patu. I flinched, but Tāwhiri grabbed her arm.

"Don't, Alani," he said. "He's awake now."

Tāwhiri held a spear in his other hand. I'd never seen him use one before; the quarterstaff had always been his weapon of choice. What was he doing with this?

And looking at Alani's patu, it wasn't one of the ones she normally used, either. Alani preferred jade, yet the patu she held was made of bone.

Alani pulled out a knife and hurled it towards me. I squeezed my eyes shut as it buried itself in the tree, less than a hair's width away from my left ear. I swallowed hard.

She glared at me. "Well, he shouldn't be."

"That's not for you to decide," said Ori. He stood on the double hull canoe, one hand holding a line tied to the mast and a foot resting on the splashguard. He looked down at me, his face impassive.

"I'm sure you're wondering why you're here?" he said.

I nodded, uncomfortably aware of how close I was to Alani's knife. Or more accurately, how close I was to *Alani.*

"She's not going to kill you," Tāwhiri promised. "But Ori said we had to do this before we leave tomorrow."

Do what? I thought. If Alani wasn't going to kill me, then why drag me out here? And what was the giant pit for? That looked like a good place to dump a body.

Ori jumped down from the canoe, grunting as he squatted into the landing. He held a spear in one hand and a staff in the other. He rested them against his shoulders.

"Tomorrow you, Alani, and Tāwhiri will board my canoe," he said. "As captain, that makes you my responsibility. But I can't focus on navigating if I have to keep the peace between you three. Seven days is a long time to be at sea with someone you hate, and I'll have none of that in my crew."

He set down the spear as Alani pulled out another knife. If Ori could see the panic this caused me, he kept it to himself.

"Alani obviously hates you," he went on. "Tāwhiri might, as well. And I've got a few things I need to say before departing. We brought you here so that we could settle our anger and leave it behind when we set sail tomorrow. Do you understand?"

I nodded, even though I wasn't sure if I did.

"You will battle me first, then Tāwhiri, and finally Alani. You may use this staff to defend yourself, but the gag stays. This is our turn to speak. You'll get yours after."

Alani raised a knife, but Ori stopped her. "Oh, and one more thing. If you try to flee or call for help, Alani will come after you."

He didn't explain any further. He didn't have to. It didn't take a lot of creativity to imagine what Alani would do to me if I tried something so foolish. I swallowed hard.

With a nod from Ori, Alani slashed the ropes, leaving the gag across my mouth. Tāwhiri pulled her away as Ori tossed me the staff. He took his stance.

"Are you ready?"

I stepped forward, bracing the staff in my hands. I nodded.

"Good."

Ori swept my legs with his spear and kicked my stomach. I felt my feet leave the ground as I flew backward, slamming into a tree. Pain exploded down my back as my head cracked against the wood. I slumped over, moaning in pain.

Ori's spear tip jabbed into my chest. I gazed up at him, too rattled to even be afraid. His brow furrowed.

"I told you, didn't I?" he whispered. "I told you that you were too hard on her, that your jealousy would hurt her."

Ori was a big guy. Tall, noble, the kind of guy who looked invincible. Yet listening to him now, he sounded so hurt. Like he was in more pain than I was. He raised his spear again, rolling it around his shoulder before planting it in the ground.

"If it wasn't for you, Masina would be here," he said. "Do you deny it?"

I shook my head. How could I deny it? Everyone knew it was my fault.

"Do you deny your jealousy is the reason why you did it?"

Again, I shook my head. My eyes burned with shame, realizing what I had done. If I hadn't made the blood deal with Mā, None of this would've happened. Masina would still be here.

Ori thumped me with the butt of his spear, prompting me to look at him. He searched my face, deep-set eyes growing more serious as he spoke. "Are you willing to become the brother she needs you to be?"

I knew the correct answer was yes, but I couldn't say it. I wanted to be the brother Masina needed, but I didn't know how. I didn't have any older siblings, and Masina was so perfect she didn't need me, anyway. I couldn't nod, but I couldn't shake my head either. Not sure what else to do, I held Ori's gaze.

Ori studied me a moment longer, then uttered a laugh. "Not where you should be, but a little bit better than where you were before," he conceded.

He drove his spear tip into the ground, then pushed against the shaft with his leg while pulling the dull end toward himself. He grunted, and the spear cracked in half. Bending over, he pried the spearhead from the ground and started to walk away.

"I still don't understand what kind of person could be so cruel," he called over his shoulder. "But I acknowledge your desire to make things right."

He was standing in front of the pit now. He glanced back at me, then held out the two broken halves of his spear.

"Forgiveness is never so simple as saying 'All is well' and letting that be that," he said. "I may need to forgive you again several times during our voyage, but for now."

He dropped the ends of his spear. They clanked against each other before landing with an almost inaudible thud deep in the earth.

Ori closed his eyes and let out a deep breath. "Toa of the Light Village, I bury my hatred for you."

I watched him in disbelief. Ori had relieved me of a burden I didn't know I was carrying. I felt lighter to know he wanted to forgive me.

Ori stepped back, cuffing Alani's arm as Tāwhiri stepped forward. He held his spear with a look of grim resignation.

I staggered to my feet, using the staff more like a walking stick as I steadied myself. Tāwhiri waited. When I was ready, he charged. I bit down on the cloth gagging me, gritting my teeth as I waited for the attack.

It didn't come.

As Tāwhiri raised his spear overhead, he brought it down over his leg, smashing it against his knee. The spear split like Ori's had. He gave a wan smile, seeing the dumbfounded look on my face.

"I do not approve of your actions," he clarified, "but I already made the decision to forgive you before all of this. I echo Ori's words that what you did was wrong, but I will not hate you for it. I know what the kind of damage a fixed hatred can bring."

He tossed his broken spear into the pit, shrugging as he nudged some dirt in with his foot. "It already happened, but Toa of the Light Village, I bury my hatred for you."

Like with Ori, I felt relieved as Tāwhiri uttered the words. I didn't have long to enjoy it, however. Because at that moment, Ori released Alani.

"How *COULD YOU*?!" she shrieked, driving her elbow into my ribcage and back-fisting me in the face. She had wrapped her patu with a cloth to protect me from the sharp edge, but that did little to soften the blows of her angered fists. She hit me with two body shots to the sides, then followed up with an uppercut. My teeth scraped against the gag in my mouth as she grabbed my arm and threw me over her shoulder. The whole time Alani couldn't stop screaming.

"What is wrong with you?" she demanded, kicking my stomach. I tried to get up, but Alani knocked me down again.

"How could you do something so *stupid*??" she punctuated the accusation with a patu strike to my shoulder. I collapsed to one knee.

Alani raged on, beating me mercilessly. "And to think of all those times she couldn't stop talking about you. Toa this, Toa that. What do you think will make Toa happy? Well, tell me, Toa. Do you. Feel. *Happy?*"

She waited for me to get up then tossed me my staff. When I grabbed it with both hands she latched on and shoved it into me. She swept my right leg and twisted. I spiraled midair as she wrenched the staff out of my grip, and landed hard on my back.

Alani dug the end of the staff into my throat. "You know she sailed to my island three times last month? And every time it was to talk about *you*! 'Alani, Toa's mad,' 'Alani, Toa's worried about his next protocol,' 'Alani, what should I get Toa for his birthday?'"

It took me a while to realize Alani wasn't hitting me anymore. Her patu trembled in her grip and tears spilled down her face.

"Toa," her voice broke, "do you have any idea how much she looked up to you?"

I wished she would hit me again. I wished she would break my ribs, break my legs, anything to get away from the disappointment in her voice. If I thought I had known shame before, it was nothing compared to this. Guilt overwhelmed me, and I cursed Alani for not using a sharper weapon.

Alani didn't let up. "I don't want to forgive you. I don't think I can forgive you. You hurt someone so pure, someone who loved you more than the rest of us did. She saw greatness in you, and the only reason I haven't killed you is because I need you to live long enough to prove her right."

"That's not the point," Ori said. "You have to forgive him."

Alani scoffed. "He doesn't deserve forgiveness."

"Then you don't deserve to get on my canoe."

Alani's eyes blazed, and I thought she might kill me in her rage towards Ori. Instead, she stabbed her patu into the earth next to my head, burying it in up to the handle.

"I don't understand people like you," she said. "I don't understand how anyone could hurt their sister. Especially you, her big brother. You're supposed to protect her the way you protect your own eyes. Instead you—"

She couldn't finish. She yanked her patu out of the ground. Dirt rained over my face, getting into my nose and eyes. Alani didn't care. She threw the staff towards me and strode towards the pit. She chewed the bottom of her lip as she held her patu over the hole, cord still wrapped around her fist. She stared at it hungrily.

"I'm going to be forgiving you more than anyone else on this canoe," she muttered. "You're cocky, you're arrogant. You're ungrateful. And if it wasn't for Ori's stupid rules, I'd cut you up so bad you'd spend the rest of your life trying to find the missing pieces."

She looked like she would curse me until the sun came up. Thankfully, Ori interrupted.

"These conditions are unbending," he reminded her. "Time is short, so I need to know now. Alani, can you forgive the man?"

"He's not a man," Alani snapped. But, even as she said it, she rotated her wrist, letting out some of the slack. Her patu dropped down several inches.

Tāwhiri rested a hand on her shoulder. "We don't forgive because we approve of what's been done. Nor do we do it as a sign of defeat. Forgiveness is simply the decision to stop letting another person hurt you."

He cupped her wrist. Alani sighed as she rolled out the rest of the slack. She held the patu by the cord; the body of it swayed back and forth.

"While I cannot even begin to fathom why you are the way you are," she said, "I am willing to forgive you for Masina's sake. I will forgive you as many times as I need to, if that's what it takes to bring her home. Toa of the Light Village I—"

Her breath caught in her throat. She bit down hard. Then the words came out in a rush.

"Toa of the Light Village, I bury my hatred for you."

She dropped her patu, watching it as it fell. Seconds later. it clanked against the broken pieces of wood from two different spears at the bottom of the pit.

Chapter 10

Alani stared into the pit, looking for all the world like she wanted to jump in and retrieve her weapon. But she didn't. She wrapped her arms around herself and let out a sigh before walking back with Tāwhiri.

Ori went back for the torch. He came back and sat cross-legged, elbows against his knees and torch burning in his right hand.

Tāwhiri pulled me up to a sitting position. "You don't have to lie there anymore, you know," he teased. "I'm pretty sure that was the worst of it. Right, Alani?"

"Not now, Tāwhiri," she huffed.

Ori tsked. "You really did a number on him, Alani." He held the torch to my face. "A few more bruises and people will his skin is purple instead of brown."

He wasn't exaggerating. Alani had beaten me so bad it hurt to sit up. She hadn't broken any bones, but every muscle in me ached.

I wiped the blood dripping down my chin, refusing to cry out. I didn't blame them for wanting to hurt me. If anything, I was surprised they hadn't hurt me more—especially Alani. Compared to what I knew she could do, she had gone easy on me.

Alani pulled out a bone knife and started fingering the blade. "You said to let it all out."

"I did say that." Ori shrugged. "And thank goodness I had the gods' blessing when I did. Otherwise Toa would be in no condition to sail tomorrow."

Tāwhiri looked up at the moon, frowning. "I thought he would be here by now."

"Does this mean we can have another round with little Toa?"

"Shut up, Alani."

Ori drove the butt end of the torch into the sand, bringing one hand under his chin. "I guess demigods run on their own time. We may as well proceed while we wait for him." He gestured at me. "You can take off the gag now."

I reached for the cloth around my mouth. My arms screamed in protest, and I couldn't stop fumbling the knots. Tāwhiri reached over and undid them for me. The cords fell into my lap, and I massaged my sore jaw.

"Thank you," I murmured.

He laughed. I frowned at him, puzzled.

Tāwhiri shrugged. "Oh, it's nothing. I just can't remember you thanking me for something before." He cocked an eyebrow. "I wouldn't mind if you did it more often."

Blood rushed to my swollen cheeks. Did I really never say thank you?

Ori rested his elbows against his knees.

"Sorry we had to meet like this," he said, "but I hope you can see now why it was necessary. A crew holding grudges is like a crew cut in half. We would never make it to the deadlands like that."

I nodded, my neck aching. "I understand."

"You took your lickings like a man," Ori noted. "I'm impressed. And now that you've heard us out, we're willing to hear what you have to say."

I braced against the pain as I curled my legs under me. Struggling not to collapse I stumbled into a bow, pressing my forehead to the earth. I felt their eyes on me and swallowed hard, not sure what to say.

Tāwhiri took my shoulders from behind and prompted me to sit up.

"We're not gods, mate," he said. "And even if we were, I don't think you'd want to pray to us."

I shook my head, unable to laugh at the joke. "You've given me more than I deserve. All of you. I—I know this is my fault, and I'm going to make things right."

Alani scoffed. "Why? So that you can be high chief?"

I winced, unable to defend myself. She was right. All my life, I had focused on becoming high chief—on claiming my birthright and becoming a great man. But now, I didn't even know what that meant.

I closed my eyes, agitated. "I just don't want that to be my last memory of Masina."

Her face, how terrified she had been when she tried to grab me. I had never seen Masina look at me that way before, like a frightened girl desperate for her brother's reassuring hand. Masina never needed protection; she never needed anything. But at that moment I was the only one who could've helped her. And I failed.

Light burned behind my closed eyelids. When I opened them, I had to squint because of the brightness. The light glowed brighter, then solidified into the shape of the forerunner. He acknowledged me with a nod, his face stern and regal.

"You seem like a boy that's ready for a change," he said.

I swallowed and looked down. "I just want to be the man I should've been all along."

"And what kind of man is that?"

One who doesn't make blood deals with demons and sends his sister to the underworld, I thought, but that hardly seemed appropriate. Besides, I wanted to be more than that.

"Someone who's not afraid to do the right thing," I said after a while. "Even when it's hard."

Masina said that during the second trial. It felt weird quoting her, but I couldn't think of a better way to put it. I didn't want the rest of the crew to think they'd have to drag me kicking and screaming to the deadlands.

The forerunner rubbed his chin. "I wouldn't mind sailing to the deadlands with someone like that."

He offered a hand. Fingers trembling I strained to take it. As his hand clamped over mine, I felt a jolt of energy. The glow radiating from him washed over me. A tingling sensation came over me as the light sank into my skin. I watched in awe as my bruises disappeared. Every cut and scrape knit itself back together and all the soreness drained out of me. I rose to my feet, unable to believe what had happened. I was *healed.*

"Thank you, my lord," I breathed.

"You didn't think we would leave you like that, did you?" Tāwhiri asked.

"I would've," Alani said.

"And we would've stopped you," said Ori.

The forerunner laughed. He reached out. The staff I had used started to glow, rolling over in the dirt before floating up to his expectant hand. He dusted it off, then held it out to me. The glow vanished when I touched it. I stared at it, not sure what I was supposed to do.

"Everyone else buried something that would hinder them on your journey," the forerunner said. "Now it's your turn. For them, it was hatred. For you, it must be your former self. Kill the old Toa so that the true chief of the Light Village may rise. Can you do that?"

His words shook me more than Alani's patu had. Kill the old Toa? How could I possibly do that? And who would I be once he was gone? Both Ori and the forerunner seemed to think I had this great potential in me—the potential to be something more than I am. I wanted to believe them, but the man they wanted me to be seemed unattainable. That kind of man, one who was brave enough to go after her and strong enough to pull her out, was someone I could never be.

"You don't have to be perfect at it," Tāwhiri said. "It's not like we expect you to be a completely different person tomorrow. All we're asking is that you try."

"Forgiving yourself is often harder than forgiving another," Ori said, "but over time, you will heal."

Doubt swam in my head. With a sinking feeling I realized those doubts wouldn't go away for a long time, even if I did promise to become someone better. And it was like Alani said; I really didn't deserve it. After everything I had done, who was I to even think I should try?

At that moment, a memory of Masina flashed across my mind. It was when she raised her cup to me at the feast. Last night it felt like a mockery. Now, however, I saw something else.

He is my quiet strength, she had said.

My grip tightened on the staff, and I hated myself for not seeing it sooner. It really didn't matter whether or not I deserved to hange. Masina was still out there, still caught in a net I had laid for her. Whether or not I deserved forgiveness, redemption, or anything else was irrelevant. If I couldn't become someone better, I would never reach her. There was no way I could kill the old Toa just for the sake of it. But I could kill him for Masina.

I knelt on one end of the staff with both knees and pulled at the other end with my arms. It took a few tries, but eventually, the solid wood snapped. I had no trouble tossing the splintered ends into the pit, imagining the Toa who had made a blood deal falling with them.

I turned to the others, "I don't know what I'm supposed to say," I admitted, "and I know I'm going to mess this up, but I'm willing to bury the old me as many times as you need me to. I won't complain. I won't get in the way. I'll do everything I can to make sure I'm not a burden until my sister is safe at home."

"Until?" Alani repeated. "So that means you're planning to be a butt again when we get back?"

I flinched. "It means I don't know how long I could keep this up."

"And that's enough for now," said the forerunner. He nodded to Ori. "You can bury it."

We shoveled the mountain of dirt into the hole. It was a weird feeling—like something had woken up inside of me. A lost part of myself that I hadn't realized was in there. I didn't know what to make of it, but I felt better. Like I really was burying the old me, the jealous brother who took things too far.

Ori patted down the loose dirt when we finished.

The forerunner looked pleased. "Well done." Then, looking up at the sky he added, "Young navigator, please wake the rest of the crew. We must prepare to leave."

Chapter 11

With the Navigator Village being an overnight voyage away, Ori and his father had only brought five men with them. Including the two of them it was the bare minimum needed to sail a canoe that size. We had the added benefit of having three extra people, but none of us were as experienced as Ori and his men. Ori tried to see if we could recruit wayfinders from the Light Village, but the forerunner said that wasn't an option. The rest of us would simply have to pick up the slack.

Neither Alani nor Tāwhiri was upset by this. Alani studied under her father's navigator, and Tāwhiri's mother made him work as a crewman when they sailed out for protocol.

I, on the other hand, didn't know anything about running a canoe. And the few times I had been on one, I was seasick every time. Whenever we left the island, Father had one of the healers sedate me for the entire trip. So much for not being useless.

Our departure was a private affair. Aside from the men needed to launch the canoe, only the high chiefs and their heirs came to see us off. When it was time to say goodbye to our parents, High Chiefess Manaia started lecturing Tāwhiri. High Chief Moe ran another safety check with Ori. Alani embraced Puana before her father pulled her away to talk battle tactics.

My father didn't have much to say, unlike the other chiefs, who couldn't stop talking. He gave me a quick hug that was little more than a shoulder tap.

"I'll do my best, Father," I said, trying to sound sincere.

He looked over at Alani and Tāwhiri, who were lining up for the push.

"Son," he said, "just promise me you'll bring her back safe."

I swallowed hard, wishing I could promise that without feeling like a liar. Thankfully, Ori called me over, and I didn't have to say anything. Ori pulled me up onto the canoe before jumping down behind his father. I helped two of the crewmembers hold the rudder in place as a group of fifty men and chiefs pushed the double-hull canoe down the pier. Ropes were tied to the two hulls in the front, and people ran ahead into the water to pull it forward.

As the canoe splashed into the tide, Ori jumped on. He pulled one of the ropes that controlled the sail. The canvas fabric billowed out, rotating with the boom as Ori and his men guided it. It caught a gust of wind and the canoe surged forward. Ori's crewmen pulled off the ropes tied to the front of the hulls. They splashed into the water to the cheers of the men and women on the shore. Alani and Tāwhiri scrambled up as the canoe lurched over another wave. Ori shouted orders as he continued to work the sail, his crewmen rushing to obey. Together they steered us out past the surf, out to where the land vanished into pinpricks of green against the pink morning sky.

Our journey to rescue Masina had begun.

INTERLUDE

Alai was the last to leave the landing bay. Long after the other high chiefs had returned, he still stood there, knee-deep in water. Staring at the spot where his son had vanished, he felt more alone than he had in his entire life. Like a childless widower. The ache left in his heart when Ta'i had died never truly healed, and in less than two days he had lost both of his children.

He clenched his fists, forcing the thought out of his mind.

No. They are not *lost.*

Toa was nobody's first choice to rescue Masina. Alai would be lying if he said he felt any different. Toa had a strong head, but his body was weak. Watching him board that canoe was like watching his only son climb into his grave.

"Standing there won't make them come back any faster," said a voice behind him. Alai recognized it as Senidra's.

"Waiting in the village wouldn't make any difference," he retorted.

Senidra laughed, now standing shoulder to shoulder with his old friend. "At least there's food in the village. But I think I know what you mean. It's hard, isn't it? Letting them go instead of us."

Sometimes Alai thought Senidra was too cheerful to be high chief of the War Village. How anyone could be that optimistic after a lifetime of bloodshed was a mystery to him. Senidra often said the same thing, joking that Alai was too serious to lead a place called the Light Village.

Alai sighed and massaged his eyes with one hand. "I'd rather sail that canoe by myself than let my kid take it to hell."

"Wouldn't we all?" Senidra's smile faltered. "Alani's my only girl, and of all my children she's the most like me. Confident, headstrong, much better at communicating with a weapon than she is with her words." His laugh turned bitter. "I never thought I'd be sending her out like this. I can lead a battle. I can get impaled during combat and still win the fight. But tell me my daughter's in pain and I can't do anything about it?" He shook his head. "It's every father's worst nightmare."

Alai winced, knowing how Senidra must've felt. He felt the same way about Masina. "It was hasty of me to allow your daughter to join this, Seni," he said. "I'm sorry."

"She'll be fine," Senidra clapped him on the back. "That wasn't a funeral canoe, Alai. Have faith in our kids. There must be something they can do that we can't."

"Precisely," chimed in High Chiefess Manaia.

Alai jumped, unaware that she was standing there.

She raised an eyebrow at him. "Do stop sulking, Alai; it's not becoming. What, do you think our children can't do it?"

Alai had expected Manaia to be in the village by now, back to business. She always emphasized being proper and maintaining appearances. Seeing her like this, waist-deep in water with her hair undone looked almost comical. Alai had never seen her look so undignified. But he didn't laugh; he understood all too well. One's own children had a way of getting them to do things they never would've done otherwise.

"It's not your children I'm worried about." Alai confessed. He hated to be the parent that couldn't believe in his child, but Toa was not a fighter. He knew nothing of survival, and Alai worried he had coddled him too much in his weakness. There was a time when Alai had truly thought Toa would grow up to be a greater warrior that he was. But then Masina came, and that changed everything. Toa's hopes of becoming the village hero died with her first breath.

Senidra nodded. "That son of yours looks like a twig with legs. But if the gods say he can do it, I won't argue. Besides, he seemed like a changed man this morning."

"It's true," Manaia agreed. "There was something different about him."

Alai had to admit that something had been different. He didn't whine or complain, like Alai thought he would. Maybe it was because he felt sincere regret at Masina's disappearance. Maybe it was because now he couldn't compare himself to her.

"They can do this," Moe reassured, stepping up to Alai's left. "They have each other, five of my best men, and a forerunner of your ancestor, Lai. I think that puts the odds in their favor, don't you?"

Alai nodded, but said nothing. Right now he didn't want to talk, and he had a feeling no one else did, either. So they stood there until the sun was well above the horizon. Then, almost in unison, the four parents waded back to shore and down into the village. Now that the sun was up and the village was awake, they couldn't afford to sit around worrying.

That was the life of a High Chief; they didn't have time to quibble or whine. They had their people to care for and a demon on the loose. The borders would need to be strengthened, and should that devil send more of her children, Alai would soon have a war on his hands. The familiar stress he carried as the high chief weighed heavily on him. But as Alai met with the village officials, all he could think about was Masina's helpless scream and Toa's stubbornness as he boarded Moe's canoe, off to face dangers that would likely get him killed.

The weight Alai carried as a high chief was heavy, but the weight he carried as a father somehow always felt heavier.

Chapter 12

The seasickness was worse than I thought it would be. I hadn't left the island since protocol meetings were held at the Navigator Village two years ago, and even then I spent the entire voyage drugged out in a hammock. Now here I was: without the sedative and on open waters. We had only been out for a few hours, yet already I had thrown up twice over the side of the canoe. A feat Tāwhiri said was remarkable, given that none of us had eaten yet.

I hoped Ori would let me take the first shift off once he knew about my motion sickness, but I should've known better. He merely tossed me a gourd and told me to check the storage compartments for excess water.

"You get seasick because you never learned how to deal with the ocean," he said. "We are now on the ocean. I suggest you learn how to deal with it."

The double-hull canoe felt smaller now than it had on land, and I understood why Ori had said everyone needed to be on good terms. There was nowhere to hide on the canoe. If two people were to stand on opposite ends of it, they still wouldn't have any problem seeing or hearing each other.

The only privacy we ever got was when an extra sheet was pulled up in order to bathe or relieve ourselves over the side of the boat. Even our sleeping quarters had to be shared, as there weren't enough for everyone to have their own.

The hollowed-out hulls of the canoe had six separate compartments. Each had a sleeping bunk in the top half, and underneath was where we kept our supplies. We partnered up with someone who would be working while we were sleeping to maximize space. The only ones who didn't have to share a sleeping compartment were the forerunner, who objected to it in spite of his status, and Alani, who bunked alone since she was a girl.

Ori had divided us into two teams to work the canoe. He hadn't included himself and the forerunner since, as captain and navigator, they would work with both teams as much as possible. The watch captain for the few hours when Ori needed rest was Alaka'i, who had been High Chief Moe's second in command.

Alaka'i and the four men that had come with him were all near their early twenties; the youngest was only a year older than Ori. That made them adults compared to us, but they were still novice wayfinders. None of them had ever been at sea this long unsupervised. In effect, we were future chiefs being led by future navigators. It would almost feel poetic if it didn't imply we were practically sailing blindfolded.

Alaka'i was twenty-one. While he was older than Ori, he was still a junior to him when it came to wayfinding. Ori has been sailing since he was seven; Alaka'i started when he was fourteen. With wiry hair and an infectious smile, Alaka'i was the polar opposite of Ori. Lighthearted where the other was serious, and much more down-to-earth. He had worked every position from cook to carpenter, and could fill in for any role if the crew.

The same could be said for all the Navigator men. Lali and Loli, two twenty-three-year-old cousins, were the best at cooking, although they argued about whose food tasted better. They both had the same dark skin and angled features, but Loli was taller and kept his long hair in a bun on top of his head.

Pule, the carpenter, was twenty. His right index finger was missing from a carving accident and he looked like he had never smiled in his life.

That left Temanu, the eighteen-year-old ship doctor. All the Navigator men knew first aid, but if any serious illness or injuries arose, they assured us Temanu was the one we wanted.

The two teams were divided as such: Lali, Pule, Alani, and Temanu worked one shift. Alaka'i, Tāwhiri, Loli, and I would cover the other. This way, when Ori needed to rest, we would have at least four men on duty. Five including the forerunner.

I climbed into all six storage compartments, verifying that they were airtight and free of excess water. When I crawled out of the last compartment, it was time for the first watch. Since I still looked nauseous, Ori decided that our team would go first. Alaka'i called for Tāwhiri to help him adjust the sheet lines. I ran to help, but Loli threw his arm out in front of me.

"Woah, there," he rumbled in his low voice. "Just where do you think you're going?"

I frowned, pointing over his shoulder at Tāwhiri. "I'm helping with the sails."

Loli made a face. He turned to the sail, then back at me. "Okay first off, they're not sails. It's just a sail. Singular, not more than one. And second..."

He stuffed me in a side hug and steered me towards the front of the canoe.

"Hey!" I shouted. "What are you—"

Loli shook my shoulders to cut me off. He pressed forward, undaunted as he took me to the edge of the deck and bodily threw me over the splashguard. I smacked into the left hull, scrambling to hold on as the canoe pitched up and down.

"What are you doing?" I cried, my hands slipping on the slicked wood as salt water sprayed my face. Bile bubbled in my throat, and I feared I might throw up again.

Loli tied a rope around one of the stays and swung himself down. His feet planted firmly against the hull as he pulled me up, ignoring my cries of protest.

"You can't help me cook if you have to empty your stomach every five minute." He positioned my hands to grip the rope the same way he was. "So hopefully this can help you get over that."

I coughed. My stomach spasmed, and I clapped a hand over my mouth. "I don't think it's working," I said, nauseated.

Loli laughed. He passed me a piece of ginger root to chew on. The taste burned in my throat and made my eyes water, but I did feel a little better.

"You'd be surprised how many people get seasick," Loli said. "I know men with saltwater in their veins who still get queasy on a voyage."

I raised an eyebrow.

"No, seriously!" he said. "In fact, we've got one in our crew. Don't tell him I told you, but Pule gets it bad. You know it's coming whenever he does extra safety checks or stands at the rudder so he can throw up behind him."

I looked back at Pule and noticed he had something in his mouth as he laid on his back. Feeling the pungent root on my own tongue, I realized he must've been chewing ginger, too. It was hard to imagine a guy like Pule emptying his stomach like I had.

"Size doesn't matter when it comes to that sort of thing," Loli said. "It's just something that affects people differently. But, that's not why we're here."

He pointed down at the water. Following his gaze, my eyes widened. There was a dark shadow gliding next to the canoe. It was half the length of the deck, triangular wings flapping in the water as it cruised along. Loli shifted his finger, pointing out more shadows like it. One of them drew closer and I made out the white spots of a manta ray.

I gasped. For all the stories I heard, all the carvings and tattoos I had seen of these creatures, this was my first time seeing them in real life. They were bigger than I had imagined, and brought the humbling sense of awe Masina described after going out with the fishermen.

"Our ancestor Kalia rides with us," Loli said with a smile.

He gripped his rope in one hand and braced his legs against the hull. Leaning out, his fingers brushed the surface of the ocean. The manta ray surged upward and Loli laughed, nodding to me as he pulled himself back up.

"Come, Light child," he said. "See if you can count how many there are."

My stomach churned as Loli walked me down the side of the hull. The wind tousled my hair and saltwater sprayed in my face. The manta rays fluttered close to the canoe. I counted six of them, each one larger than a grown man. Peering into the deep, I watched them curl backward, their gilled bellies reflecting the sunlight above. One leaped out of the water, pectoral fins flapping before it splashed back down. My grip on the rope loosened as I let go with one hand, pointing excitedly with the other.

Loli sat down on the hull, feet dangling over the side. "See? The ocean's not so bad."

I leaned away from the canoe and let my fingers run through the water, eyes on the manta rays. "Not at all."

We sat there for the better half of an hour. Loli told me all about the ocean and the creatures that lived there. He also told me how wayfinders relied on ocean swells to navigate. It didn't cure my motion sickness, but knowing the constant movement kept us on course was comforting.

Eventually, Alaka'i came looking for us. Seeing Loli on his back and me with my feet in the water, he crossed his arms in a sign of mock anger. "Having fun?"

Loli wagged his eyebrows. "We were, but then you showed up. So I guess that's over now, eh?"

Alaka'i shook his head. "You know, if you're going to adjust the stays by the safety net, I need you on the board by the safety net. You're no good to me down there."

"Sorry boss." Loli said, winking at me. "But you have to admit, the Light child looks better than before."

Alaka'i snorted. "He's got more color in his cheeks, I'll give you that. Still, Loli. Don't teach him any of your bad habits. For now, you two take over for Tāwhiri at the fishing lines. I need to see how well he can put a bowline on a bight."

We crossed to the other side of the canoe, then climbed under the navigator's chair to a small cutout deck. Tāwhiri was sitting there, holding two fishing lines loosely in each hand. He looked bored as he drummed his fingers against the mo'o of the canoe.

Loli hopped over the railing. "Eh, Wind child," he said. "Ka'i needs you on the deck."

Tāwhiri threw his arms in the air. "Praise the gods!" he said, dropping the fishing lines and scrambling up top.

Loli picked up the lines, shaking his head as he turned them over.

"No wonder he wasn't catching anything," he said. "Look how short the lines are."

I couldn't see what he was talking about, but Loli insisted they needed to be recast. We reeled them in, looping the coils of fishing line around our arms. When the hooks resurfaced, I was surprised to see the bait was picked clean off.

"You see?" Loli tsked. "Our Wind child was feeding the little fishes for free."

He disappeared above deck before returning with fresh slices of squid, which we pierced through the lines Tāwhiri had been holding. Loli showed me how to tie off the first one, then had me finish the other three. This time, he made sure we left out twice the slack that Tāwhiri had. Bigger fish, he explained, were skittish around canoes. That was why we needed a longer line to lure them in.

"Your knots aren't bad, Toa," he said. "You'd make a fair fisherman."

I laughed. "I don't have the muscle for that."

Loli raised an eyebrow. "Since when do you need muscle to throw a hook in the water?"

I shrugged, not sure how to answer. I didn't know Loli before today, but he must've been there for the trials. He had to know what kind of person I really was.

"You think rather poorly of yourself, don't you?" Loli observed.

I cringed. "Why shouldn't I?"

Shame welled inside me. I wanted to help, but even I knew I was only here because the gods commanded it. If it weren't for that, the others would've left me behind.

"You shouldn't because you already did the forgiveness ritual," Loli said simply. The conviction in his voice made me fumble the lines, and I was grateful we had tied all of them to the ship for security. I looked at him, unconvinced.

He turned his palms up. "The old you died, remember? So stop digging up his grave."

He went back to the deck.

I fingered a line in my hand, staring out at the brilliant blue of the ocean all around me. This was the longest I had ever stayed awake on a canoe before. It made me feel small, but not in the way that I felt small next to Masina. Out here, she'd look pretty small, too.

I wrapped the line around my fingers, giving a few lazy tugs. I imagined the hook wiggling with at the end of the line and wondered if any big fish were swimming by. Masina said she preferred diving to line fishing because it was less guesswork. Now I knew what she meant.

The line snapped around my hand, and I lurched forward. Coarse fibers bit into my skin, and I cried out as I braced my legs against the railing. There was another tug as something threatened to pull me overboard. I strained with all my might against it.

Loli!" I shouted. "Loli! Help!"

Feet pounded behind me as Loli appeared. His head jerked back in surprise. Then he clapped his hands and let out a whoop.

"What did I tell you, boy?" he cheered. "We'll make a fisherman out of you yet!"

He called for the others as he grabbed the line. Soon Lali, Tāwhiri, Ori, and Alaka'i were there. They crammed inside the lower deck and we pulled together. Alaka'i jumped over the catwalk to pull from the outside. Whatever we had caught thrashed at the end of the line.

"This feels heavy!" said Tāwhiri. "Loli, are you sure *Toa* caught this?"

"It's not caught until it's in the canoe," Ori grunted, "Keep pulling!"

We wrestled with the fish until the sun reached its midday zenith. The air was ripe with sweat, and before long we saw a massive ahi shoot out of the water, less than ten feet away from where we were. My mouth fell open. That thing was as big as I was!

We pulled with renewed vigor. Alaka'i called for Alani to ready her knife from above. With every inch of line reeled in our excitement grew. The ahi continued to jerk and pull at the other end. Then the water glowed silver as the it neared the surface.

On the count of three, we heaved it onto the catwalk. The canoe vibrated as the fish beat against it. Lali and Loli pinned it down while Alani brained it between the eyes. She sank her knife in deeper, then pulled it out. The ahi beat its tail once more, then grew still.

"Praise to the ancestors," Alaka'i breathed.

Up close, the silver-scaled fish was bigger than I had imagined. It was longer and wider than I was. And as everyone struggled to pull it inside, I wondered if it was heavier, too.

Once we had heaved it onto the deck, Ori called for a moment of prayer. We bowed our heads and closed our eyes as he honored the ahi for giving us life, then offered his thanks to the ocean goddess Kalia and to the light god Havaiki.

"You see?" Loli said, winding me as he slapped me on the back, "You're not useless at all. The gods must think highly of you to give you such a big fish on your first try."

I laughed uneasily. "Either that, or they felt sorry for me."

"Doesn't matter to me. Pity or praise we still get a big fish," Loli chuckled. "But if your theory is true, then it's a good thing you skinny, ah? If you looked more like me, you might've pulled up something smaller."

"It's still just a fish," I said, embarrassed at the praise.

"Just a fish?" Loli was amused. "Wait until we cook it. You'd be amazed at how much good food can help people."

Loli had already started a fire in the stone oven we had in the middle of the boat. He told me how it was done as he rinsed the ahi so that I would be ready for the next meal.

The stone chest was like a makeshift 'umu. It stood elevated on four stacks of flat rocks and had a canvas on each side to protect it from the wind. The long side facing me had a latch on it, acting as a door. Inside there were two shelves, the bottom one much skinnier than the top. The bottom shelf was where we stoked a fire to heat it up, and the food went on the top.

In their preparations last night, Loli had cooked ulu and kalo as they packed, just in case we ran into a situation like this. While I was watching the fishing lines, Loli ignited a pulu to heat up the rocks in the 'umu while Tāwhiri grabbed the premade starches to warm them up.

Per Loli's request, I fetched extra coconuts and some onions. I sliced the onions as Tāwhiri and Alaka'i husked the coconuts. Loli fileted half of the ahi, dicing it into tiny cubes and setting it into a bowl. He called for me to bring him salt, green onions, tomatoes, and a cucumber. I fetched and rinsed all of these for him, watching as he chopped them with an expert hand. He mixed them with the raw fish, then doused the whole thing in fresh coconut milk.

Everyone wanted to eat it right then and there, but Loli beat them away with his spoon—saying it needed time to marinate. When it was ready, he had me divide the raw fish evenly into ten bowls. For the finishing touch, we pulled open the stone 'umu and gave everyone some hot ulu and kalo to go with their meal. I poured drinks of fresh water and coconut juice while Loli set the bowls in a circle.

As everyone sat down to eat, Loli spread his arms like a proud parent. "Lunch is served!"

The crew offered a quick prayer, then let out a cheer as everyone dug into their food. There were moans of pleasure, and I watched everyone's faces light up as they filled their bellies. I reached for my bowl, only to have Loli whack me with his wooden spoon.

"Ow!" I complained.

He glared at me. "What do you think you're doing?"

I looked down at my bowl. "I'm...eating?"

Loli closed his eyes and sighed. "Oh, great Kalia, help me to teach this one."

I started to feel defensive, but Loli pointed to the other half of the ahi, which laid butchered and uncovered on the deck.

"Were you gonna leave that for the flies?" he asked.

"There's no flies out here," I grumbled. Still, I knew what he meant. We couldn't leave a fish like that out to spoil, especially since we didn't know when we'd catch another one like it.

Besides, Loli added, we weren't the only ones still working. Ori and Alaka'i were steering the rudder; the forerunner stood in his chair and called adjustments to them. Like us, they would eat later. There was always something to do on a canoe.

So while Temanu shouted his compliments and Lali strummed his 'ukarere, I stayed with Loli. We sliced, salted, and seasoned filets he said would sit for a few hours before we marinated them. Loli showed me how to cover and store the fish in a cool, dry place where it wouldn't spoil. Once that was done, and I could repeat back to Loli everything he had taught me, he finally let me eat.

Lali and Tāwhiri made room for me in the circle, their bowls empty as they clapped me on the back.

"That was some fish you caught, Toa!" Tāwhiri laughed.

"And it was sooooo good." Temanu drooled.

"I can't wait to see what's for dinner!"

Lali nudged Alani. She jostled her food, but stayed composed.

"What do you think?" he asked her. "Does it satisfy your appetite?"

Alani plucked up a cube of raw fish and popped it into her mouth, chewing silently. I bit the inside of my cheek as her eyes flicked up at Lali, then to me.

She nodded. "It's good."

That was it. No praise or even a smile. But I knew the true value of her words. Alani didn't give away compliments; she made people work for them.

I exhaled in relief. Her mouth quirked into what might've been a smile, then she looked away.

I nursed the bowl in my lap. The fish was warm and the ulu had gone cold, yet it was the best meal I could remember. Looking back on my life I couldn't recall any moments like this, surrounded by friends talking and laughing, all of them enjoying a meal I had made.

Sitting with them now, our mission didn't feel as impossible as it had before. I couldn't swing a war club or kill a pig, but I could still be useful. I could cook, I could catch a fish—

"Oi, Light child!" Loli called. "You gonna help with these dishes, or what?"

And I could also wash the dishes.

INTERLUDE

Mā was beginning to think Alai′s daughter was more trouble than she was worth.

Even without her corporal body, the girl ravaged Mā′s home and killed every demon she had on hand. Mā was still fuming about that; she could make as many minions as she wanted, but they still took *time*. She was already rushing to breed them by the thousands; now, she had to add an extra eighteen to the list.

Mā had heard tales of the great Masina, the pearl of the Light Village. Yet watching a ten-year-old behead a monster twice her size wasn't something Mā was used to seeing. With a little redirection, she could bring the living world to its knees.

If only she'd stop crying.

Despite all her strength, Masina was a little girl who couldn't handle the situation she was in. He arms hugged her sides as she sat cross-legged on the cave floor, rocking back and forth. She hadn't moved from that spot for hours.

"I want to go home." she whimpered.

Mā massaged her temples "You've already said that."

Masina sniffed. "So can I go, then?"

"No," Mā snapped. "Look around, child. This is your home now."

She gestured at the cavern they were in. Black clouds plumed along the walls and curled against the ground. Cages stacked by the hundreds filled the room. Each contained the souls of the vengeful, the wicked who sought justice through Mā's dark magic.

Masina shook her head, wiping her nose with the back of her hand. "This isn't home. I want my dad and my brother. And Ori, Alani, and Tāwh—"

"You've said that before, too." Mā cut off. She rolled her eyes; every time the girl added more names to the list of people she wanted. "And as I may remind you, again, you don't want them. Especially your brother. He betrayed you."

Masina glared at her. "You're wrong about him," she said. "He loves me."

Mā sighed. *Here we go again.*

"Child, your brother sold your soul to me so that he could keep his title," Mā said. "He's not coming for you."

"Yes, he is," Masina said stubbornly.

"He's the reason you're here," Mā reminded her. "He cared more about winning than he did about you. The smart thing for him to do now would be to let you die so that no one can fight him for his title." Mā shrugged. "That's what I would do if I were him."

In reality, Mā was surprised to hear the little sun warrior was with the rescue crew. The complicated things, and Mā didn't like it. She wondered what the light god was playing at—sending such a pathetic opponent after her.

"Lā would never hurt me," Masina insisted. She folded her arms tighter, as though that emboldened her statement.

"Never?" Mā slithered across the floor. Masina shrank a little, and it thrilled the demon to see the child could feel fear. She touched the wall behind Masina and it dissolved, swallowing Masina in a cloud of darkness. Mā circled her as she spoke.

"Tell me, Masina." she said. "Who put those ugly bruises on your face?"

Masina brushed the dark splotch on her cheek. Doubt flickered in her eyes, but only briefly. It was there for a second, and then gone.

Masina set her jaw. "That was your fault," she said. "You tricked him! You made him think trusting you was the only way to win the trials. If it wasn't for you, this never would've happened."

She wasn't entirely wrong; tricking the boy had been part of the plan. So had the initial raid that interrupted the last protocol meeting and cast even more doubt on the boy. But if Masina really thought her brother would protect her, she was sadly mistaken. Mā almost pitied her.

Oh child, she thought. *How very wrong you are.*

She really wasn't going to give up on him. Even after everything he had done, Masina still trusted her brother. He could drive a knife through her heart, and Masina would die saying he was trying to kill a bug. Attacks against the boy would not persuade her; Mā would have to try something else.

She paused, shifting her tail so that she was staring down at Masina. Masina jutted her chin defiantly, and Mā raised an eyebrow in amusement. Such insolence. With a little more hatred, she could be great. Power like this was wasted on the innocent.

Perhaps this could remedy that. "Very well then, child. Believe what you want. Let's say that your brother would never hurt you."

Masina smirked triumphantly.

Mā held up a finger. "But did it ever occur to you that you might be the one hurting him?"

Masina looked like she'd been slapped. Her face contorted in rage and a burst of light shot from her spirit, giving her enough color that she almost looked alive again. Mā recoiled, the light hitting her skin like a hot iron. She fell to the floor, smoke curling off her burned skin.

So much power...and all of it in the hands of a child.

"I would never hurt my brother!" Masina spat.

Mā ground her teeth. Rage boiled inside her, but she forced herself to calm down. Masina, she reasoned, was still useful to her. She uncoiled her tail, allowing Masina to see the blisters smarting against her rubbery skin.

"Oh, but you are hurting him," she said, wincing against the pain as she pushed herself up. "Your very existence is an insult to him. Tell me, Masina, haven't you ever wondered why you're so strong? Has it never bothered you that no one, not even the bravest warriors in the Light Village, could never do what you do?"

Masina inhaled sharply. Her brightness dimmed like a blown-out candle. She tried to recover, tried to put her brave face back on, but Mā knew she had her.

Masina furrowed her brow. "What do you know about it?"

There was a definite hunger in her eyes. Masina was more stubborn than a wild boar, but even she understood there was something unnatural about her. Something that, for whatever reason, no one ever bothered explaining to her.

Mā grinned, flashing her pointed teeth as she summoned the darkness around her. The cool touch of the mist eased the sting from her burns, and within seconds she was healed. She sighed with relief. It had been a gamble, but she was correct; Alai had never told his daughter the peculiar nature of her powers. Perhaps he did it to protect her. Maybe he was genuinely afraid of her.

Whatever the reason, Mā was grateful for it. Now she could use the revelation to seal the Light Chief's fate. It was all she could do to keep a straight face as she started spinning the tale to crush her soul.

"It's the reason why he hates you, you know," she said. "And it's the reason why he'll leave you here to die."

Chapter 13

"Pull harder, Toa, come on," Ori urged. "If my little cousin can adjust the sheet, you can do it, too."

"I bet he wasn't adjusting it by himself," I grunted.

Before stepping on this canoe, I always thought a sheet was a piece of fabric. But out here, it was the rope that ran across the sail, and needed constant adjustments to keep us on course.

"Hey, less talking more pulling," Loli said. He stood behind Ori, the two of them feeding me slack from their end of the sheet. "And for the record, she did pull the sheet by herself. She dislocated both her shoulders, but she still did it without complaining."

Adjusting the sheet was a four-person job—with two people pulling while the other two fed them slack. But Loli had asked that I pull by myself today. Said it was a good "teaching moment."

I threw the sheet around my back, wrapping my wrists around it to grip it tighter. The course fibers rubbed against my palms, but that was a pain I was used to. As I leaned back into the sheet, the boom and the spar holding up the sail slowly began to pivot left.

"There he is!" Alaka'i said, smiling.

"Keep going, Toa," Ori said, his eyes on the sail. "Loli, let's give him some slack."

Loli loosened his grip, and the sheetline grew less taut. My muscles groaned as I squatted back, pushing against the rope that ran across my back.

"A little more," Ori murmured. "A little more....Okay, hold her there."

I froze mid-squat, stumbling to one knee as I tried to stay in place. Across the deck, Ori turned to the forerunner, who was up in the navigator's chair behind me.

"What do you think?" he asked.

The forerunner stood on his elevated chair. He looked out past the end of the canoe, taking everything in from the sun above to the rise and fall of the deck against the ocean. His face was passive, but moments like these were crucial. As navigator, the forerunner was constantly making calculations. Compensating for leeway, calculating our distance traveled, observing ocean swells and celestial lights—all of that kept us on course.

He closed his eyes, and nodded. "Better. You can tie her off and adjust the rudder. You remember how the swells should hit, captain?"

Ori nodded, then turned to us. "You heard him, men. Tie her off."

We tied the sheet into a knot at each ends of the canoe, securing the sail as it adjusted to the change in pressure and sucked us forward. I exhaled in relief, my arms aching. The Navigator men made it look easy, but moving parts of a canoe this big was exhausting.

Ori crossed the deck to Alaka'i and Tāwhiri by the rudder. The two of them scooted back so that Ori could grab the front of the massive oar, and together they steered to the right.

"That's it, right there!" Ori called out when they were in position. "Hold her steady, men. I'm going to secure it."

Reaching for the coil of rope we kept near the right hull, Ori tied it down next to the railing. Tāwhiri moaned as he flopped onto the deck.

"Every time I do that, I swear I'm being pounded into poi," he said.

Loli smiled. "If that were the case, I think you'd be kalo juice by now."

He was referring to the bruises welling on Tāwhiri's side. He, Alani, and I all had them; some of the Navigator men had them, too. When it came to steering, smacking into the rudder repeatedly was unavoidable.

When we first pushed out, I had underestimated how heavy the rudder was; it looked like a stick poking out at the back end of our canoe. But when Alaka'i put Loli and I on steering rotation, I felt the full weight of it. Feeling mischievous, Loli had let go, and I flew off the canoe as the rudder flopped behind me.

"Oh, I'm sorry, Light child." Loli chuckled as he pulled me back. "I just had to see if that would be as entertaining in real life as it was in my head."

I thought that would get me kicked off rudder duty, but if anything, it just made Loli more determined to prove my size didn't matter. I thought that was easy for him to say; Loli could pick up three of me with one hand. But he pointed out how Alani and Temanu could steer even though they weren't that big or strong. He didn't care that I was inexperienced; he just wanted me to pick up the slack.

Loli rolled his shoulders, stretching them out. "You know what's great to do after something like that?" he asked me.

"Take a nap?" I said hopefully.

Loli laughed. "Nope, even better." He nudged the stone 'umu with his foot. "What are we making for dinner?"

I smiled and ran to get the ingredients. Everyone rotated jobs on the canoe, but Loli and I always cooked. We spent the bulk of our time on duty prepping meals and planning what to cook for the next one when we weren't.

I could see now what Loli meant when he said good food worked wonders at sea. Mealtimes were a highlight of the day, something everyone looked forward to. We spent so much of our day working, or trying to stay out of each other's way. Breakfast, lunch, and dinner were the only times we really got to bond as a crew.

Everyone was so appreciative every time Loli and I set out the bowls and plates. And while Loli joked it was because nothing made food taste better than an empty stomach, the others seemed to genuinely love what we cooked for them: pan fried mahi mahi, hearty stews, buttery lau lau with hot fa'i.

The only thing I enjoyed more than cooking was watching everyone's reaction as they ate. Weary faces lit up and slumped shoulders straightened after a good meal and a few stories from the Navigator men. And the same people whining about their jobs before eating went back to it joyfully with a full stomach.

By a stroke of luck, Tāwhiri's octopus trap had pulled up a squid, which I planned to make into some old-fashioned fe'e. Loli started the fire as I sliced the squid. After eight meals of cooking with Loli, I could now salt, season, and sauté all kinds of seafood—all while cutting on a rocking piece of wood. Loli never had to check on me anymore.

About an hour later, we served up another successful meal, one that smelled so good we coaxed our sleeping crew members out of their bunks.

"You know the food is good when it starts to wake people up," Loli said, nudging me. My chest swelled with pride, once again beyond thrilled by our own cooking.

After dinner, Loli went to collect water for the dishes and I started scraping food scraps into the chum bucket. It was part of Loli's fishing strategy; by throwing a bag of chum in the water next to the fishing lines, we could lure in more fish, and the ones that were big enough to bite down on the hook would be the ones we ended up catching. It was simple, yet ingenious. This way we could se up our food scraps while increasing our chances of catching something.

"Either that is a fascinating bucket of chum, or someone is getting distracted," came a voice.

Startled, I flipped around to see the forerunner standing behind me. He wasn't as tall as Ori or broad like Alaka'i, but his presence made me shrink. We hadn't spoken since the forgiveness ritual. Like with everyone else on board, I tried to stay out of his way.

"Apologies, my lord," I said, dropping my head. "I meant no offense."

He smiled, unaffected by my shyness. "None taken. Come, Toa, I'll help you finish."

I nearly dropped the bowl in my hands. The forerunner wanted to help *me* to make *chum*? Could I get struck by lightning for this?

"It's alright," I said hastily. "I should've been faster. I apologize for not—"

He cut me off with a shake of his head. "What are you apologizing to me for?" he said. "I'm not your taskmaster; I'm your navigator. If you think that means I need to be pampered, I must be doing something wrong."

He smiled again. For a moment I stood there with my mouth open, shocked at how casual he was. All my life, I had been taught to honor authority in all its forms. My father, the elders, high chiefs from the other villages—even children a month older than me deserved my utmost respect. It was shameful to treat someone of rank like an equal. Now here I was, trying to respect someone above every rank imaginable...and he didn't want it.

Looking at him now, I noticed the forerunner wasn't wearing the formal attire he had at the god pool. Instead he wore a simple sulu like the rest of us. He didn't have to do that; even if he was acting as navigator no one would've thought twice if he had kept his divine apparel. But he hadn't.

The forerunner picked up a soiled cutting board and motioned for me to pass the knife. When I didn't, the dirty utensil glowed white as it floated up to him. Embarrassed, I kept my head down and ran the empty dishes to Loli, praying he would switch with me. He didn't, of course; he was too busy arguing with Lali about whose fe'e tasted better. Grumbling inwardly, I went back to the forerunner, who hummed as he cleaned out a bowl.

"You seem to be enjoying yourself," he said after a while.

I nodded, not sure if I should speak. Protocol mandated that children should be seen and not heard. Then again, protocol also mandated that heavenly didn't gather scraps for chum, yet here we were.

He lifted an eyebrow. "It's not a sin to speak, you know."

"M-my apologies," I murmured, my voice cracking. My cheeks grew hot. Nobody had ever covered this in a protocol meeting, but something told me I wasn't exactly showing god-appropriate behavior. "Apologies, my lo—"

He sighed. "More apologies? If this is what it's like to be a god, I think I'll quit now. All these formalities."

He shuddered. A laugh escaped out of me, and I tried to disguise it as a cough. Then I realized I didn't know which was worse—laughing or coughing in front of a demigod.

The forerunner smiled. "Ah," he said. "I see that you are, in fact, human." His shoulders were relaxed and his smile genuine, reminding me of when I met Loli.

"Is this normal?" I blurted.

He laughed. "For a servant to be serving others? I should think so. Do not let my abilities fool you, Toa. I am nobody special."

"Hard to say that compared to the rest of us," I murmured. For the love of Havaiki, the man could *glow*!

But the forerunner shook his head. "I'm sure the fish in the sea thought the same thing when they first saw birds flying overhead. But once they realized their feathered friends couldn't swim..." he shrugged, rinsing the bowl in his hands.

I looked up at the sky. The sun was melting into the horizon with the first pinpricks of starlight poking through the heavens. It was beautiful.

"If I were a fish," I said, "I think I would still be jealous."

The forerunner nodded. "And if I were a bird, I might be as well. Birds can't swim with the manta rays or dive into the deep like other animals can." He paused, then shook his head. "But enough of that. Tell me about this sister of yours."

The sudden mention of Masina came as an electric shock, and I was reminded once again it was my fault we were out here. Loli insisted I let the old Toa die, but that was hard to do when his follies still hounded me.

"She's definitely the bird out of the two of us," I said. "Although I guess she could be the fish, too. Masina loves being in the ocean."

I told him what an excellent diver she was and how much she loved going out with the fishermen. The forerunner asked how she had learned so quickly, and I replied she hadn't really "learned" at all. For Masina, fishing, hunting, and fighting came as naturally as breathing. She never had to think; she just did it.

"She means a great deal to you, doesn't she?" he asked after I had told him about Masina's newest hobby, lei-making.

My mouth quirked in a smile, remembering her face as she held up her first kahoa lei.

I made it myself, Lā! I love you!

"She is the better one out of the two of us," I said. "I may spend the rest of my life catching up to her."

The forerunner nodded. "I used to feel that way about my older sibling, too."

I frowned. "You have siblings?"

The forerunner laughed. "No, the gods just snapped me into existence and realized what a mistake that was. No family should ever be punished by my presence."

Seeing the way my cheeks colored, his smile widened. "I'm kidding! But to answer your question, yes. I have siblings. I also have parents, auntys, uncles, and lots of cousins." He looked up at the moon, his smile sagging. "You think you've got it bad? Most of my siblings have achieved the rank of godhood. Try living up to those standards."

"Oh, I—" I didn't know how to respond. For an immortal demigod I had never expected to hear him say something so...human. Maybe the gap between gods and humans wasn't as wide as I had thought.

The forerunner shook his head, as though coming out of a dream. "Forgive me for souring the mood. Perhaps it was a mistake to tell you such things."

I shook my head, grateful he had confided in me. I wanted to tell him this, but already the forerunner was passing dishes to Lali, who had relieved his cousin of duty.

"Thank you for your diligence during the third watch, Toa," the forerunner said with his back turned. "You ought should rest. The next six hours will go by very quickly."

He picked up a rag and started to wash. Lali raised an eyebrow at me, and I turned up my palms. At least I wasn't the only one who thought the forerunner was acting strange. But, knowing better than to argue, I corked the chum bucket and stowed it away. My head barely touched my pillow before I fell into an uneasy sleep.

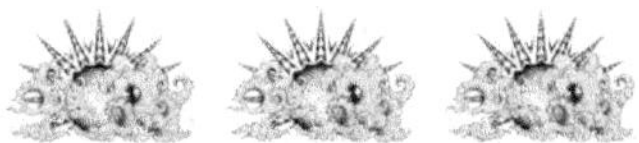

I woke up when I heard the music. It was faint, the sound of it dancing above the canvas covering my bunk. It was dark. Veiled moonlight shone through the fabric, and my foot thudded against the hull as it pulsed through the waves. I almost went back to sleep when I heard it again—music. It sounded like humming.

My eyes widened; I knew that song. More than that, I knew who was humming it. How could I not? This was how she woke me up every morning. I threw back the canvas, peering out onto the deck. My heart stopped.

It was Masina, climbing a stay tied to the mast. Her long hair flowed behind her as she shimmied up and threw her legs over in a side-straddle, her foot twisting around the line beneath her to hold her in place. She held on with one hand and stretched out the other, swaying back and forth as though she were about to fly. All the while humming that familiar tune.

I stumbled out of my bunk, feet heavy as I forced myself to walk. The moon shone bright against the sky with shards of starlight scattered across it. No one else was on the deck. A part of me wondered where the crew was as I staggered towards her. She had her back to me, her arms open out to the ocean. The wind lifted her hair, revealing the kaulima on her left arm.

"Masina?" I breathed.

Above me, Masina tensed. She pulled closer to the rope and pressed her cheek against it. Then she brought her free arm around the stay, flexing her foot as she slid back down. She touched silently against the deck.

"Hello, brother," she said, not looking at me.

Her long hair shadowed her face, but there was no mistaking her. I knew that hair, knew those toned arms and the gown she wore. It even smelled like her: the subtle scent of pikake flowers mixed with coconut oil. Nobody was this good at imitation; this was my sister.

I let out a surprised laugh, excited and a little overwhelmed. "Masina, I don't believe it! You're here!"

I stepped towards her, but Masina retreated. Her shoulders hunched.

I froze. Masina had never tried to run from me; usually it was the other way around. Her shrinking from me was like Ori trying to give up sailing. It wasn't natural.

My smile evaporated. "What's wrong?"

"Nothing," Masina said, hesitating. Then she shook her head. "Everything? I don't know, it's all so confusing. But Lā, you shouldn't be here."

"Why not?" I said, making a face. Then I realized what she must be thinking and I laughed. "Because you're here? I guess that does change things. We don't have to waste our time at sea, anymore. We can go home now."

I stepped forward again, but Masina moved down onto the catwalk, maintaining her distance. She gripped the stay, drawing an invisible barrier between us.

"That's not it," she said, her eyes still downcast. "I'm not...I'm not really here, Lā. I just came to warn you."

As though to confirm her words, the ship lurched, spraying saltwater onto the deck—saltwater that passed straight through

Masina's body as though she were nothing more than a cloud of mist.

Or a ghost.

I sank to my knees, all emotion draining out of me.

Oh, gods, please no, I prayed. *PLEASE no.*

"Masina," I whispered, "are you...are we...?"

The words wouldn't come. Masina hugged the rope in the crook of her elbow and pressed both palms to her eyes.

"I'm not dead," she said. "But I don't think I'm alive anymore, either."

A tear slipped out of my eye, trickling down the side of my face. "Where are you?"

"Close," Masina said. "But not too close. And I'm not exactly far away," she shook her head. "It doesn't matter. I just came to tell you I'm going away, now. And you won't have to worry about me bothering you anymore."

"What?"

Masina had always been my ʻopihi—sticking to me like a sea urchin no matter how many times I ripped her off. And despite that, she never complained. It never occurred to me that, at some point, Masina might get tired of it. That if I pushed her hard enough, she wouldn't want me anymore.

"No, Masina, it's not like that," I said, sitting back on my knees as I tried to search her shadowed face. "I know I messed up, and I'm doing everything I can to fix it. We're coming for you. Me, Ori, Alani, and Tāwhiri. We've even made new friends in the crew, and we all care about bringing you home."

Masina stooped lower as though the words pained her. I scooted forward, panic swelling in me at the thought that my sister might not come home with me. Not because of demons or some curse we couldn't break, but simply because she didn't want to.

Masina crouched on the catwalk, looking smaller than I had ever seen her. "It's okay, brother," she said, her voice muffled as she spoke behind the railing. "You don't have to do that. It's dangerous, and things are only gonna get worse."

"No, I want to," I said, agitated. "Masina, I mean it! I'm not that person anymore," my voice cracked. Masina flinched as though I had hit her. "I just want to bring you home."

Masina lifted her chin, moonlight spilling onto her face. I gasped when I saw her. Angry welts peppered her nose and cheeks. Her left eye was blackened, and a bruise ran from her right cheek down to her jawline. Hatred surged inside of me. Who *dared* lay a hand on my sister?

But as Masina's lower lip started to tremble, I remembered where those injuries had come from. Cuts she had gained from scraping the ground as she rolled away from me. A black eye from a blow intercepted with her club. And the worst one, the bruise that took up a quarter of her face, from when I had hit her so hard her body flipped midair. These were injuries I had given her during the third trial.

"Masina, I—" I started, but my own shame choked back my voice. What could I possibly say to her? Sorry? Did I really think sorry was going to make up for this?

Masina's chin drooped to her chest, and her body started to blanch. Her black hair and dark skin faded until they matched the silvery glow of the moonlight above. Her clothes changed with her, turning that same pale silver, making her look more ghostlike than ever. The cuts pulsed red, the bruises stuck out darker and more hateful than they had before, and when Masina looked at me tears of moonlight welled in her eyes.

"It's okay, brother," she said. "Don't look for me. I know you don't really want to."

She let go of the rope, her body wraithlike as she drifted away. I cried out as I lunged for her. But Masina's transparent fingers passed straight through my own, and she vanished.

Chapter 14

Ori stood at the prow, his little finger and thumb measuring the distance between Hina and Tane, two stars in the Celestial Siblings line. All stars in that line rose and fell along the same path in the night sky, making them ideal for navigation. If those stars aligned with his hand when he stood at the prow, they were still on course. If not, it meant they were drifting, and needed to make adjustments.

Thankfully, the stars aligned perfectly. Hina shone at the tip of his pinky, and her brother star Tane rested below Ori's thumb. Hovering above the horizon was Lia, the third star in the constellation. Ori lowered his hand, satisfied they were still on course. Behind him, Alai spoke.

"Um, captain?" she asked.

"Yes, Alani?" he said, not turning. He was going through his usual mental checklist, the one he obsessed over to make sure he didn't get everyone killed. The first item for the evening shifts was to measure the stars. Ori triple-checked, holding his hand out to make sure Hina and Tane hadn't moved. Stars aligned? Check.

Ocean swells?

He rubbed his feet against the deck, feeling the pulse of the canoe rocking against the waves and nodded. Check.

Morale?

Ori thought about the crew. They had plenty of food and water. Nobody was sick. And so far as he could tell, everyone got along fine. Even Toa and Alani were—

"Captain!" Alani called, this time more insistent.

Frowning, Ori looked back at her. Alani stood aft of the sheet with Pule, and walking drunkenly in front of them was *Toa*.

His eyes were closed. Ori watched dumbfounded as he stumbled across the deck, muttering to himself. His hands moved as he talked, and he seemed to focus on one of the stays on the right side of the canoe. Ori followed his gaze, but nothing was there.

Temanu, made a face as Toa nearly stepped on his saina leaves. "Hey!" he complained, looking up at Toa's sleep-disturbed face. He glanced at Lali. "I'm not the only one seeing this, right?"

"What's wrong with him?" Pule asked.

Alani prodded him with the butt of her knife. Toa twitched but didn't wake up. He paced in a small circle by the catwalk, muttering to himself.

Lali made a face. He looked at Toa, then to the rope he was mumbling at, then back to Toa. "It looks like he's having a very important discussion with that rope over there. Not to say that there's anything wrong with that, I mean I like that rope, too. It's a nice rope."

Pule scoffed, "It's not *that* nice."

Ori stepped through them, nudging his crewmen aside as Toa fell to his knees. His face twisted in agony, as though he were pleading with an invisible tormentor. Ori called for Temanu, asking for an assessment.

Temanu rested the back of his hand against Toa's forehead, then pulled away as Toa started waving his arms agai., "He doesn't have a fever," he said. "He's probably just sleepwalking."

"I don't know if this counts as sleepwalking," Lali said, "It looks more like he's possessed."

Light glowed behind Ori as the forerunner peered down from his chair. He crouched beside Toa as he looked up at their navigator. "There's nothing...otherworldly about this, is there?" he asked.

"Oh, there is," the forerunner said grimly. "It's not possession, but I'm afraid it's something I shouldn't interfere with."

Ori furrowed his brow. "Shouldn't?"

The forerunner nodded, climbing down from his chair, "Do you remember how you said that forgiveness is never simple? It looks like our little chief is re-learning that lesson. He is being forced to acknowledge the consequences of his actions. And that's something every man has to learn for himself."

Alani tilted her head. "So you're saying that this,"—she gestured at Toa—"is caused by guilt?"

"Partially, yes." The forerunner knelt in front of Toa, who was reaching for something by the catwalk. He sighed. "Don't let his eagerness or enthusiasm fool you; this boy has not forgiven himself. He may not be able to for a long time."

Toa started to whimper, and a tear slipped down his right cheek. Ori had never seen anything so pitiful in his life, except for maybe when Masina came to him after the chief trials. He didn't think he could take any more.

"Can you stop him?" he asked the forerunner.

The demigod shifted uncomfortably and looked away. "She's almost done."

Whoever "she" was, the forerunner didn't say. Everyone on duty was silent, their eyes averted as Toa continued to pine for someone or something that wasn't there. Moments later, he let out a strangled cry and collapsed to the deck, sobbing.

That was what did it for Ori. He couldn't leave anyone in his crew like this, not even if they deserved it. He grabbed his shoulders. "Toa," he said, "Toa! Wake up!"

Toa's eyes flew open and he tried to jerk away from Ori, but he pinned him down. Toa writhed under his grip.

"Umsorry!" Toa yelled, his voice slurred. "Idnt meanut! I'm sorry!"

Ori shook his head. "Toa, relax. It's just us."

But Toa wasn't listening. He continued to struggle, growing more and more frantic as Ori tried to calm him down. Not sure what else to do, Ori pinned arms to his sides and stood up, lifted Toa overhead.

"Toa, *that's enough*!" he yelled.

Toa's eyes went wide, and he stopped struggling. He stared down at them, looking from one perplexed face to another.

"Look at me," Ori said. Toa's head snapped to face him, now looking more confused than afraid. Ori felt the tension drain out of his arms. He raised an eyebrow at him. "You good now?"

Toa nodded, and Ori set him back down. Toa sank to the deck and pressed his palms to his eyes. Ori waved for the crew to return to their positions. They obeyed, each glancing nervously at Toa as they passed. Even Alani looked concerned. That was good; she was forgiving him.

Ori knelt down, resting a hand on Toa's back. "Are you alright?"

Toa shook his head. "What happened to me?"

"You would know better than us," said Ori. "We just saw you walk out of bed with your eyes closed."

Toa winced. "Sorry."

"Don't be," Ori said. "Stranger things have happened at sea."

He clapped him on the shoulder, but Toa didn't look up. He had that sunken look in his eyes, one Ori knew meant he didn't want to be here. Ori's frown deepened; emotional turmoil was dangerous. Nobody liked to talk about it, but feelings of anger or deep sadness could be just as damaging as broken bones. Sometimes more.

"Toa?" he asked. "Do you need to talk about it?"

He shook his head. Ori wanted to insist, but thought better of it.

"Okay," Ori said. "I respect that. But I still want you to get checked." he called Temanu. "Make sure he's okay. Give him the sedative if he can't sleep."

"Yes, captain!"

"Try not to overthink tonight," Ori said, standing up. "We can look into it more if it becomes a problem, but for now you need your sleep. The next watch begins in two hours."

Toa nodded before scooting over to where Temanu was waiting for him. Ori silently envied that Toa would be going back to sleep; he could count on one hand how many hours he'd slept in the past three days. Even now, his eyelids felt heavy and his body ached. But Ori would never complain. This was part of his burden to bear as a captain. Someday, it would bleed into the burden he would carry as high chief.

So as Temanu dabbed sedative potion under Toa's nose and Loli snored in his bunk, Ori took over at the rudder so that Lali could help Pule adjust the sail. The star Tane was drifting to the right, and the swells were hitting at the wrong angle again. Those needed constant monitoring to avoid lateral drift, and Ori was one of two people on board who could correct it.

He yawned. A captain's work was never done.

Chapter 15

I didn't tell anyone about Masina—partly because I didn't know if they would believe me, but mostly because I wasn't sure if I believed it myself. Temanu said I was sleepwalking; did that mean the whole thing was a dream? A vision?

Whatever it was, it was too painful to think about. I knew no one expected much from me, but somehow hearing Masina say it herself made it a million times worse.

Loli nudged me with his elbow, shaking me out of my thoughts. "Oi, Light child," he said. "Watch how you're cutting. We're making lomi, not onion poi."

He was referring to the way I sliced the onion he'd given me. Loli had asked me to dice it into cubes, but I had minced it to the point it was starting to look like mush. If it weren't for last night I might've laughed; it really did look like poi.

"Sorry," I said. "Should I get another one?"

Loli waved the thought away. "May as well see what we get with this one. Set that aside and start on the other vegetables. Try not to make those into baby food, eh?"

I gave a half-smile. "I'll do my best."

With today being our fourth day at sea, Loli said we needed to finish off our most perishable foods, which was why we were serving lomi style ahi for dinner. I wanted to make lau lau to go with it, but we had used up all of our kalo leaves before on the second day; they wouldn't have lasted much longer than that.

It wouldn't be long before Loli and I would be trying to invent a million ways to cook sweet potato and tapioca. And that was when the real challenge would begin for us as cooks; it was easy to be happy when we ate like chiefs three times a day. Swap that for boiled tapioca every meal, and the mood would change very quickly.

"Hopefully, we'll have your sister on board when that happens," Loli said. He propped open the lid on the stone 'umu. "I'm sure the crew will be so happy to see her they'll eat anything we put in front of them."

I winced, thinking about how "happy" Masina had been to see me last night.

"That might be sooner than you think," Ori said behind us. He and the forerunner were climbing down from the navigator's chair. The forerunner seemed nervous, but Ori looked relieved.

Loli lifted his eyebrows, "Well, don't keep us waiting. Tell us the good news; how far away are we from eternal damnation?"

The forerunner managed a smile. "Closer than I hope you'll ever have to be again. Men like you are too optimistic for the underworld, Loli."

"Listen up, crew!" Ori called out. "Come closer, all of you. I want everyone to hear this."

"We can already hear you just fine," Alani called back. She was on the opposite side of the deck, hanging her laundry on the line she had made before walking over. She slipped a knife out of her dress and started twirling it between her fingers.

Once everyone was within earshot Ori cleared his throat.

"Based off our calculations the deadlands are close," he said. "We should arrive two watches from now. Once we do Alani will run point on a scouting mission to help us come up with a plan."

Alani dropped her knife. "Ori, are you saying what I think you're saying?" A watch shift was six hours long. If we only needed two to get to the deadlands...

Ori broke into a rare smile. "Men and woman," he said, "tomorrow we rescue Masina!"

The crew erupted into cheers.

"This is almost too easy," Tāwhiri laughed. "I thought we would've at least come across a sea monster or something first."

"Eh, don't jinx it," Alaka'i warned. "I've been on voyages that went south in the wrong ways. Trust me, this is better."

Loli clapped me on the shoulder.

"What do you make of that, Light child?" he said, "You'll have your sister back in no time."

"That's—that's great," I said, forcing a smile. In my mind all I could see was Masina's spirit with tears of moonlight spilling down her cheeks.

Don't look for me, brother. I know you don't really want to.

I clenched my fists. I didn't know how I would do it, but somehow I would prove to her that wasn't true. Somehow, I would get her to come home—even if it meant taking her place in hell.

After everything that had happened, I owed her that much.

Chapter 16

The next watch flew by. All hands were on deck, everyone eager to keep the canoe moving as fast as possible. Now nearing the end of our fifth day at sea, we prepared for the real challenge of bringing Masina home. Alani did combatives with Tāwhiri. Pule ran multiple safety checks, and I helped Loli with our rations. Lali and Temanu were on permanent standby near the rudder, ready to make any adjustments to avoid lateral drift.

"Lo, Lali, bind the sheet," Ori said. "Ka'i, Pule, steady on the rudder. There's a storm brewing out west, and I don't want us to hit it."

"Looks like a big one," Alaka'i grunted, noting the dark splotch of gray in the distance. "What are the odds that's our welcoming gift from a certain demon?"

I shuddered, thinking of the black clouds that took Masina. Could the demon Mā create storms with those? Would she use them to keep us from the deadlands?

But the forerunner was shaking his head. "I wouldn't worry about it," he said. "She can possess, contort, and manipulate, but she can't control the ocean. That power belongs to the goddess Kalia and her representatives."

The Navigator men pressed a fist over their hearts at the mention of her name. Their heads bowed in unison as each offered a silent prayer to their patron goddess.

"That's a relief," Tāwhiri said when they were done. "Sounds like the worst she could do, then, is try to push us in there."

He laughed, but no one else did. We glanced at the forerunner, all of us wondering the same thing. *Could* Mā do something like that?

He shrugged. "I wouldn't put it past her. Among many things, she can be quite...persistent."

I shuddered, remembering the chief trials. How long had Mā been planning that? And even now as we neared the deadlands, were we still playing into her hands?

"How do we know when we're at the deadlands?" Alani asked, unwrapping the knives she had used for practice with Tāwhiri. She had a few bruises from his quarterstaff, but it was nothing compared to the welts smarting against his arms. Tāwhiri didn't complain; he knew the welts were Alani's equivalent of a love tap.

"Green," the forerunner replied, a faraway look in his eye. "You'll see a lot of green."

"Green?" Alani raised an eyebrow at me. I shrugged, not understanding any better than she was.

"He means a green light," Ori clarified. "One that's most visible at night. Once the sun sets, that'll become our mark."

"But why is it green?" Alani persisted. "Shouldn't it be black? Or marked by skulls and dead bodies?"

The forerunner laughed, his solemn face breaking into a rare smile. "That's a mortal stigma," he said. "Death and life are connected; death leads to new life and in many ways is what gives it value. They're two halves of the same whole, and green is the color they share."

As he said it, the sun dipped below the horizon, a green light flashing in its place. It was directly in line with our canoe, pulsing with the rise and fall of the waves. My heart leapt to my throat. We were closer than I had thought.

The forerunner sighed. "Men and woman, behold the deadlands."

The entire crew roared with cheers of delight. I did my best to imitate it, forcing a smile when Loli thumped me between the shoulders. I stood with him at one end of the sheet, Pule and Alani waiting at the other.

"You ready, Light child?" he asked.

I nodded, not sure if he was talking about shifting the boom or saving my sister. Either way, I was about as ready as I would ever be. In front of us, the green light was drifting left, and my grip tensed on the rope in my hands.

"Fix your line, men," Ori said to the crew members on the rudder, "Eyes on the—"

He was cut off as the canoe lurched to the right, jerking so fast the left hull rose out of the water. I skittered across the deck and smacked into Ori, whose knees buckled as the canoe slammed back down. Behind me, Loli braced himself against the spar. Pule and Alani were flat on their backs. The two of them scrambled to their feet, Alani's eyes darting about as she slipped a knife out of her dress.

The canoe slowed to an awkward stop, the sail unable to catch the breeze. We bobbed perpendicular to the green light of the deadlands, the prow pointing west.

Ori pulled me up. "Are you alright?"

I nodded, my heart racing. "What happened? Did we hit something?"

Alaka'i scoffed. "You're in a crew full of Navigator men and you thought we'd hit something? In the middle of the ocean? Good gods, Toa, I'm almost offended by that."

"Then what happened?" Ori asked, raising an eyebrow at him and Tāwhiri at the rudder.

Alaka'i held up his hands. "I don't know, captain, but I can promise you it wasn't us. Even I can't make that kind of turn."

Ori frowned. "Then who—"

He was cut off again as the canoe shot forward. It cut through the water so fast the wind whistled in my ears. I lost hold of Ori as I flew back, scrambling to grab the sheet before I flew overboard. I tried to right myself, my feet leaving the deck every time we bounced against the waves. Behind me the green light of the deadlands was shrinking, fading away as we were sucked towards the storm.

"What's going on?" I yelled, my voice cracking over the wind.

"I don't know!" Alani yelled back. "It's like we're in a riptide."

"It's not a riptide," the forerunner called. "It's her. Look at the water."

I looked over the railing, my blood running cold. Sure enough, the water surrounding our canoe was an unnatural shade of black. It didn't reflect the moonlight or move with the rise and fall of the ocean. Instead it was a thick trail of black mist, one that led straight to the storm clouds. In the opposite direction the light of the deadlands looked even smaller, drifting away like Masina had in my vision.

Ori gritted his teeth, pushing off the spar to grab onto the rudder. "Oh no. You. Don't," he grunted. "Manu! Get behind me. Everyone else to the sheet. That slimy eel won't get away with this."

We did as he said, the forerunner jumping behind me while Lali and Pule went to help Loli. It was hard to hear Ori's commands over the wind, and his mouth was barely visible in the darkness, but we did it. We shifted the boom while Ori's team pulled hard on the rudder, angling our canoe to catch the cross breeze.

The canoe lurched as we spun out of the black riptide. Nobody relaxed until that unnatural stream was well behind us, and the deadlands were visible again. Once we saw the green light pulsing against the horizon everyone collapsed to the deck, exhausted.

"Take that, you old hag," Tāwhiri gasped, punching his arms in the air.

Alaka'i swatted his head. When Tāwhiri complained, he said, "'The worst she could do is try push us into the storm,' eh?"

Tāwhiri rubbed his head sheepishly. "Sorry."

"I wouldn't relax yet, men," Ori called. "She tried to derail us once; she might do it again. Lali, keep an eye out up front. Everyone else, stay put."

No one spoke as Lali slid into place by the safety nets, our eyes glued on the deadlands as though they might get ripped away again. As the green light of the entrance pulsed nearer, I started to relax. Maybe the worst of it was over.

Something rammed into the right side of the canoe. The force of it sent tremors down the deck.

Alaka'i threw his hands up. "Good gods," he said. "Now what is it?"

The canoe shook again as something hit us from the left hull, eliciting gasps of surprise. I peeked over the edge, but saw nothing. All eyes turned to Ori, awaiting orders.

"Hold her steady," Ori said to the rudder men. He glanced at the forerunner, who called to pivot the boom towards the wind. The canoe slowed beneath us, rocking to an uneasy stop.

Two more shoves came under the canoe, one on each side. I fumbled the sheet as the deck bucked side to side. My eyes fixated on the glowing entrance to the underworld, anxiety welling inside of me. We were closer than before but still not where we had been before the riptide. I didn't know if I could handle getting thrown off course again. Every minute we were delayed was another minute Masina spent in hell.

The forerunner left the rudder, peering over the catwalk. His brow furrowed as he stretched out his hand.

"Havaiki, help me," he prayed. The light that shone off him pooled into his hand, and he poured it into the water. Like liquid sunshine, it illuminated the depths below us. He swirled his fingers in a loop, and the liquid light stretched into a circle around our canoe. Its glow intensified.

Across the deck, Temanu gasped.

"There!" he cried. "I saw it!"

Everyone leaned right to see what he was pointing at, but then Lali yelled from the safety net, "There's another one over here!"

"We've got two by the rudder!"

"One more under the left hull!"

More underwater shoves came. They weren't as violent, but it was hard to stay on my feet with the deck bucking beneath me. The forerunner dripped more light into the water, and I saw a shadow dart under the canoe, its eel-like tail flapping behind it. I thought I might be sick.

"Oh, Hana. What have you done?" the forerunner said, his voice barely audible. He clenched his fist and daylight exploded in the water, lighting up the ocean. My blood ran cold.

There were hundreds of them—hundreds of the half-eel, half-human things that had attacked the village. Where the others had wings, these had webbed hands and gill slits in their necks. Their vertical pupils glared up at us as they snarled through mouths lined with fangs. They huddled under the canoe, shrinking away from the light. The water bubbled as they hissed and wriggled their tails.

"Ori?" I asked.

Ori's eyes were wide, but he shook himself out of it. "Stay the course," he said. "Don't let her scare you. Remember, we're here for Masina." He looked like he wanted to say more, but the words were lost as more demons rammed the canoe. The deck shook, and I heard wood splintering.

Pule cringed. "That's gonna leave a mark."

Alani and I strained against the sheet as Loli and Temanu fed it to us. The boom swung outward, catching the cross breeze and sucking us forward. We tore past the daylight the forerunner had created. He closed his fist, extinguishing it.

More shoves came—like a thousand underwater thunderclaps pushing us back to the storm. Ori's voice went hoarse as he screamed for us to adjust. Not that he needed to, we could feel the drag, the unnatural pull as the demons tried to force us off course. I clenched my teeth, rope biting into my hands as I held the sheet with a death grip. We could *not* afford any more delays. Not with the deadlands in sight and the knowledge my sister was inside.

Come on, I thought. *Come ON! I can't let her down again!*

The forerunner speared rays of light through the demons, but it wasn't enough. The canoe started turning in a circle, sail flopping from the awkward changes in wind pressure. We were slowing down.

Demons jumped on the deck. Alani abandoned her post. She didn't look back as she pulled out her knives, cutting them down before they could hurt anyone. Tāwhiri followed suit, leaving the rudder to grab his quarterstaff.

With Alani gone, I lost my footing. I slipped on the deck, struggling to right myself as the sheet yanked me forward. Ori ran behind me, cuffing my waist with one arm and grabbing the sheet with the other. He walked us back, setting me down to take Alani's place.

"Thanks," I breathed.

"Don't mention it," he said, glancing back at the rudder. Alaka'i and Temanu were the only ones there now. They widened their stance, trying to compensate for the extra weight and turbulence.

All the while, the forerunner lanced through demons, his spears of light cutting back and forth underwater. He hissed in annoyance.

"There's too many I can't see," he grunted. "I need to go deeper."

Before any of us could register what he had said, the forerunner dove into the water. He kicked down, killing more demons with the light-lances he created. He saw us gaping at him and motioned for us to keep going.

"He'll be fine," Ori called, "Steady, men. Let's make the most of the time he's giving us. Lali, how's the front?"

I looked up from the sheet as Lali scanned ahead. He was silent for a few moments before nodding.

"All clear!" he shouted back.

Ori looked relieved. "We just might outlast these devils," he said. "Pule, switch with me. I think it's better if I—"

He didn't finish the sentence. At that moment, a demon leapt out of the water, quicker than any manta ray I'd ever seen. It was small, no bigger than a piglet. I hardly noticed it as it wound its tail around Ori's neck. Then it clamped its teeth over his jaw.

Ori screamed. The demon let go and tried to slither away, but Alani hurled a knife that impaled it to the right hull. Ori crumpled to the deck. His body convulsed, and his eyes rolled back in his head.

Everybody froze. For a moment we forgot about the demons, about the deadlands, and about the storm we were supposed to be avoiding. All eyes were fixed on our captain. Of all the people to get hurt, nobody ever expected it would be him. Now that he was writhing on the ground....

Alaka'i dropped the rudder and ran to him. Tāwhiri looked like he wanted to join him, but another wave of demons crawled on board, forcing him to join Alani.

Temanu yelped. In his panic, Alaka'i had left him alone at the rudder, and Temanu didn't have the strength to hold it by himself. The giant oar tilted, lifting Temanu off his feet. He flipped upside down, fingers slipping as he wrapped his legs around the rudder. He grunted, using his body weight to adjust it. Under different circumstances, it might've worked. But another shove hit the left hull, and he lost his grip. The green light of the underworld started drifting out of alignment. We were getting off course.

Loli peeked down at the water, still glowing from the fading light the forerunner had poured into it. His eyes went wide.

"Kalia, help us," he prayed.

I looked over the catwalk. My skin crawled. Demons swarmed under the hulls like ants over rotting food. Their webbed hands dug into the wood, eel-like tails whirling in unison. It was like a giant, slimy hand was scooping us out of the water. Pushing us off course. Taking us away from the deadlands and into the trap Ori had told us to avoid.

We were heading straight for the storm.

Chapter 17

Everyone abandoned their posts. There was no point in staying; unless we found a way to get rid of those monsters, we weren't going anywhere. Temanu rushed to Alaka'i, who pinned Ori down to keep him from rolling overboard. Pule and Lali went left to help Tāwhiri. Loli and I went right with Alani.

Alani slashed through demons with the same precision Loli used to gut a fish. She was good, but for every demon she cut down, three more slithered into place. All the while, the green light of the underworld was fading, and I tried not to think about how far away we were getting from it.

"Any ideas?" she grunted, hurling a knife that speared a demon to the catwalk. She leaned forward and snatched the handle, shaking off the carcass.

I stepped behind Loli, who was beating away demons with his club. I looked out at the water, watching the flashing lights where the forerunner was fighting.

"What about fire?" I said, pointing. "Those things seem to be afraid of light."

Alani paused, watching the forerunner's murky form underwater. In spite of how long he'd been down there, he hadn't been bitten. None of the demons were even trying—they scattered from his light like rats caught near an open flame. She nodded.

"Worth a shot," she said. "See if you can get one started."

I turned to go, and that was when I heard it. Laughter. High-pitched and mocking, almost jubilant. All the blood drained from my face. I knew I shouldn't be surprised; these were, after all, *her* creatures. It would only make sense that their mistress was nearby.

Still, when I saw the demon Mā poke her oily head out of the water, rage boiled inside me.

"Alani, there!" I said, jabbing a finger. "Kill her!"

Alani hesitated. She frowned at me. "Kill who?"

"*Her!*" I screamed, angry at Alani for playing dumb with me. "Kill her! Kill her *now*!"

"Kill her now," Mā mimicked, her voice dripping in arrogance. "Oh, it doesn't look like she can hear you, little chief."

"Loli—!"

"Don't waste your time," Mā said, flicking her wrist. Demons swarmed beneath her, piling up on one another in a makeshift throne that lifted her out of the water. She waved a hand over Loli's face, but he didn't react. He kept swinging his club, striking down at the catwalk.

Mā turned to me. "You see?" she said, "No one else can hear me. I'm only here for you."

I clenched my teeth. "What do you want?"

"To make you a deal," Mā leaned forward, eel tails wriggling beneath her as she did. "How's this for a trade: I will spare all of your friends and your precious canoe in exchange for your life."

"My life?"

I stared at her, not sure what she was playing at. She couldn't possibly have anything to gain from me dying. Then again, if she was asking for it, maybe she did.

I blinked, shaking my head. "What's in it for you?"

"Just that," she said, holding up a hand. "Promise."

I scoffed. "And you never break those."

She shrugged. "I don't. But you do."

I winced. She had me there. Still, this wasn't right. "My sister—"

"Is no longer your concern," Mā snapped. "And believe me, I almost wish she was. She's a terrible house guest, but no matter."

She gestured behind me. "Look at your friends. Wouldn't you agree they could use a little mercy right now? A little compassion?"

She was right again. The crew was in chaos. Ori convulsed on the deck, Alaka'i looked like he wanted to give in to his anxiety while Temanu dug through his bunk for medicine. Lali, Pule and Tāwhiri were battling demons on one side of the canoe, Loli and Alani doing the same on the other. The forerunner dashed back and forth in the water. All while the storm inched closer.

I balled my fists, my insides churning. Could I really put an end to all this?

"Don't you think you've put them through enough already?" Mā asked, her tone gentle. "You couldn't save your sister, little chief, but you can save them."

She held out her hand, and my fingers twitched to reach for it. Alarms sounded in the back of my mind, but they were fading quickly. We had been here before. Back when she pulled me out of Mother's garden and I made the blood deal—but this was different. This time, I wasn't making deals for myself. And If really could save the others...

I lifted my arm, my body shaking as I reached for her. Her grin widened, fanged teeth straightening in her mouth to look human.

"That's it," she coaxed. "Just a little more."

I leaned forward, my insides going numb. I really was going to do it; I was going to die. The thought didn't scare me nearly as much as it probably should have.

It's for the best, I thought. *I'm not cut out for this, anyway.*

"Toa! *DON'T!*"

The words electrocuted me, and I looked up just in time to see the forerunner leaping out of the water. He lunged for Mā, who blinked at him. He tackled her, her throne of eels melting as they went under.

Light exploded beneath us, stronger and brighter than any I had seen that night. The ocean rumbled, as though lightning had struck beneath the surface. The force of it blinded me, and I stumbled on the catwalk. It was so bright that I could still see it with my hands pressed over my face.

Even after it started fading, I was still blinking spots out of my eyes. Loli, who leaned against the railing, was doing the same. Tufts of steam rose from the ocean, and with it drifted the dead bodies of demons. The canoe slowed as more bodies appeared. Their bulbous eyes were unseeing, and smoke curled from their charred, fanged mouths. I stared at the spot where Mā had been, but she was gone.

The light winked out as the forerunner floated to the surface. His eyes were closed, and the soft glow that usually emanated from his skin was gone. He moaned, brow furrowed as though he were trying to wake himself up.

For a moment, all I could do was stand there. My arms went limp, my head ringing with Mā's words.

You could end this, little chief..."

A hand rested on my shoulder—Loli's. "Stand back, Light child," he said. He had tied a harness around his waist and secured it to the railing. He walked down the side of the hull and threw the forerunner over his shoulder. He laid him on the deck, pressing two fingers to his neck to check his pulse, then rested them under his nose.

"He seems okay," he said. "Probably just needs rest."

He threw the forerunner over his shoulder again and headed for his bunk. Alani and I checked on Ori. He looked like he was getting worse. His seizures were worse than they had been seconds ago. Alaka'i and Tāwhiri were both pinning him down out of fear that he would pitch himself overboard.

"Hang in there," Tāwhiri said as Ori kicked. "We'll get those leaves for you real soon. Just sit tight."

"Are you talking to him or me?" Alaka'i grunted. Ori twisted away so forcefully that he elbowed him in the face. Alaka'i stumbled back, blood dripping from his nose.

Across the deck, Temanu popped out from his bunk, raising his arms overhead. In one hand he held a clump of red-heart leaves. The other held a bottle of sedative.

"Got 'em!" he said, "Can someone make me a fire?"

Before anyone could answer the canoe pitched, tilting dangerously as we rolled down a giant wave. I lost my balance, skittering against the deck before smacking into the spar. I tried to grab on, but then the canoe tilted in the opposite direction, slowing down as it rode up another wave. Thunder boomed, and rain started pouring down in thick angry sheets.

"The leaves have to wait, Manu!" Alaka'i yelled, "Just give him the potion. We've got other things to worry about."

He was right. Despite the forerunner's intervention, the storm was upon us. Waves rose like mountains with winds so strong they threatened to rip us off the canoe. There was no way we could make a fire like this, let alone set up a spit for Temanu to roast his leaves on.

Temanu tossed me the sedative. I uncorked it, coating my fingers before dabbing it under Ori's nose. He stopped seizing, arms and legs collapsing to his sides. His brow worked fitfully, and his body twitched, but he wouldn't roll overboard now.

Alaka'i stood, bracing himself against the railing. "All hands to your stations!" he yelled. "Pule, take Manu and Tāwhiri to the rudder. Head for the east!"

Everyone others struggled to obey his orders. Waves slammed down from overhead, pounding against the deck, and blinding us with the rain. But somehow, we did it. I helped Lali, Loli, and Alaka'i gripped the sheet as Pule, Manu and Tāwhiri.

"Hold," Alaka'i called. "Hold!"

"N-n-no," came a voice. "Don't."

The voice was small and came in a series of stutters, but everyone stopped when they heard it.

Alani was still kneeling next to Ori, who had pushed himself up on one elbow. He struggled to open his eyes, but he raised a trembling hand.

"It's t-too late," he stammered, "Can't run now."

Alaka'i dropped the sheet and ran to him. "What should we do, captain?"

"Pull up the boom and lower the spar. Pro—" Ori clenched his teeth, straining from the effort to speak. "Protect the crew."

He collapsed again. Alani barely broke his fall, keeping him from hitting his head on the deck. She kept him up on his left side, eyes fluttering underneath closed eyelids.

Alaka'i bent over, pressing his nose to Ori's before sitting up. "Yes, captain," he murmured. Then he whirled around, facing the rest of us. "You heard him! Tie the boom to the spar and bind them to the deck. Secure the mast! We can't run from this storm, so we'll have to wait it out."

Temanu and Lali carried Ori into his bunk. I tied down the stone 'umu with Loli before helping to take down the sail. We rolled it up tight and bound it to the side of the canoe. Once all of that was done, we each tied on a lifeline. With nowhere to hide, we crouched low to the deck, trying in vain to find shelter from the sea boiling around us. Waves like mountains tossed our canoe, pitching us up and down, slamming the deck with blow after blow of angry saltwater.

I curled up next to Alani, feeling more helpless than I ever had in my entire life. She tried to say something, but I couldn't hear her over the storm. Loli threw his arms over us, head bowed as he squeezed us into his sides. I closed my eyes, fear and anger and regret eating away at me. I should've taken Mā's deal. If I had, none of this would've happened.

This was all my fault.

Chapter 18

Morning came.

My sides ached, and my skin felt raw under the lifeline. The ocean was so peaceful, sunlight glittering against the water as it lapped against the canoe. I blinked at it, feeling the familiar rise and fall of the swells. Could this really be the same ocean we suffered through last night?

I squinted at the horizon. The green light from the deadlands was gone. The sun hovered low where it had been. My stomach sank, remembering the storm and the chaos leading up to it. I thought of my run-in with the demon Mā and her offer to take me for the crew.

Guilt swelled inside me, but I forced it down, reminding myself that nothing good ever came from a deal with Mā. Besides, one night off course couldn't be that bad; we would make up that time easily. And when we got back to the deadlands, things would be different.

Alani was still sleeping. She lay huddled on the fishing deck, resting fitfully. I pulled out a blanket from the bunk I shared with Lali and draped it over her. She let out a deep breath, shoulders relaxing from the added warmth.

The rest of the crew was already working. Pule and Tāwhiri held the rudder while Loli and Lali raised the spar with Alaka'i. Loli waved when he saw me.

"Morning, Light child!" he said. "Did you sleep well?"

"I've had better nights," I said, massaging the back of my neck.

Loli nodded. "I would be concerned if you hadn't. See if you can help Temanu; that might get the kink out of your bones."

The ship's medic was heating up the red-heart leaves in the stone 'umu. He smiled when he saw me coming.

"Thank Kalia that you learned how to tie good knots," he said as I sat next to him. "Had we lost this, I don't know how we could heal our captain."

"How is he?" I asked, glancing at his covered bunk. I couldn't see him under the canvas, but the mental image of him writhing on the deck still made me squirm.

"He's stable," Temanu said. "Once we get these on him the juice will kick in soon enough." He pulled out the leaf he was roasting and passed it to me. "Press this to his left jawline. Let me know when the bite marks appear."

I lifted the canvas over Ori's bunk. His ehu hair was matted with sweat and his breathing came in labored gasps. His muscles still spasmed, and he was burning up with a fever.

I felt a stab of pity. Ori was the guy who had been invincible. Now here he was, bedridden with a life-threatening illness. I pressed the warm leaves to where the bite had been. Ori hissed in pain.

"Sorry, Ori," I said. "I know it hurts, but it'll draw out the poison. You'll be back to bossing us around in no time."

"T...Toa?" he wheezed.

"It's me." Then, thinking of something Loli might've said, I added, "Sorry we couldn't send in the girl of your dreams or something."

Ori let out a dry cough that might've been a laugh. He grabbed my wrist. His fevered hand felt hot against my skin.

"Crew?"

"They're okay," I told him. "Thanks to you, captain, they're all okay. We lost a few coconuts, but that's about it."

The truth was we'd lost more than that. Nobody confirmed that for me, but Temanu's medical supply looked smaller than it had before, and I knew for a fact things were missing from my bunk. I worried about what else had washed out in the storm, but Ori didn't need to hear that now.

He exhaled in relief. I couldn't help but laugh, thinking of how odd it was. Here Ori was, practically on his deathbed, yet all he could think about was us. Deadly poison be damned; he would never put himself before his crew.

Ori's brow wrinkled. "Sorry."

I frowned. "What did you say?"

"I'm. Sorry," Ori said through clenched teeth. "Got bit. My fault."

I rolled my eyes. "Ori, if you say that again, I'm putting hot rocks in your bunk. You've got nothing to be sorry for. It's not your fault you're allergic to poison like the rest of us."

Ori coughed another laugh, and I felt his jaw relax under the leaves I held to it. I smiled, grateful that he still had a sense of humor. I gripped his wrist.

"You did good, Orr," I insisted. "We're alive because of you. It's not your fault you got bit, and it's not your fault we got distracted. But if it wasn't for you, we would've tried to sail through that storm. And who knows where we'd be after that?"

Ori didn't say anything, but he let out a rattled breath. Somehow I knew that meant he understood. He rolled his head away from me and I felt the leaves grow damp. I peeled them back, not surprised but still unsettled by the bite marks that now circled Ori's jaw. Purple puss seeped out of the holes perforating his skin, and I dabbed at them with a clean cloth, shouting to Temanu. He was there before I could finish a sentence, armed with more leaves, ointment, and bandages. Ready and willing to patch up his captain.

As Temanu drained the puss, he asked me to check on our other patient. "He's been unconscious longer than I thought he'd be," he said, frowning. "I'm not sure how to diagnose him, but maybe you'll notice something I missed."

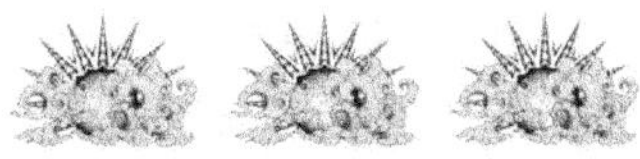

When I looked in the neighboring bunk, the servant of Havaiki was on his back. His skin didn't glow, and I was reminded again of just how human he could look. His eyes creaked open when he heard me.

"You're awake," I said. "That's good."

"Is it?" The forerunner lifted his right hand, examining his fingers with a look of disgust. "I think I'd rather be sleeping."

"Eh, sleep so'o," I told him, using the word that meant *too much* in our village. I was sure my ancestors would cringe to hear me say that to a forerunner, but I didn't care. He seemed more comfortable when we didn't give him special treatment, anyway.

He lifted an eyebrow. "And you just might be talking so'o."

I laughed. "If you can be sarcastic you can't be that sick," I said. "How are you feeling?"

"Pathetic." The forerunner didn't sound angry, or annoyed. It was more like a resigned fatigue, as though he expected nothing more of himself.

I frowned. "For what? You killed at least two hundred demons last night. If it wasn't for you we would've been dragged into the storm."

"Sounds like you were dragged into it, anyway."

"True," I admitted. "But we had time to prepare for it. You bought us that time. Who knows where we would've been without it?"

The forerunner sighed. "Have you come to give me a pep talk, little chief?"

"No. I've come to be your doctor." I folded my arms. "So if you could kindly describe your symptoms, I'll make a diagnosis and we'll call it a day."

The tiniest hint of a smile tugged at his lips. He closed his eyes. "Do you remember me telling you that I have siblings?"

I frowned, surprised at the question, "Yeah...why?"

"You're starting to remind me of one in particular."

I grinned. "Thanks!"

"It wasn't a compliment."

I scowled, toying with the idea of putting hot rocks in *his* bunk. "Is sarcasm one of your symptoms? Or is this your version of self-medication?"

He shrugged, staring past me to the open sky. "It's more like I'm enjoying the benefits of a rather debilitating condition. I only recently regained control over my voice, so I'm taking full advantage of it."

I tilted my head. His speech was coherent, but nothing he said made sense. I thought about getting Temanu, but the forerunner kept talking.

"It's one of the limits of my powers," he said, not looking at me. "What you saw last night is something I can only do for a limited time. If I go too hard or too long with it, the magic dries up. In severe cases, I lose feeling in my entire body." He gestured at himself. "Like so."

I was stunned, the realization hitting me like a boulder. "So that— that light you had, the thing that made you glow. That was your powers?"

"Yep."

"But they're gone now?"

"Indeed."

I gaped at him, unable to believe that he wasn't more upset by this. "So you're...you're a mortal!"

That explained his mood. By helping us last night, the forerunner had sacrificed his godhood. Had he lost his place in the heavens because of us?

But the forerunner looked confused. "What? No, I'm not a mortal. What are you talking about?"

"But you just said—"

"I said my powers are gone now, yes," he corrected. "That doesn't mean they won't come back. I've pushed myself like this before. Usually I just need a day or two for that magic to renew itself. It's not that different from the way mortals recover from bruised bones or a minor illness."

"And you'll go back to normal?" I snapped my fingers. "Just like that? You'll be alright?"

"Of course." The forerunner tilted his head at me. "Are *you* alright? If I didn't know better, I would think you were the one that needed attending to."

You have no idea, I thought. The idea that divine powers could recharge or could come back...I doubted the forerunner understood what that meant for me. By the gods, I wasn't even sure if *I* knew what that meant for me.

I shook my head. "Do you need anything?"

"I'm alright," he said, watching me with intrigue. "Do you?"

I didn't answer, opting instead to bow as I replaced the canvas. When Temanu asked, I told him the forerunner needed rest, and wouldn't be out for two days.

Temanu grimaced. "That's the same for Ori. If I had been able to treat him right away, he'd be fine by now. But that wound had a long time to fester. Even when he's well enough to walk, there's no telling when he'll be able to work again." He massaged his temples.

"I can't believe this; we're down two men. And of all people, it had to be the captain and the navigator."

I nodded. "It's going to be a rough few days without them."

They were our strongest men at sea. Ori kept everyone together, and the forerunner kept us on course. Not having them with us was like trying to function without a head and a heart. The only way to do it was if you were already dead.

Alakaʻi worked the rigging of the sail as he called to Lali and Pule to shift their angle on the rudder. He then switched places with Loli, who had been adjusting the front stays, so that Loli could run back to the stone ʻumu where breakfast was cooking. Behind their hurried footsteps and raised voices, Alani's head poked out from the fishing deck. Her bed hair and bleary eyes were clear proof that she had just woken up.

Loli looked at me as he pulled tapioca out of the ʻumu. He yawned. "So, are you a doctor or a cook?" he asked.

I shrugged. "Both, I guess."

"Good," He tossed me a knife, "Then please grab me another tapioca root, and try think of something we can make to go with it. If ever there was a time we needed a hot meal to boost the morale, I would say it's right about now."

"How big of a morale boost do we need?" I asked, reaching for the tapioca in the storage bin.

"Aside from the fact that we lost our captain and our navigator?" Loli glanced at Alakaʻi, who lifted his chin in approval. Grimacing, he turned back to me. "Alakaʻi calculated our position this morning to see how far off course the storm blew us last night. Pule, Lali, and I confirmed it while you were helping Temanu. We know where we are now."

"Okay?" I was only half-listening, still thinking about what could complement the tapioca. Grilled onions with coconut milk was always an option, but the crew probably needed more than that. Maybe we could go with a simple breakfast, and I could drop the lines to catch something fresh for lunch.

Loli closed the 'umu before walking over to crouch next to me. He called my name and I turned to him, arms full of coconuts that needed husking. His expression was grave as he rested a hand on my shoulder.

"I'm sorry, Light child, but the storm pushed us two days off course. With a fully functioning crew, we could be in the deadlands tomorrow night. Being the way we are now, though, I'm not sure how long that will take."

Chapter 19

Alani did not take the news well. She didn't scream or start breaking things the way I thought she would, but from the shattered look in her eyes, I knew she was devastated. We all were. What should've been a joyful reunion had ended in disaster. Now we didn't have a captain or a navigator, and we were two days off course. Which, Loli warned, was being optimistic. In our crew's current state, it could take four days to get there. Maybe five.

Alaka'i called for a crew meeting during breakfast. Out of respect to Ori and the forerunner, we sat in a circle near their bunks. Even if they couldn't move, it felt wrong to meet without them. Ori drifted in and out of consciousness as Temanu changed his leaves. Loli rolled back the forerunner's canvas and propped him up against the hull. He sat next to him so that the forerunner would have someone to lean against.

"With Ori out, I guess that makes you acting captain, eh, Ka'i?" Lali said as he popped a piece of tapioca in his mouth.

Alaka'i made a face. "I wish it didn't have to be that way, but it looks like I am."

"What do you need from us, then?" Loli asked.

Alaka'i rubbed the back of his neck. "I guess Ori would do a morale check, or something right about now?"

Alani moaned. "Please don't. I really don't want to talk about it right now."

Tāwhiri agreed, his expression hollow. "We were right there," he said. "We were *right there!* We should be with Masina right now."

Hearing her name tore at my insides. Did Masina know we had come for her last night? Would that change anything between us if she did?

Pule downed his coconut juice in one gulp. "Well, we're not," he said coldly. "Face it, everyone. That rescue attempt was a failure."

Temanu scowled. "Thanks for that."

"What, you think I'm wrong?"

"No, but I think you're being a real—"

"Stop it," Alaka'i waved a hand to cut them off. "I need to think."

We ate in silence as the watch captain rubbed his chin, his eyes on the horizon. When he finally spoke, he chose his words carefully.

"We've got a lot of ground to make up," he said. "And not just with distance. Lali, you said our food supply took a hit?"

"We lost about a third of it," Lali said, grimacing. "Which I take responsibility for since I didn't secure that extra storage compartment we had."

Alaka'i let out a breath through puffed cheeks. "How much do we have left?"

"We have enough food for five days," Loli said. "But our sickmen might use all our water before then."

Temanu nodded. "He's right, especially about the captain. People need more fluids when they're ill."

"How long before he recovers?" Alaka'i asked.

"I would give him three days," Temanu said. "He had all night for the venom to mess up his body. It's going to take a while for him to get over it."

Alaka'i winced. "And Pule? How's the canoe?"

Pule shrugged, "We're sinking."

Tāwhiri gasped. Alani looked dumbstruck. My eyes darted around the deck, half-expecting to see water seeping up from the hulls.

Loli stood up and whacked Pule on the shoulder. Without his support the forerunner flopped forward. Loli barely grabbed him before he fell face-first into his food.

"Don't say it like that, Pule," he said. "You gonna scare people with that kind of talk."

Pule made a face. "Okay, fine. We've just got twelve slow leaks in the hulls, five on one side and seven on the other. And since we're getting all kinds of luck lately, my resin washed out in the storm, so I've got nothing to fix it with. Does that sound better?"

Loli whacked him again. "No, it doesn't. Come on, Pule, you're terrible at this."

Alaka'i ran his fingers through his hair, his brow crinkled in concern. "Alright," he said. "Now that everyone knows where we're at, there's one more thing we need to discuss." He glanced at the forerunner. "The attack last night. That was the demon, ya?"

The forerunner nodded, his left arm limp at his side. "She is fixed in her hatred," he said. "She wants you to fail, and she will do whatever it takes to make that happen."

Alani gripped her knife in the chambered position. She looked like she wanted to stab it into the deck. Alaka'i tapped her shoulder and motioned for her to hand it over. Grudgingly, she complied.

Alaka'i tossed the knife up and caught it. "Do you know how many of those things she has?" he asked the forerunner. "Those eel things that were in the water?"

The forerunner shook his head. "It's impossible to know. She can make as many as she wants; she's likely replacing the ones we killed right now."

Tāwhiri scowled. "Now that's just cheating."

"So we need to be ready for another attack." Alaka'i nodded. "Anyone got any ideas?"

"This sounds like her area of expertise," Loli said, lifting his chin at Alani. "What do you say, War child? Think you could come up with something?"

Alani, who already had another knife in her hands, lifted her eyebrows in acceptance. "It would be my pleasure," she said. "I might need help making weapons, though. The storm took a lot of the ones I packed."

"Pule and Tāwhiri can help you," Alaka'i said. "We've still got some wood and Pule's carving tools. See what you can make with that."

Tāwhiri smiled at Alani, who gave a shy nod.

"Alright, then." Alaka'i swallowed the last of his tapioca and leaned against the mast. He looked up at the sail, then at all of us. "Alani, Tāwhiri and Lali to the sheet," he said. "Once we're underway, Pule and Tāwhiri can grab their tools." He pointed at the rudder. "Loli, let's have you, Manu, and Toa over there. Temanu, you know what to do after that."

He looked down at the forerunner. "Toa said you need sleep to get your strength back?"

The forerunner nodded, looking embarrassed.

Alaka'i pressed a finger to his chin, thinking. "With all due respect, then, would you be alright resting until you're back to normal?"

The forerunner cringed, but nodded. "I won't be of much use until then," he said.

"Thank you." Alaka'i turned to Lali and Pule, nodding towards the forerunner. "Make sure he's comfortable before you do anything else."

The forerunner was almost pitiable as Lali and Pule laid him in his bunk. The parts of his body he could move were stiff, his discomfort visible. But he didn't complain as they arranged his bed before replacing the canvas cover.

I heaved the rudder with Loli and Temanu, the three of us working in unison as Alaka'i watched the steady rocking of the canoe. Lali and Pule helped Tāwhiri and Alani adjust the sheet. The boom shifted to catch the cross breeze, and we were on our way.

Chapter 20

As predicted, the next forty-eight hours were miserable. We hardly slept, and aside from the times Loli forced us to sit down, we barely ate. Everyone was too busy working. Our crew had gone from ten active members to eight. But with everyone working double-duty, it felt more like we had gone from ten members to five.

"No, Whiri, that's not how the spear's supposed to look!" Alani said as Tāwhiri carved. He sat near the splashguard, jaw working as Alani nagged him.

Alani paced the deck, too stressed-out to realize how much she was bothering him. "You know it's supposed to have a straight head; serrated edges will ruin it."

Tāwhiri scowled. "Don't call me Whiri," he snapped. "And it's not serrated; it's just really hard to carve out here. In case you forgot, Alani, we're on a rocking boat in the middle of the ocean."

"Well, figure something out!"

"How about this, then. You be the carpenter, and I'll be the crybaby throwing knives all day," Tāwhiri fired back.

Alani pulled out a knife. "Say that again."

"Okay," Tāwhiri threw down his tools and stood up. "How about you—"

"Stop it, you guys!" I said, stuffing myself in between them. I had a wooden spoon in one hand, and it looked pathetic against Alani's knife. She narrowed her eyes, the tip of her blade leveled at me.

"Out. Of. The way. Toa," she spat.

"Yeah, Toa," Tāwhiri said, bumping my free arm. "Let her come. I'd love to see how well she fights on a boat again. We saw how well that went at the deadlands."

Alani swung. Panicked, I tried to shove Tāwhiri out of the way, but it was like pushing a mountain. I stumbled as a pair of arms seized Alani around the middle.

"Enough!" Alaka'i roared, swinging her up and away from me.

Alani screamed. She kicked in his arms, but Alaka'i held her. He twisted her wrist, and her knife clattered to the deck. She wrestled out of his grip, flipping around to face him. Alaka'i was holding her knife by the blade. She glanced at it, then looked back at him. Her eyes were bloodshot and murderous, but he remained calm.

"We don't point knives at our friends," he said. "That isn't going to help Masina."

Alani dug her fingers into her hair, grunting. She looked like she was about to scalp herself.

Alaka'i tossed me the knife and rested a hand on her shoulder. "You know it's not your fault, right?"

Alani didn't say anything, but her eyes spoke volumes. She felt guilty.

Alaka'i gave a wan smile. "I think I know how you feel," he said. "Take a break, Alani. Switch with Lali at the rudder."

Alani complied, sliding in place behind Pule. She wrapped her arms around the oar and hugged it to her side, listening to the subtle changes Pule asked her to make.

"Thanks for getting rid of her," Tāwhiri grumbled. He started to sit back down, but Alaka'i waved him forward.

"Oh no, breezy boy," he said. "You get over here."

Frowning, Tāwhiri set down his toki and walked over. When he was within arm's reach, Alaka'i whacked him on the back of the head.

Tāwhiri's hands flew up. "Ow!"

"What's the matter with you?" Alaka'i said, hands on his hips.

Tāwhiri opened his mouth, then seemed to think better of it. It was one thing to fight with Alani; she and Tāwhiri were the same age. But Alaka'i was older than both of them, and he was our watch captain.

"She's trying to make sure our next trip to the deadlands goes better than the last one," Alaka'i said. "I don't know if you remember, Tāwhiri, but you didn't do so well that night, either."

Tāwhiri winced, guilt flashing across his face. Alaka'i's scowl relaxed as he sighed and pulled Tāwhiri into a side hug.

"We've got enough things going wrong right now, okay?" he said. "The rest of us are working twice as much so that you and Alani can come up with a plan. When you act like that, it makes us feel like we're wasting our time. You understand me?"

Tāwhiri nodded.

"Good. Take over for Pule so you guys can talk it out. When you've calmed down, you can come back here."

Alani didn't look any happier about it than Tāwhiri did when he stood at the rudder, but neither complained. Watching them strain to keep the rudder in place, I understood what Alaka'i was doing. By putting them alone on the rudder, they had no choice but to work together; they couldn't sit and fume about the other person's faults.

Pule took Tāwhiri's spot and started whittling. Alaka'i faced the front of the canoe. He laced his fingers behind his head and let out a sigh.

"What's wrong?" I asked, looking out past the prow with him. We were nearing the end of the first watch. It was another chill morning with a strong breeze to pull us forward. The past two days had been so calm—it was crazy how peaceful the ocean could be when life was so hectic on deck.

Alaka'i wiped a hand down his face. "I never thought being captain would feel like babysitting." He glanced over at the left hull, "Ori made this look easy."

"Yeah," Loli said, scraping a tapioca root behind us. "He did have a full crew, though."

Ori's absence still weighed heavily on the crew. And while no one did it to offend Alaka'i, we all found ourselves looking for Ori at times, only to remember he couldn't help us. He was getting better, but Temanu didn't think he would be out of his bunk anytime soon. He was still too weak, and could only stay awake for minutes at a time.

"Pule," Alaka'i called, "how long has it been since the last bail?"

Pule shaved off a chunk of wood, thinking. "Maybe twenty minutes. I'll give it another ten before I check again."

Alaka'i looked down at me. "Was it your turn to bail next?"

I shook my head. "Loli and I went last. It's yours and Alani's."

The twelve holes in our canoe were another major source of stress. We didn't worry about sinking, but the leaks slowed us down. Loli had covered them with a paste made out of ulu, but it was only a temporary fix. We still had to empty out everything in the compartments four times a day to scoop out the saltwater pooling in the hulls. And nobody liked doing that because, not only was it monotonous, but it also reminded us of how little supplies we had left.

Outbursts like the one between Alani and Tāwhiri were not uncommon; we were all getting on each other's nerves. Everyone was tired, hungry, and worried that we would sink before arriving at the deadlands. Poor Alaka'i spent more time keeping the peace than he did acting as watch captain.

I wasn't doing much better, myself. The past two days had drained me both physically and mentally. With everyone else either caring for the sick or making weapons, Lali, Loli, and I became Alaka'i's main crew members. Cooking used to be our main responsibility, now it was the only kind of down time we had anymore. Even simple things like doing laundry or taking a shower had to be alternated between the three of us while preparing our next meal.

The rare times I wasn't on deck or in the kitchen I was with Temanu, occasionally taking over when he needed to rest. I felt sorry for our doctor, who looked guilty whenever it was his turn for a break. Ori's leaves needed to be changed regularly, and he had to take the oral dosage three times a day. Then Temanu gave routine stretches and exercises to the forerunner. This increased blood flow and mobility, and would hopefully have him on his feet soon. Both men also needed to be fed and hydrated, which wasn't easy to do with Ori since he spent more time asleep than awake.

Adding to Temanu's workload was that, after our first sleepless night, Alani and Tāwhiri started coughing. Then other crew members showed signs of getting sick, and Temanu took it upon himself to make sure everyone was getting the minimum two hours of sleep during their breaks. Even now, as he came back from treating Ori, he pointed his roll of bandages at Pule accusingly.

"What do you think you're doing?" he said.

Pule frowned. "Carving."

"Yeah, I don't think so," Temanu snatched the toki out of his hand. "I don't even want to see you look at a piece of wood until you get some sleep. I've already got two sick men; if you add yourself to the list, the first thing I'm giving you is a big fat dose of 'I Told You So!'"

Despite the tension I couldn't help but smile. Temanu chased Pule like a grumpy aunty, not the least bit intimidated that Pule was six years older and a full head taller than he was. Temanu was the only one who got away with talking back since he always did it as a doctor.

"Alright, fine," Pule said, backing away from his tools. He lifted the canvas over his bunk and looked back at Alaka'i. "Wake me up when we get to the isle?"

Alaka'i nodded, as Pule disappeared under the cloth. He then looked up at the navigator's chair. "How much longer?"

"I'd give it an hour," the forerunner said. "We're not that far away."

Pule's head popped out from under the canvas. "Does that mean I can skip the nap, then?"

Temanu growled. "Don't make me drug you."

In the two days since we had been blown off course, the only visual sign of progress we had was the forerunner, who was well enough to come out of his bunk. His legs were numb and he was markedly lightless, but he could sit in the navigator's chair without any problems. Someone, usually Loli or Alaka'i, had to stay close by in case he fell out. He didn't say much, but he seemed happier.

"An hour?" I said, my eyebrows shooting up. "Are we really that close to the deadlands?"

The thought should've excited me, but I only felt dread. Showing up to the deadlands like this was laughable.

But Alaka'i shook his head. "We're not going to the underworld yet. There's an island we need to stop at first."

"What?" Alani let go of the rudder. Tāwhiri fumbled to hold it without her. She crossed her arms, looking furious. "You're taking a detour? And you didn't tell us?"

I didn't always see eye-to-eye with Alani, but she was right. Since when did Alaka'i keep secrets from us?

"I did tell you," Alaka'i said. "I told everyone this morning. You and Toa were all falling asleep at your posts."

Alani looked at Lali and Loli, who both shrugged.

"It's true," said Lali.

"I was going to tell you, but you were drooling," Loli teased.

"Why are we stopping?" Alani asked, her scowl deepening.

"Because we're tired and weak, and our canoe is sinking beneath us," Alaka'i said. "If we want to have any kind of fighting chance, we need to make repairs."

He was right, and everyone knew it. We needed rest badly. Right now none of us cold think straight, let alone fight off a bunch of demons. Still, Alani didn't look convinced.

"How long will this take?" she asked.

Alaka'i shrugged, looking over at the right hull. "Pule?"

"At least twelve hours," Pule called, voice slightly muffled under the canvas. "But could be overnight. Depends on how fast we find everything we need."

Temanu threw his hands up. "You're supposed to be sleeping!"

"What for? Sounds like I'll have to get up soon, anyway."

"I know it's a setback," Alaka'i said, looking apologetic as he turned from one crewmember to another, "But we need this—and not just for the repairs. It'll set us up for success when we reach the deadlands. If we sailed straight, we would get there by nightfall, and that's when the demon Mā is strongest. By stopping, we can time it to arrive at sunrise."

"That would even the odds a little," Temanu said, nodding, "Still, I'm surprised at you, Ka'i. Usually you would've told us sooner."

"Don't blame the watch captain," said the forerunner, "The stop was my idea. Last night I saw signs of land, and told Alaka'i."

"You've been there before?" Lali asked.

The forerunner laughed once. "You could say that."

I glanced back at Alani. She didn't look happy about it, but there was resignation in her face as she grabbed the rudder. In front of her, Tāwhiri nodded.

Loli held up the tapioca root he was peeling. "You know, I think a quick stop might be good for us. If nothing else, we'll have something to eat besides baked tapioca for lunch."

Minutes later, the island appeared, rising above the horizon as though it were emerging from the sea. Mountains of green stretched upward, and the ocean faded from dark blue to turquoise as it neared the white shores. We steered the canoe past the atolls surrounding it, not stopping until we felt the hulls rub against the sand.

"Men and woman," said the forerunner, "welcome to Faletahi Island."

"Glory to Kalia," Alaka'i said reverently. We bowed our heads as he offered a prayer of gratitude to the gods, giving thanks for the blessing we had to make it this far. He then asked for the strength and wisdom we needed to make it to the deadlands, as well as for a blessing on our captain.

When we finished the prayer, Alaka'i wrapped his right hand around his left fist, bringing both up under his chin, thinking.

"I don't want us to be here any longer than we need to be," he said. "We need food, water, and whatever Pule needs for repairs. So who's going to get what?"

"I'll stay here," said Pule. "I can finish carving those weapons while I wait for supplies."

Alaka'i frowned. "But Pule, if you're here, who's going to get supplies for you?"

"I'll get it," Lali said, raising a hand. "It's ulu resin, ya Pule? We need ulu for our food stock, so I can tap a few trees while I'm at it."

"Does anyone live on this island?" Temanu asked. "I have some herbs I need to gather, and don't want to trespass by accident."

The forerunner shook his head. "There is only one other person besides ourselves on this island, and believe me, she wouldn't mind at all. This place exists as a refuge for weary travelers. We can take as much as we need."

Tāwhiri looked surprised. He squinted into the bush growing inland. "Who is she?" he asked, "The woman that lives here? Do you think we'll run into her?"

"We might." The forerunner shrugged. "She knows when she has visitors, but rarely ever appears to them."

He didn't explain any more than that, and no one felt the need to pry. This island provided respite, but time was of the essence.

The rest of us quickly divided our assignments. Alaka'i and Alani would go inland to hunt. Loli would stay with Pule so that he could start a fire to cook over.

That left Tāwhiri and I to find fresh water. I helped him throw our drinking gourds and bamboo shafts into two nets, which we tied and threw over our shoulders.

I jumped off the catwalk after Alani, foam splashing as I landed in the whitewash. My feet sank into the sand, tickling me as I tread behind the others. It felt weird to be on solid ground again. After a week at sea, I was so used to the constant motion that my legs wobbled, and it took a few minutes for the land to feel truly solid again.

I walked with Tāwhiri along the shore. Beneath our feet the wet sand molded to my toes and along the soles of my heels, leaving imprints of my footsteps behind me.

"You see those birds over there?" Tāwhiri said, pointing.

I followed his finger, looking up at a flock of five white birds flying ahead, all with thin long legs and pointed beaks. They looked like the kind of birds normally found near the marshlands.

"What about them?" I asked.

"I saw more like them on our way in," said Tāwhiri. "They were circling a bay not far from here. I think there might be fresh water there."

I raised an eyebrow. "You got that from watching birds?"

He shrugged. "Birds have to drink, too."

We rounded the bend and were met by jagged rocks that marked the edge of the beach. Since they were too sharp to climb over, we would have to go around. I followed Tāwhiri as he picked his way through the bush, occasionally calling out a warning when he saw spiders, sinkholes, or poisonous frogs in the trees. Fumbling the bag over my shoulder, I stumbled to keep up with him.

"I bet you're excited to see your sister tomorrow, yeah Toa?" Tāwhiri said as he hopped over a fallen tree trunk.

My answer was lost as I walked through the spiderweb. I spluttered, wiping the sticky fluid off my face. "Sorry," I said, blinking the gunk out of my eyes. "What did you say?"

"I said I bet you're excited to see your sister." Tāwhiri sniggered, taking my bag as I scrambled over the log. "Have you thought about what you'll say to her?"

The vision I had of Masina flashed across my mind. I thought of her face, ghostly white and ruined by the pain I had caused her. My muscles tensed, and I felt my heart shrink inside of me. What would I say to her when we found her tomorrow? Was there anything I *could* say, after everything that had happened?

"Toa?"

I shook my head. "I don't know. I just want to make sure we get her back first."

It was a lame excuse. One that, thankfully, Tāwhiri decided to run with. His face was solemn as we walked toward the edge of the trees, spotting another bank of sand up ahead. As we left the bush, Tāwhiri spoke up again.

"You've changed a lot since we left," he said, looking back at me. "Do you realize that?"

"Me?" I frowned, not sure what he meant. I did feel a little different. But in some ways I still felt the same. I wasn't stronger, faster, or smarter by any means. And deep down, there was still a part of me that resented my sister. Not because of what she had done to me, but because of what had made her so strong in the first place.

"You seem happier," Tāwhiri said. "Less stressed. I don't know if that's because we're out of the Light Village, or because you're not comparing yourself to Masina, anymore. Either way, I think it's something you should keep up when we get back."

"Yeah, sure."

He was right about that. My days with the crew had been some of the happiest of my life. Loli suggested I visit the Navigator Village to learn more about wayfinding. A part of me wondered if I could live there permanently. Maybe it wouldn't be so bad if Masina took the title and I left the village.

We went around another bend that opened up to a bay area. The birds Tāwhiri and I saw were circling a reef about fifty feet out from the shore. They landed in line with a cluster of birds surrounding the shallow waters. Twig-like legs submerged, I watched as they dipped their elongated beaks under the surface, waiting for a few seconds before pulling them out.

There were several mini-flocks of these birds like throughout the bay, all of them in near-perfect circles as they took turns dipping their beaks in the water. It looked like they were drinking straight out of the ocean.

I frowned, trying to make sense of it. "Are they eating something on the reef?"

"No..." Tāwhiri waded into the water, watching. Some of the birds closest to us took off. They flew to another spot further away from us, joining the circle of birds over there. Giving Tāwhiri another sideways look, they resumed their game of pecking at the saltwater.

Tāwhiri waded deeper, reaching out with his arms as though he were searching for something. Whatever it was, he must've found it because he broke into a huge grin.

"They're drinking," he said.

I raised an eyebrow. "They drink saltwater?"

"No." Tāwhiri ran back towards his bag and pulled out a gourd, "There's fresh water over there, but I think you have to dive for it," he looked at me, "Wait here with our things, I'll be right back."

He dove in, making the birds scatter. When he resurfaced, his smile was bigger, and he held his gourd up with one hand before swimming back to shore.

He passed it to me. "Drink up."

I waited for him to laugh as I brought the gourd to my lips, but instead of the expected brine I tasted cool, refreshing water. My eyes widened and I tipped the gourd, taking greedy gulps, feeling energized as the cold liquid ran down my throat.

"You see?" Tāwhiri said, wagging his eyebrows. "I told you there's water down there."

"I'm sorry I doubted you," I said. "How did you find it?"

"It's like an underwater well," Tāwhiri said. "It comes up from the ground in certain places. And since freshwater is colder than saltwater, it wasn't hard for me to find." he picked up another gourd from his bag. "Do you want to try? We can fill up faster that way."

I grimaced. "I still don't know how to swim."

"Oh yeah," Tāwhiri shrugged. "No problem, then. You can wait here and make sure no one steals our water. I'll take care of this."

Not wanting to be completely useless, I rinsed out all our drinking flasks, passing an empty one to Tāwhiri every time he came up. We filled up four gourds and three bamboo flasks that way, when Tāwhiri came up gasping.

"Toa!" he yelled. "Toa, come quick!"

I ran out until I was waist-deep in the water, frowning as he kicked towards me.

"What is it?" I asked.

Tāwhiri shook his head as he stood, running his hands over his face. "This is going to sound crazy," he said. "But there's two people down there."

My mouth fell open, horrified at the grisly image. I swallowed. "You found two dead people down there?" I said. Thinking of the water I just drank, I thought I might be sick.

But Tāwhiri shook his head. "They're not dead. Actually, I don't know if they're even people. They look like they could be gods, or something," he grabbed my arm. "It doesn't matter. They need to talk to you. Let's go."

"Wait, Tāwhiri," I complained, twisting my arm away from him. "I don't even know what you're talking about. And if these people are down there, how am I supposed to get to them? You know I can't swim."

Tāwhiri did not look sympathetic. "You'd better figure it out then," he said. "Because believe me, you'll want to hear them out."

I frowned. "Why?"

Tāwhiri held up the gourd he had in his other hand. When I saw it I froze. Looped around the top was something I recognized immediately. A wooden bracelet, a kaulima worn by women around the tricep. I knew the crescent moon patterns etched into this one as well as I knew her face.

This kaulima belonged to Masina.

Chapter 21

I took a deep breath and dove in. My eyes stung from the saltwater as the world melted into a turquoise blur. Tāwhiri gripped my wrist and kicked down; I flailed my legs to keep up with him. The sunlight above grew dim, disorienting me the further down we went.

In the darkness ahead I saw a light dancing in the water. As my eyes adjusted the light grew, expanding as though it would swallow me. I reached out to it, but then Tāwhiri jerked on my arm.

Suddenly, we were falling. Falling through empty air as though we had kicked to the surface instead of the ocean floor. I screamed. My stomach clenched, and I started flapping my arms, as if that would somehow get me back in the water.

"Woah, take it easy," said a voice. "I got you."

Someone caught me and set me on dry ground. Gasping, I rubbed saltwater out of my eyes, blinking. We were still underwater, but it wasn't a cave like I might've guessed. It was more like a giant bubble, though how one this big ended up down here I had no idea. Looking up, I saw the waves rolling over us, and beyond that the blurred image of the sun. Fishes of all colors swam back and forth. One of them—a fat manini—swam straight into the air bubble we were in. It flopped clumsily in the sand, gills working as it tried to breathe.

I picked it up, cupped it with two hands, and nudged it back into the water. I wasn't sure who was more surprised, the fish or me. As I watched it dart away, I realized that I wasn't wet anymore. My skin and hair were completely dry.

"And Tāwhirimatea's child said you couldn't swim," laughed a voice, different from the one I heard earlier.

Whirling around, I felt my breath catch in my throat. Tāwhiri was on his knees, and I prostrated myself beside him. Standing in front of us were two of the most beautiful women I had ever seen. Tāwhiri was right; they had to be goddesses. No mortal could be this beautiful.

The one on the left was taller, with flowing hair and skin the color of koa wood. She must've been the one who caught me. Light radiated off her as though she were a star personified. Standing beside her was a younger woman who looked around Ori's age. Her curly hair cascaded down to her waist, and she had a tiare flower tucked behind her ear.

"Hello, little chiefs!" she said. "Welcome to my home."

My eyes widened, still fixated on the ground. *Her home?*

"Just look at them," said the other one, tsking. "Too terrified to speak. Rise, sons of Havaiki and Tāwhirimatea. Time is short, and we must counsel with you before sending you on your way."

We obeyed. Mindful to excuse ourselves first, Tāwhiri and I rose to our feet. Looking down at myself, at my dirty skin and ragged sulu, I felt ashamed to be standing before them. My haggard appearance hardly seemed appropriate for the situation. With the way Tāwhiri shifted from one foot to the other, I could tell he felt the same.

"I am Tahi," said the one with curly hair. "The forerunner of Kalia."

"And I am Hina, daughter of Havaiki," said the other goddess.

"Hina?" I asked, surprised. I wondered if it was rude for me to speak, but the goddess nodded her consent. I cleared my throat. "That's—that's the name of the star we've been following," I said. "One of the Celestial Siblings."

It felt stupid pointing that out to her. Being a daughter of the light god, she must've known all about the stars, especially the one named after her. But she didn't look annoyed as she lifted her chin in acknowledgment.

"It's true," she said. "When my siblings and I achieved the rank of godhood, our father celebrated by giving each of us a star in the heavens."

"So there are five of you, then?" Tāwhiri asked. There were five stars in the Celestial Siblings, which logically meant Havaiki had five children.

But Hina shook her head. "There's a few more. However, now isn't the time to discuss it."

Tahi nodded, her smile faltering. "It's true," she said, glancing at me. "Your sister is running out of time."

"So you've seen her, then?" I asked, pointing at the kaulima around Tāwhiri's gourd. "You got this from her, didn't you?"

Hina nodded. "Yes. Her spirit is strong, but her body is failing. If you cannot reunite her spirit and body by tomorrow night, she will remain in the deadlands forever."

My insides shriveled at that. I pictured Masina's spirit, pale and ethereal, drifting through the deadlands until the end of time. The wounds from our battle permanently etched into her face.

"What must I do?" I asked, my throat dry.

Tahi held up a finger. "First, don't lose hope. The deadlands aren't far from here. Getting to the entrance will be easy; the real challenge begins once you're inside."

I thought of how badly we had failed the first time we went to the deadlands. If that was Tahi's version of easy, I wasn't sure I wanted to know the "real challenge."

Tāwhiri looked from Hina to Tahi. "What should we expect when we get there?"

Tahi opened her mouth but then faltered. She shared a look with Hina, and the two of them came to a silent agreement.

"It's...too soon to say," said Hina. "But that is not why we are here. We brought gifts to help you on your way to the deadlands."

My eyes widened. Divine help was exactly what we needed right now. Thinking of everything we needed, I wondered what the goddesses had for us. Was it food? Water? A special resin for our canoe?

Tahi looked up at the ocean rolling overhead, then behind her. It was like she was looking for someone. She frowned at Tāwhiri and I. "Where is Marama?" she asked.

Tāwhiri and I frowned. "Who?"

"Hina's brother?" Tahi held a hand over her head. "About this tall? Close to my age? Looks like he takes himself way too seriously most of the time."

"You mean the forerunner?" Tāwhiri asked.

Now that I thought about it, I didn't really know his name; we only ever used his title.

"Wait a minute," I said, looking at Hina in disbelief. "He's your brother?"

"Don't sound too surprised, Toa," Tāwhiri muttered. "How many people do you know that can glow?"

I shook my head, not sure why that bothered me. Of course the forerunner—Marama—could glow, and he always had a regal air about him. But there was a big difference between sailing with a heavenly errands boy and the actual son of Havaiki. He wasn't a mere forerunner, he was royalty of the highest order. Why hadn't he told us?

Hina folded her arms. "He's still on the canoe, isn't he?" she asked.

Tāwhiri nodded. "It's not his fault. There was an accident, and he still can't walk because of it."

"He could've made it," Hina said. "All it would've taken was a call to Tahi. Or he could've asked one of you to carry him here."

I tried to imagine the forerunner letting Tāwhiri carry him piggyback style through the bush. It was easier to picture Loli shaving his head.

Tahi sighed. "Let the man keep his pride, Hina. You know how hard this is for him. I don't blame him for not wanting to be here."

"Yeah, because he knows he needs it more than anyone else," Hina grumbled.

Suddenly I remembered the conversation the forerunner and I had a few nights ago. He told me his siblings had impossible standards. Looking at Hina, I wondered what it was that made him feel so inadequate compared to her. She could've been older, yes, but she had the same formal air about her and she didn't glow any brighter than he did. Did her abilities put his light-lancing to shame?

"Forgive me if this isn't polite," Tāwhiri said hesitantly, "but why did you want us here?"

"Forgiveness isn't necessary because that question is entirely appropriate," Tahi said with a wink. "As for the answer, we are here to offer retrials for our sun warrior."

I looked up, blinking. "Me?"

"What are retrials?" Tāwhiri asked.

Hina waved a hand dismissively. "It's exactly what it sounds like. We are giving you the chance to redo your chief trials. We're not testing to see if you're ready to be a high chief, but we still need to know if you're better now than you were then. Not just anyone can have divine assistance; you have to be worthy of it."

"We were hoping that Marama could be here to vouch for you," Tahi said, sighing. "But it doesn't matter. We can do it without him. Are you ready?"

No, not really, I thought, thinking of how much better it would be if I just swam back to shore and let Tāwhiri get the divine assistance. And remembering how badly the trials had gone the first time...

I let out a deep breath, steeling my nerves. Now wasn't the time to fall apart; I needed to do this.

"Okay," I said. "What must I do?"

"Splendid!" Tahi clapped hands together. "If you could kneel for me like you did at the first trials, we can get started."

I sat on my knees with my hands in my lap. Tahi motioned for Tāwhiri's gourd. He passed it to her before sitting behind me to act as a witness.

Tahi uncorked the gourd and pressed it into the side of the air bubble, filling it up. Bringing the gourd to my head, she tipped it slowly, letting the saltwater trickle down my face.

"With the sacred water of Faletahi," she said, "I wash you of your guilt, anger, sorrow, and regret. Hereby declaring before the gods that you are relieved of your pain from your first trials." Tahi smiled gently. "Only time will tell what kind of man you truly are," she said, corking the gourd and setting it down.

I stared up at her, tasting salt as I blinked water out of my eyes. Those hadn't been the words Orator Ra'i had used; they sounded much more compassionate.

Tahi stepped back, letting Hina take the lead. She regarded me as she knelt down, looking me in the eye. "The trials, as you know, are divided into three tasks," she said. "Each one will test the will of your heart, mind, and strength. No man can truly serve another without all three. The first two trials will be conducted here; tomorrow you can prove your strength at the deadlands."

I nodded, preparing myself for the trial of the mind. At the village, the high chiefesses asked questions about the history and politics of our people. Those were easy enough to answer.

Hina glanced off to the side, gathering her thoughts. When she looked back at me, her expression was somber. "Do you find this agreeable?"

"Agreeable," I said, my voice faltering.

Hina inclined her head at Tahi, who knelt beside her. Tahi tucked her hair behind her ears, her smile sagging as she looked at me.

"The trial of the mind is to test your intelligence," she said. "No god or demigod in the heavens would ever help a fool. However, instead of bombarding you with trivia, I have but one question. I am not interested in how well you know politics, or agricultural calendars. I need to know how well you know yourself."

I laced my fingers together, my stomach pinching inside of me. How well did I know myself? There wasn't exactly a lot to know. Tahi might be disappointed by my answer, but at least I couldn't get it wrong. I chewed the inside of my cheek, waiting for her to start the trial.

"Toaolelā," she asked, using my full name. "Why did you hate your sister so much?"

My eyes flew open, her words hitting like a splash of cold water. I felt my insides shrivel and my hands grew hot. The weight of her question pressed down on me, and I trembled at how I would answer.

"Toaolelā," she said again. "Why did you hate your sister?"

I swallowed, wishing she could've asked something else. *Anything* else. I hadn't thought about this for years. My hatred towards Masina was so ingrained into me that I had accepted it as a part of myself; I stopped thinking about why I hated her, I just did. Of course I knew the answer, but did I dare say it out loud?

"Masina was always stronger than me," I said, my tongue like ironwood in my throat. "She was beautiful, faster, and much more likable. I knew people wanted her to rule instead of me, and I hated her for that."

I felt Tāwhiri's stare on my back, and wished I could evaporate on the spot. What must he think of me right now? What would any of them think if they could see me here, whining about how unfair my life had been? Shame burned in my eyes, and I almost hated Tahi for asking me that.

Please accept it, I thought. *Please take my answer and let it be over.*

But Tahi brought a hand under my chin, prompting me to look at her. Tears were brimming in her eyes and she shook her head.

"I'm sorry, Toa," she whispered. "But you know that's not true."

Panic exploded inside of me. My lower jaw started to shake and I felt a chill pass through my chest, like the cold hand of dread wrapping around my heart. A lump welled in my throat; it was all I could do not to fall apart. I met Tahi's gaze, my eyes going moist as I blinked at her.

"Please," I said, my voice cracking. "I promised I wouldn't tell."

Nobody knew the real reason why I hated Masina all those years—no one except for my father. It was a secret we swore to take to our graves. We knew it was for the best, but that didn't mean I wasn't tempted to start the rumors. Masina would not have been nearly as loved if the village knew where her powers had come from. And in my envy, I would've loved to see her lose it all.

Now, however, all I could think about was myself—what I had done, and more importantly what I hadn't done. The guilt and shame of it was too much to bear. I had masked it as hatred for my sister, when it was really an even deeper hatred for myself. I blamed Masina for a lot of things, even the death of our mother. But the truth was none of that was her fault.

A tear slipped down Tahi's cheek. "I can't help if you don't tell the truth," she said. "And I already know what happened. I know what it is that you need to say to me."

Another wave of guilt slammed into me. I thought I might break. She *knew*? How could she even consider helping me, then? Didn't she realize what I had done?

Tahi reached out and took my hand, squeezing it in hers. Her touch eased my anxiety, giving me a kind of comfort I hadn't felt since my mother was alive. When she spoke, her voice was filled with compassion.

"I know it's hard," she said. "I know you've buried this for so long, you forgot it was there. But this will make you a better man, and it will help you understand your sister. So, tell me, little sun warrior. Why did you hate her so much?"

She let go, clasping her hands in her lap and watching me with those patient eyes. I didn't want to say it, but I knew she was right. This was a part of myself I needed to face.

"Because," I said, the word coming out like a croak, "Masina—Masina wasn't always the strong one. It used to be me."

"And you regret that, don't you?" Tahi asked, tears now flowing freely down her face. "The night she was born, that decision you made. You regret it more than you'd like to admit."

The weight of her words threatened to crush me as my mind went back to that night. That night I made a decision that changed not only Masina's life, but mine as well. For years I've been running from that guilt, that unbearable shame that I made the wrong choice. But now, I could run no longer. I jerked my chin up and looked Tahi in the eye, hating myself as I forced a nod.

"Yes," I said, my voice wooden, "I regret that night. I know I shouldn't, but I regret it."

Tahi rested a hand on my head before cradling my cheek. When she smiled at me, there was no anger or hatred in her eyes.

"Well done," she said. "You pass the first trial."

Chapter 22

Tahi filled Tāwhiri's gourd with freshwater. She gave it to me, advising that I drink. I refused at first, but she insisted.

"We still have one more trial," she reminded me.

Grudgingly, I raised the gourd to my lips, taking a sip. It did make me feel a little better; at least I didn't feel like I was about to start sobbing anymore. I took another gulp, then passed it to Tāwhiri. I didn't look at him, but I could feel his curiosity burning into me, and I was grateful he knew better than to ask. Talking was the last thing I wanted right now. My head was spinning, and I felt both relieved and guilty at the same time.

I had told part of Masina's secret, the one I promised not to tell anyone. Even Masina didn't know anything about it. Tahi said she already knew the story, but a part of me still felt like I had betrayed my father. It seemed that, even when I was trying to make things right, I couldn't help but disappoint him.

Tahi switched places with Hina, letting her take the front as she sat cross-legged behind her. She nodded her encouragement, but Hina's face was somber. She twirled her wrist.

There was a puff of light, and a small burlap bag appeared in the air over her hand. Inside it was something round that looked like a mango or a papaya. Light shone out of the top, and Hina pulled the drawstring tight, sealing it off. She set it in her lap, clearing her throat.

"The trial of the heart will be as simple as the first, consisting of a single question," she said. "As you already know, a man without a good heart is nothing more than a tyrant."

I nodded, my nerves on edge as I wondered what she would ask. I failed the second trial with High Chief Moe, but that had been relatively painless. But after Tahi's trial, I didn't know what to expect anymore.

Hina studied me, fingering the bag in her lap. "When you did this with Moe, he warned you that the council had already decided who they thought had a better heart," she said. "In like manner, Tahi and I have also made our predictions for this trial. I'll still give it, but know that I have my suspicions about your heart."

I swallowed hard, my shoulders tensing. High Chief Moe and the council thought Masina had a better heart than I did. It felt like favoritism at the time, but they hadn't been wrong. Would things be any different this time?

Hina held out the bag to me. Frowning, I took it from her. It wasn't heavy, and had a plush texture to it. Like it really was some kind of fruit. I looked up at Hina. She motioned for me to open it.

I undid the string and was nearly blinded by what rolled out. I pinched my eyes shut, squinting as the light faded. When I could finally get a good look at it, I saw what looked like a golden-white mango. It was so plump I had to hold it with both hands. Light pulsed from it, and I felt an overwhelming urge to peel back the skin and take a bite.

"This is the fruit from the ninth heaven," Hina said as I stared at it. "They say it is where my father first gained his powers. One bite is enough to restore a demigod to full strength. Feed this to Marama, and he will be back to normal."

"Wonderful!" Tāwhiri shouted.

I looked back at him, frowning. To his credit, he folded his arms and looked ashamed of his outburst. He cleared his throat.

"I misspoke," he said. "Please continue."

I rolled my eyes, looking back at Hina then down at the fruit in my hands. "So if we give this to the forerunner, he can help us when we get to the deadlands?"

Hina nodded. "Correct."

I waited for her to say something else, but she only stared at me. There was no malice in her eyes, but suddenly I felt like she was watching me the way a spider watches a fly. I glanced down at the fruit again.

"So, what's the challenge?" I asked.

"One bite of that is enough to speed up Marama's recovery," Hina said. "But if a mortal were to eat the whole thing, they would be granted the same measure of power."

She let her words hang in the air, leaving me to fill in what they meant. Instinctively, I felt my grip tighten around the fruit, my nails digging into the skin, nearly puncturing it.

My tongue went dry. "You're saying, that if I eat this, I can...I can be—"

"Like a god," Hina finished. "Yes. You will have the enhanced strength and speed that Marama has. You will be able to manipulate light. You will have a connection to the ninth heaven that is reserved for only the greatest of heroes." She hesitated. "You could become the sun warrior of the Light Village."

My hands twitched, jerking the fruit up to my mouth, but I forced them back down. It couldn't be that simple. Could it? This had to be a part of the trial, which meant there was a reason I wasn't supposed to eat it. But looking at the fruit...at its supple skin, and smelling its sweet aroma...I couldn't deny that I was tempted. I could be as strong as I was when Mā had possessed me. Only this time, it would be done the right way.

I shook my head, forcing my eyes away from it as I tried to concentrate. "What's the catch?" I asked. "Are you saying that I should eat this instead of the forerunner?"

Hina turned her palms up, her face expressionless, "I am saying it's your choice. You could eat that and gain the strength of ten men, possibly twelve. You could go on to single-handedly save your sister if you wanted to. Then you could go back to the Light Village, and no one would ever question your right to rule."

I rolled the fruit in between my hands. That didn't sound bad, at all. This whole time I had secretly wondered how I could help Masina. Alani had offered to show me sparring techniques, but we never had the time for it. Plus, I knew it was hopeless to try and squeeze ten years of training into a week-long trip. But with this...

"He hasn't eaten it yet," Tahi noted, a hint of pleasure in her voice.

Hina nodded. "That's a good sign. Tell me, Toa, what do you think you should do with that fruit?"

"What if we both ate it?" I blurted, desperately trying to come up with a third option. "If I ate half, and the forerunner ate the other half, then we would both be strong."

Tahi chuckled. "Say what you want about the boy, Hina, but he is not lacking in creativity."

"I wish it were that simple, Toa," Hina said with a small smile. "But it's one fruit per person. If you try to split it, it won't work for either of you."

Of course, I silently cursed. *Because that would be too easy.*

"Would it be so bad if Toa ate it?" Tāwhiri asked. "The forerunner said he'll get his powers back, anyway. By the time we get to the deadlands, we could have two demigods in the crew instead of one."

A demigod, I thought. That was something I could get used to hearing.

Hina shook her head. "Marama would still be weak by the time you arrived. He would most likely overexert himself again, and could end up impeding your progress."

"Besides, there's more at stake here," Tahi added. "If Toa eats this fruit, he will become a warrior, but he will lose Masina forever."

I gasped, dropping the fruit like a hot rock. It sat in my lap, still pulsing light, but now it reminded me more of an octopus trap.

"What do you mean?" I asked, "If I eat this, I'll be strong enough to save her. That's the whole point, isn't it?"

But Tahi denied it. "I'm not talking about her life. I'm talking about something much more precious. There is something very special about your sister, Toa, and it's more than what you already know about her. I know you can't see it, but she needs you the way you are right now. If you eat that fruit, you might be able to pull her out of the deadlands, but you will lose her in ways you can't possibly imagine."

"So here's our question, Toa," said Hina. "Will you eat this fruit and become the warrior you've always wanted to be, or will you give it to Marama with the hope that it'll save your sister in the long run?"

I picked up the fruit, surprised at how heavy it felt now. One bite—one bite was all I needed to be strong again. I could save Masina and return home a hero. Tahi said Masina needed me the way I was now, but how could that be? Masina had never needed me; she was so much stronger than I was. What could I possibly do for her that she couldn't do for herself?

Like a flash of lightning, Masina's ghostly image flickered across my mind. I thought of her face, pale and ruined by injuries I had given her as tears of moonlight spilled down her cheeks.

It's okay, brother. Don't look for me. I know you don't really want to.

The fruit was less than an inch away from my lips now, and my jaw quivered as I tried not to bite it. What was I doing? Weren't we in this mess because I had tried to be stronger than Masina? Even if I did rescue her, wouldn't I be setting myself up for the same thing, all over again? I wasn't sure if Masina needed me to be this way, thin and gangly. But I did know I shouldn't have this kind of power. I didn't know how to handle it.

Summoning every ounce of willpower I had, I pulled the fruit away from my mouth. "Tāwhiri!" I shouted.

Behind me Tāwhiri let out a startled gasp as he scrambled to his feet, "What is it?" he said, eyes darting around. "Is there a shark coming?"

I stuffed the fruit in the bag and pulled the drawstring tight. With heavy arms, I held it out to him, forcing myself not to look at it.

"Take this back to the forerunner," I said, my voice wooden, "Tell him and Alaka'i I'll be back with our water soon."

"Wow..." Tāwhiri sounded surprised as he took the bag. "I'll get this to him," he said. "Thank you."

He ran, diving straight through the air bubble and kicked up to the surface. I watched him go, wondering if I had done the right thing. That seemed to be the theme for the trials, today; was I any better today than I had been when we left the village?

"Told you he would do it." Tahi said.

I looked at her. She smiled as she tilted her head to Hina, who raised her eyebrows.

"I didn't doubt it," she said. "But it is good to know we were right."

"Does this mean I pass, then?" I asked, rubbing the back of my neck.

"Unless you plan to swim after him, I should think so." Hina nodded her approval. "Well done, little light chief. Your second trial was a success."

Chapter 23

I gulped down the rest of the water from Tāwhiri's gourd. I felt...odd. Better than I had after Tahi's trial, but still empty. I had just given up my chance to be a warrior again, the thing I'd wanted since Masina was born. Tahi said I didn't need that power to save her. I really hoped she was right. There was no going back now; skinny Toa would have to be enough.

"How are you doing?" Tahi asked.

"Alright," I said, looking down at my bony fingers. How these hands could ever be more useful than a pair of strong arms was beyond me.

"That's good," said Hina. "I know it's hard to believe, but that form you wear is quite powerful. When the time comes, you'll see what we mean."

She held out her hand, motioning for the gourd. I passed it to her, and she slipped off the kaulima, cupping it as she traced the rim with her fingertip.

"This isn't part of the trials," she said, "but out of curiosity, what do you hope to find when you get to the deadlands?"

I frowned. Wasn't that part obvious? "I'm...going to find my sister."

Hina tilted her head, contemplating this. She tossed the kaulima into the air. Tendrils of light snaked around the wooden frame before sinking into it, as though the kaulima was a dry cloth dipped in water. It floated down to Hina's hand. She passed it back to me, the light fading when I touched it.

"Hold onto that," she said. "When you get to the deadlands it'll make it easier to find your sister."

"Thank you," I said.

Tahi smiled. "You really have become a better man," she said. "One whom I would be happy to help."

I bowed low to them. "You've done more than I could've possibly hoped for. We are eternally indebted to you for that."

Hina let out a derisive scoff. Startled, I looked up, wondering if I had offended her. But her smile was playful; she looked like she might laugh.

"That's cute," she said. "He thinks this is all the help we're going to offer."

Tahi hugged her sides, looking amused. "After everything you've been through, Toa, I think you deserve a little more than a fruit you couldn't eat and an old bracelet."

"No, really, I—" I started, not sure how to finish. Was it rude to tell a goddess to stop giving you things?

Hina lifted her chin smugly. "You what? You don't want our help? Got it all under control, do you?"

My face grew hot, and I wished I hadn't said anything. I had a hard enough time maintaining formalities in protocol, let alone in front of two goddesses.

Tahi laughed. "I think I can see why she's so attached to him. Give him the space to grow, and he really can shine."

"He'll need that," said Hina. "Especially where he's going."

She and Tahi stood up. Tahi offered me a hand, pulling me to my feet. The generosity of the act was not lost on me. Servants always stood up first. By helping me up, Tahi was giving me a level of respect I did not deserve.

"I refilled your water and sent it back to your canoe," Tahi said. "There's also another gift waiting for you there. Something that'll make it easier to cut through those demons."

I nodded gratefully. "I wish that I had more to give you."

"Then don't fail," said Hina. "We're all counting on you, Toa. Now would be a terrible time to get cold feet."

I swallowed hard, the weight of her words pressing down on me. Now more than ever I wished we had Masina. I couldn't fight against demons, but she could.

I bowed to Hina and Tahi, excusing myself as I started to walk backwards away from them. When I was at a respectful distance, I turned around, thinking about how I would swim to the surface, when Hina called out to me.

"Oh, and Toa?"

I spun around. "Yes?"

Hina furrowed her brow. "There's something Marama isn't telling you, something I think you should know before you get to the deadlands. He bears you no ill will, but I worry his motivations may impair his judgement. "

I nodded uncertainly. "Okay," I said. "Is there...anything you want me to tell him?"

Hina's frown deepened. "Tell him it wasn't his fault. And this won't change what happened."

I nodded, even though I didn't know what she meant. With questions swimming in my head, I thanked them again and jumped through the bubble. Following the faint light, I gripped Masina's kaulima and kicked up to the surface.

A chill wind prickled the top of my head as I broke through, inhaling greedily. Heart thudding in my chest, I tilted my head back and closed my eyes, letting my feet float up as I caught my breath. It was evening now. The sky melted from blue to golden pink as the sun dipped behind the mountains.

I blinked in surprise; Tāwhiri and I came here around lunchtime. Had I really been down there that long? Shaking my head, I made the swim back to shore. Despite my inexperience in the water, it wasn't as hard as I thought it would be. The water seemed to be leading me forward, and I wondered if somewhere in the deep Tahi was pushing me.

Were it not for the forerunner's glow or the sound of Lali's ukarere, I might've thought there was another shipwrecked crew on this island. The group singing around a cozy fire was too cheerful to be my crew mates. None of them were grumpy or sleep-deprived; instead, they were laughing and singing like old friends. Music danced through the air, accompanied by mouth-watering aromas that made my stomach rumble.

A pot was propped up over the fire; Loli stirred its contents as he hummed. He waved when he saw me, bright smile standing out against his dark skin.

"There you are, Light child!" he said, clapping me on the back. "I was beginning to worry about you. But, just like Lali, here you are—showing up as soon as the food is ready."

"Eh, I helped cook," Lali protested. "And I gathered it, too. So I don't know what you're talking about."

"Oh yeah? You know where we're gonna gather your food from, Lali?"

"Where?"

Loli pulled down his eyelid. "Right here."

I ducked as Lali threw a banana skin at his cousin. Loli caught it with one hand, laughing.

"You all seem to be in a better mood," I said, remembering how it used to be like this every night. Had that really only been three days ago?

"A good day on dry land will do that to you," Lali said, passing me a ripe banana. I peeled it open and took a bite. The sweetness of it made me want to melt; we hadn't had fresh fruit in days.

Then, remembering what my assignment had been, my eyes widened. "Tāwhiri," I started. "The water. Tahi—"

"Already here, mate," Tāwhiri said, smiling. "It all came floating back here when I arrived. I think she spoiled us, because there were more gourds in there than we had set out with."

I sighed in relief. I glanced at our canoe, which was no longer resting on the shore. It bobbed several feet out, and I knew someone must've tied the anchor line. That was odd; had everyone pushed off while I was gone?

Following my gaze, Tāwhiri nodded at the forerunner, "It was all him, mate," he said. "You should've seen it; he picked up the canoe so that Pule and I could fix the bottom."

My mouth fell open. I stared at the forerunner, who was weaving a basket with Alaka'i. "He *picked* it up?"

"Like a child's plaything," Tāwhiri said. "He grabbed the right hull with one hand and the whole canoe started glowing white like he does. And he just held it there—balanced a two-ton canoe and told us to take our time with the repairs." he shook his head. "It was like something out of the old stories. He looked like he could've held it up there all night."

I was amazed. Hina had said he would be stronger, but I didn't realize he would be *that* strong. I felt a flare of jealousy thinking how that could've been me holding up the canoe, and tried to shove the thought aside.

"And water's not the only thing she gave us, mate," Tāwhiri added, pointing with his chin. Just off the coast our canoe bobbed up and down with the water, but grounded against the shore was something else. Something that also sported a double-hull and a crab-claw sail.

I thought my eyes would bulge out of my head. "No way," I breathed. "*Another* canoe?"

"She floated up here not long ago," Loli said from his pot. "Nearly gave me a heart attack; I thought it was manned by ghosts," he chuckled.

"She's a beauty, though," said Pule, "Marama said we had permission to name her, and everyone agreed to call her the *Inati*."

I popped the rest of my banana into my mouth as I stood with Tāwhiri, walking over to examine the new canoe. This one was noticeably smaller than the one we arrived on, with the triangular sail opening diagonally over the deck rather than standing straight up. While all ten of us could comfortably sit or stand on this canoe, it looked like it was meant for a crew of two to three people. If needed, one person could probably alter the sheet and the rudder by themselves. I rested my hand against one of the hulls, offering a prayer of thanks to the gods.

"This could make all the difference at the deadlands," Tāwhiri said. "Our canoe was too bulky to outmaneuver the demons. But this one will be much, much faster."

I winced. "Does this mean we're leaving our old canoe?" Maybe it was silly, but somehow that felt like leaving behind a crew member.

Tāwhiri made a face. "Oh, gods no. It just means we'll have two canoes to work with instead of one. That opens up all kinds of possibilities."

We walked back to the others. I picked up a coconut leaf to help Alani, who was making dinner plates. "How was the hunting?" I asked her.

She laughed. "It wasn't even hunting. It was more like we went up to the mountains and the gods said, 'Here, have some food.'"

I arched an eyebrow, "It can't be that easy."

"Actually, it can," Alaka'i called across the flames. "I'm not even kidding, Toa. It was so easy to find a pig when we went up there. There were farmlands that had these huge sections of livestock. We saw pigs, cows, horses, and chickens—all of them fat and healthy.

Marama said we could take what we needed as long as we worked the land for a few hours."

The forerunner shrugged. "It's the same principle you learned back home; take care of the land, and the land will take care of you." He finished his basket and tossed it up in the air.

"But still," Temanu said, pouring coconut oil into a bamboo flask, "I think this island is too good to us. Ulu farms, kalo plantations, everything we needed practically gift-wrapped before we got here. There was even a garden full of medicinal herbs. Don't get me wrong, I'm thankful, but—" hH shook his head.

I smiled. I could see Tahi taking pride in a place like this. One where weary travelers could come to be rejuvenated and leave to finish their voyage with honor. She had even provided a way to give food and water while making people feel like they had worked hard to earn it.

"Do you think she'll be joining us?" Pule asked the forerunner.

Marama shook his head. "Tahi is generous, but I doubt she will attend tonight. She has other responsibilities to attend to."

Hearing him say that reminded me of what Hina had said, about something Marama was keeping from us. I opened my mouth to ask him about it, but then he looked me in the eye. His gaze was severe, and I could've sworn he gave a small shake of his head. I looked away, startled. Had he known what I was going to ask him?

Alani finished her plate and pulled out a knife to trim the edges. "Tāwhiri says you met our hostess?" she asked.

I nodded, allowing her to take the conversation in a different direction. "I think you'd like her, Alani," I said. "She's really nice. She even gave me this, said it'll help us find Masina."

I showed her the kaulima. Alani's eyebrows creased as she took it from me.

"I gave her this," she murmured. She pressed it to her lips, then let out a sigh. "One more day. One more day, and we can finally put this behind us."

Lali stopped strumming and Loli looked up from his pot. A soft reverence passed through the crew as we contemplated what that would mean. We had endured so much together, and after tomorrow it would all be worth it. I swallowed, remembering what Tahi had said about Masina needing me the way I was, and prayed that I would be able to deliver.

Seeing that I was almost done with my plate, Alani offered me her knife. I nodded my thanks and shaved off the excess fronds, setting my finished plate on top of hers.

We wove in silence until Loli announced it was time to uncover the 'umu. As we shrugged off the banana leaves, a gust of steam blew up in my face, making me salivate. Next to the roasted pig was the ulu, kalo, fa'i, and roasted tapioca. On top of that were rolls of palusami. The salty-sweet scent from the coconut milk mixed with the pork and seemed to melt my insides.

Loli quartered off the pig, dividing the best parts into the two baskets Marama and Alaka'i made. These would be left as offerings to Hina and Tahi. We added the juiciest vegetables we could find with it as well as the sweetest-smelling palusami. Alani tucked a plate and a flask of coconut juice into each of them, then Marama and Alaka'i went inland to make the offering.

When they returned, Marama announced the offering had been accepted, and we were allowed to eat. Pule blessed the food, thanking the ancestors and our patron gods for helping us make it this far. He prayed that the food would give us the strength we needed to conquer death tomorrow, and we bowed our heads in agreement as he finished.

"Okay, men and woman," Loli said rubbing his hands together, "let's get to work! This pua'a isn't going to eat itself."

We heartily agreed. I filled up my plate next to Tāwhiri, careful I didn't take too much of anything and accidentally rob someone of the chance to enjoy it. There was more than enough food to go around, but I could tell Loli had been careful not to make more than was needed. According to him, wasting food was the most serious unpardonable sin. Murder was a close second.

Night had settled, and our circle around the bonfire tightened against the cold. Alani asked Pule how well the spears would fit into the frames, and Pule replied they would work just fine. Lali said the palusami tasted sour, to which Loli declared he was souring it with his own breath. I relaxed in between Tāwhiri and Temanu, a part of me wishing things could stay like this forever. Next to a warm fire on a moonlit night, it couldn't get much better than this.

Alaka'i broke the mood when he sat up straight, his eyes squinting. "Eh, Pule," he said. "Look at our canoe. Do you see what I'm seeing?"

Pule frowned, turning to look over his shoulder. His expression shifted from confusion, to disbelief, then back to confusion. "What in the name of Kalia...?"

The rest of us strained to see what they were looking at. At first, my eyes darted to the *Inati*, but it was fine. When I heard Alani gasp, I whipped around to face our original canoe, the one floating offshore. It was hard to see after staring at the fire. But as my eyes adjusted, I could see what had caused the alarm.

I scoffed. "Is that...is that a guy on our boat?"

My description hardly did it justice, but nevertheless there was indeed a guy standing on our boat. One who tottered on the deck like a drunkard. He spotted us and started waving, his face shadowed by moonlight as he yelled something that was lost in the wind. He must've realized we couldn't hear him, because he dove into the water and started swimming to shore.

I felt Tāwhiri tense next to me, and Alani slipped out her knives. Swallowing hard, I wished I had a weapon. Not that it would've done me any good; I still had no idea how to use them.

As the stranger paddled closer, Alaka'i warned us to be ready. "We haven't found anything dangerous on this island," he said. "But I'm not sure if this will change that."

Temanu readied his axe. When the stranger arrived on the shore, he didn't attack anyone or make any threats. Instead he paused in the whitewash, resting on his hands and knees in exhaustion. He coughed up saltwater, and I felt a stab of pity for him, even if I wasn't sure what he wanted. But as he rose to his feet, a collective gasp rippled through the crew. This wasn't a stranger at all.

"Where are we?" he asked, running a hand through his sopping wet ehu hair. "This is not the Light Village. The unfamiliar connects us with the divine, but I don't think this is what the orators meant."

Alani was the first to react. Tossing her bone knives aside, she ran up to him with a childlike enthusiasm I had never seen from her before. For once, she looked less like a warrior and more like a thirteen-year-old girl. She threw her arms around his neck, laughing as he scooped her up.

"Ori!" she exclaimed. "Ori, it's you! You're okay!"

Ori smiled. And it wasn't his usual half-smile or an emotionally muted smirk, but one that radiated pure joy. He looked thin. The bandages on his head needed to be changed, but he was here. It was like he'd come back from the dead.

Ori set Alani down and kissed the top of her head. Temanu grabbed a blanket and threw it around his shoulders. He dried off his face and made his way around the crew, embracing each of us in turn as we told him what he'd missed.

"You've accomplished so much on your own," he said after hugging Loli. "Thank you all for taking care of me. I'm...sorry I couldn't be with you sooner." He looked pained, obviously ashamed he had been unable to help his own crew.

Alaka'i pressed his forehead to Ori's before pulling him into a hug. "Actually, captain," he said, "you are right on time."

INTERLUDE

Masina stared into the wooden bowl, watching the lights inside contort into the image of her brother. She watched him talk animatedly with Ori as he loaded supplies from a smaller canoe onto a bigger one. He walked with his back straight and had an ease about him Masina had never seen before. She bit her lip, telling herself that this was good. It was good that he was happy.

She just wished he would realize how much happier he would be without her.

Turn back, she thought, watching the crew gather for a prayer before dividing into two groups. Lā, Ori, and another man stayed on the smaller canoe. Everyone else boarded the bigger one. Masina recognized the light radiating from the third man's skin, and her heart sank.

Please turn back.

Masina twirled her fingertips through her hair, noting how transparent they looked. She knew it wouldn't be long before she faded away completely. She prayed that would happen before her brother could find her. She didn't want him to see her like this.

A woman's hand rested on her shoulder, and Masina felt her slide next to her on the floor, staring into the bowl with her.

"There, now," she said, comforting Masina as she relaxed into her embrace. "It's alright."

Masina's lower jaw began to quiver. "I really don't want him to come."

The woman shushed her, brushing the hair out of her eyes before cradling her head. Masina clung to her, wondering how she could possibly love her after everything that had happened. After what Masina had done to her.

"He'll be alright, love," she said, kissing her forehead. "And so will you. You'll see."

Masina didn't think she would. She closed her eyes and turned away from the bowl and the shifting lights inside of it, not wanting to watch her brother sail to his death.

The lightweight design and crab-claw sail allows this canoe to
be faster and more agile than its European counterparts.

Chapter 24

The *Inati* was a lot faster than I thought it would be. Ori knelt by the paddle he used as a rudder, angling the sail to make the tiny skiff zoom forward. We cut through the water so fast that Ori had to double back several times. I knew that Ori could've kept an even pace with our old canoe if he wanted to. Him sailing around in circles and drawing figure eights in the water was probably his way of testing out our new boat.

Either that, or he was just showing off.

I knew it was childish, but I couldn't resist making faces at Alani as she sharpened her knives, or as Loli held the rudder every time we circled around them.

"You're laughing now," Loli said, patting the rudder. "Just wait until it's your turn."

Ori wanted everyone to take a turn on the *Inati* so that he could teach us how to sail it. I had an hour to learn, then I would switch with someone else. Having two canoes altered the work schedule we had, but nobody seemed to mind.

Ori tried to show me how to steer the *Inati*. But like with so many other things, I didn't have enough confidence for it. If I wasn't fumbling the sheet, I was forgetting to steer, and after nearly flipping the canoe, Ori took the oar and suggested I get a feel for the speed instead.

When my hour was up, Alani threw me a line before she hopped onto the *Inati*. After her it was Tāwhiri, then Pule. The rest of the crew followed.

By the time Lali finished, the sun had reached its midday peak. Marama estimated we had four hours before we reached the deadlands. Alani requested a meeting, and Ori pulled up the sail as Marama secured a line connecting the two canoes. He tied a bowline so that he and Ori could cross over before letting out the slack so that the *Inati* wouldn't bump into the rudder or hit one of the hulls. The tiny canoe trailed behind like a baby duck chasing its mother.

Watching the *Inati* bob up and down, I realized I didn't know the name of our original canoe. It never bothered me before, but now that we had the *Inati*, it felt almost criminal not to know it.

I mentioned this to Ori, who raised an eyebrow in surprise.

"You mean you don't know?" he asked.

I shook my head. "Should I?"

Ori tilted his head to the side, thinking. "I guess not. You were really young when she was named." He rested a hand against the mast, as though he were greeting an old friend. "This canoe was blessed two weeks after Masina was born. My father and his craftsmen had just finished it when we heard about your mother.

Because of that, he thought it fitting that this canoe should be named after her. Your father approved, and even came to our village for the blessing."

My eyes went wide. "You mean, you mean that—"

Ori nodded. "You've been sailing aboard the *Ta'ifetū*. This is the canoe that will help you save your sister. Well, one of them."

I touched my fingertips to the mast, surprised at the reverence I felt. The memory was faint, but I did remember my father leaving with his advisers. He didn't tell me where he was going, only that I needed to take care of Masina until he got back.

I looked over my shoulder, thinking of my father. What was he doing now? Had life gone back to normal in the village, or did more demons attack when we left? Suddenly I wished I could be with him, if only to support him in war.

We met aft of the splashguard where Pule and Tāwhiri prepared to unveil the weapons they'd been working on. Pule brought out a spear while Tāwhiri set up a wooden frame for it. The frame went up to Tāwhiri's hip, and had a long shaft to load the spear in. It rested on a triangular base that could rotate from side to side, and had a separate switch to angle it up and down. As Pule slid it into place, Tāwhiri explained how it worked.

"Alani said she needed crossbows, but we didn't know how to make those. So instead, we took what Pule knew about spearfishing to come up with this." He pointed at the cords that ran around the back end of the spear. They hung loose before, but with a loaded shaft they were pulled taut. "These cords give tension like your basic three-prong and are locked in place by a mechanism under the loading dock." He tapped the underside of the shaft holding the spear, which had a cord dangling down from it. "This switch down here is what releases it."

"That's smart," I said, impressed at their ingenuity.

Temanu frowned. "But does it work?"

Tāwhiri wagged his eyebrows. "See for yourself."

Pule pointed the mount away from the canoe. He knelt, bracing his shoulder against the frame before pulling on the trigger cord. There was a loud crack as the spear shot forward, leaving a trail of bubbles in the water before it lost momentum. Pule and Tāwhiri must've used ironwood when they carved it, because it didn't bob back to the surface.

"Nice!" Alaka'i exclaimed.

Lali whistled. "If only we had this sooner. Think of the fish we could catch."

There was another rope attached to the spear, one different from the cords used to give it tension. This one was strung through the shaft like a tail. Pule tugged on it to reel the spear back in.

"We added lines to the spears to make them retrievable," he said. "It's a little bit thinner than the tension cords, so don't get them confused if you end up shooting." He compared it to the cords that ran down the loading shaft, showing us the difference between them.

"Pule also thought it would be smart to keep the spear tip simple," Alani said, showing us how the wooden spear came to a straight point. It wasn't serrated, and didn't have a separate stone head tied to it. "That way, we won't waste time trying to get demons off after we've speared them. A few good shakes should do the trick."

Ori raised an eyebrow, "Should?"

Tāwhiri turned his palms up. "Sorry, captain, but we didn't have any demons to test it on."

"I like it," Loli said. "When this is over, we can use them to catch dinner."

Alaka'i ran a hand along the frame, appreciating the craftsmanship. "How many do you have?"

"We made three," Pule said. "Two for the rudder, and one for the safety net since those areas were hardest to protect," he paused, glancing at Ori. "But that was before we got another canoe?"

"Don't worry about it," Ori said. "It's an ingenious invention, but a little too bulky for the *Inati*. Wouldn't you say so, Alani?"

She nodded. "The spearguns are meant to be long-distance weapons, and that'll be hard to do on such a small canoe."

"Who will use the guns?" Temanu asked.

"Definitely Pule," Alani said. "And we were hoping Lali and Loli could take the other two? They have more experience with spearguns than the rest of us, and they're big enough to handle the recoil when they shoot."

Loli nudged his cousin. "You hear that? I think she just called you fat."

"Speak for yourself!" Lali said, thumping Loli's belly with his fist.

Alani explained our revised strategy for the deadlands. Last time, we got sucked into the storm because everyone was busy fighting monsters. But we didn't need to kill them all; we just had to get to the entrance. Staying on course was our main priority.

"Everything we do needs to focus on the end goal of keeping both canoes moving forward," she concluded. "I went over tactics with Ori and Alaka'i, and they said they might have a few tricks for that."

Alaka'i held up a fist. "It's going to be a bumpy ride, but we'll get there."

Alani glanced at Marama. "As for that other thing we discussed?"

He nodded. "I can help. No problem at all."

Alani looked relieved. She let out an even breath as she pointed to the top of the mast. Tied to it were four long ropes that drooped into thick coils on the deck.

"I'm not sure how often we'll use these," she said, "but we have extra lines in case we need to transfer from one canoe to the other. Since the Navigator men will focus on sailing, the rest of us might need to go back and forth if demons swarm one of the canoes."

I was impressed. That was a good idea. I couldn't see myself swinging from those ropes, but Alani and Tāwhiri had the agility for it. And with Alani being our best warrior, she probably needed to be on both canoes. For all her snark and salty attitude, Alani showed promise as the future high chief of the War Village.

"But again, these are just a precaution," Alani went on, fingering one of the extra lines. "I don't think any of us will use them except for Toa."

I blinked at her, startled. "What, me?"

She had to be joking.

But Alani wasn't laughing. "Toa, out of all of us, you're the one who needs to get to the deadlands the most. If we have to split up, you need to be on the canoe going to the underworld. That's non-negotiable."

The entire crew had their eyes on me. I squirmed under the attention. Alani, like everyone else, believed there was something only I could do to save Masina. Tahi and Hina had said the same, but I couldn't see what that was. Now that we were here—now that we were hours away from death itself, I really hoped they were right.

Ori broke the tension. "I'll take Toa and Alani with me on the *Inati*," he said. "The rest of you stay on the *Ta'ifetū*." He looked at each member of his crew. "All hands to your stations, and pray to the gods. Everyone hopes to rest with the ancestors someday, but I'd rather we didn't do that tonight."

Chapter 25

We started seeing the carcasses an hour later.

Tāwhiri spotted the first one from the catwalk. His surprised yelp was so loud, we heard him on the *Inati*. As the Navigator men crowded next to him, Ori swung the canoe around to see what they were looking at.

The misshapen half-man, half-eel body of the demon looked eerie against the calm sea. Time exposed to the elements had left its charred flesh sun-bleached and bloated with water. And there were more like it, more bodies that bobbed in the water, like grisly markers left along a mountain trail.

Ori steered the *Inati* to the *Ta'ifetū*, drawing close enough that Alani could brace against the catwalk. She looked like she might be sick.

"If I didn't know anything about wayfinding," Loli said, "I would ask myself whether she was being polite, or trying to lead us into another trap."

"You call this polite?" Lali said, his nose wrinkled in disgust.

Alaka'i frowned. "These shouldn't be here. The last time we were in this spot, the waves were like mountains. These should be miles away by now."

"Not only that," Ori said, pointing at the trail with his oar. "But look at the line they're making. There's no current pulling in that direction." He looked to the forerunner, his brow furrowed. "What's happening here?"

Marama folded his arms, staring morosely at the sea of floating corpses. "Think of it as a welcoming gift," he said. "It's her way of reminding us who we're dealing with."

Temanu shivered. "I thought she wasn't as strong in the daylight."

"She isn't," Marama agreed. "You've seen what she can do under a full moon; this is a far cry from her best."

"What's her deal, anyway?" Tāwhiri asked, squirming as Ori used his oar to push away a body that was drifting too close. "I know she had issues with Toa's dad, but even then this seems extreme."

He had a point. I never really questioned why Mā had kidnapped Masina; I was more focused on getting her back. Now that Tāwhiri had brought it up, I realized I had no idea why Mā decided to take her in the first place.

"That is a wise question," Marama said. His lips pressed into a thin line. "One that has a complicated answer. Hana has always had a grudge against the Light Village. She is a being of darkness; Havaiki is the light god. They naturally conflict with one another."

"That doesn't sound so complicated," Alani said.

He made a face. "There's more to it than that. Something...something happened between her and the light god's family. Rather than overcome it, she turned her hatred against his descendants, determined to end his mortal line forever."

A carcass thudded against the hull, and Pule pushed it away with a spear. I shuddered at the squelching noise he made when the spear prodded into the rotting corpse.

Ori frowned. "That doesn't make sense. Why would she come after mortals if the problem started with gods?"

"For the same reason why any of your families would be a prime target for your enemies." The forerunner grimaced. "If you really want to destroy a man, you take what's important to him, and the gods are incredibly proud of their mortal children."

"But what could've been so terrible?" I asked. "What could've happened that made her hate a village full of people she's never met?"

Marama tensed, and while I didn't know how I'd done it, I knew I had crossed a line. He snatched Pule's spear and jabbed it into the water. A shock of light flashed from it, zipping to the nearest carcass. It evaporated as the light passed through it. The trail of light continued to zip from body to body, dissolving each of them in turn as it shot away from us like an underwater lightning bolt.

Marama handed the spear back to Pule. "We don't have time for this. There are more pressing matters to attend to."

I watched the light streaking through the water, growing smaller and smaller as it raced away from us. Just when it was about to disappear beyond the horizon, I saw a flash of green light shoot up in the air.

Ori saw it, too. He set his jaw, his grip on his oar tightening. "Marama's right," he said. "We need to focus. It won't be much longer now." he hesitated, then added, "Tāwhiri, bring your quarterstaff and switch places with Toa."

I jerked away from the catwalk as Tāwhiri retrieved his weapon. "Switch places?" I blurted. "But why?"

The question was out of my mouth before I could stop it. I cringed, wishing I hadn't said anything. It wasn't my place to question Ori; as the captain he always had the final say.

Ori regarded me, his eyebrows knit together. "Tāwhiri is a better fighter," he said finally. "Sorry, Toa, but you're better off helping Loli where you can use what you've learned about sailing. If you came with us, you'd only g—" He caught himself, clearing his throat. "You're better off here."

I winced. Ori had been kind to correct himself, but gods; it still made me feel worthless.

I should've eaten the fruit.

"Don't worry, Light child," Loli said, pulling me onto the catwalk. "We'll put you to work. You know how it is; there is always something to do on a canoe."

I shrugged. "Yeah, sure."

"Toa," Alani said abruptly. "Wait."

I turned around. She pulled something out of her apron and handed it to me. It was an obsidian knife, a few inches longer than the bone ones she normally used. She had wrapped a cloth around the blade and I slipped it off, admiring the smooth finish and the serrated edges.

"I know you're not much of a fighter," she said. "But it's better than nothing. Knives are most effective when used by someone who relies on wit rather than brute strength, someone who can outthink an opponent. So, it should be perfect for you."

I wrapped the cloth back around the knife and tucked it into my waistband. "Thank you," I said, surprised at the veiled compliment.

It occurred to me how far my relationship with Alani had come. Just a week ago she was kicking my shins and calling me sunspot. Now she treated me like any other member of the crew. I could see that in the way she bowed her head and brought a closed fist to her lips before raising it in a salute.

"Fight for love," she said.

I saluted her back, uttering the words her village was famous for. "Fight with honor. Should blood be spilt, may it only be the blood of your enemies. And let it be done in the name of peace."

Alani raised an eyebrow. She looked impressed, and I earned my first non-malicious smile from her. I spent years studying the customs of the War Village, but this was my first time to say the warrior's prayer outside of a protocol meeting. The prayer took on a new meaning when used before an actual battle.

Ori stuck his oar in the water and tugged on the sheet. The *Inati* lurched forward. Alaka'i called for me to help with the sheet of our own sail, and we followed them.

I took over for Loli at the rudder, sliding into place behind Lali. He sat with his legs dangling over the fishing deck, examining the speargun next to him.

"It really is a shame we didn't have these sooner," he said, pulling the mechanism that allowed him to raise the spear up and down. "Think of how much easier it would've been to catch our dinner with one of these."

I nodded. "True, but think of all the holes we might've punched into the canoe by accident." By "we," of course, I was thinking more about myself. I wouldn't put it past Loli to make me use one of these during his little teaching moments.

Loli chuckled. "I'll give you that one."

I hugged the rudder to my side with both hands, throwing my bodyweight against it to keep it in place. I pictured the massive paddle head in the water, and tried to imagine Loli using the speargun to pick demons off of it.

"Do you think you can keep those things away from the rudder without hitting it?" I asked him.

Loli brought one hand to the trigger and stared down the shaft. "Shouldn't be too hard," he said. "It really is like a giant three-prong, and I was using those before my parents let me hold a kitchen knife."

He took a few shots to get a feel for it. The first two went wild, one coming dangerously close to the left hull, but Loli was able to adjust by his fourth shot. When he felt comfortable with it, he took over for me at the rudder so that I could find something to use for target practice. With limited options, I settled for a few coconut-frond plates that had dried out. I threw one out. Loli let it float for a few seconds before spearing it through.

"Psh!" said Lali. He was looking over his shoulder as Loli reeled the plate back in. "Weak shot. Look how far off-center you were."

Loli stuck out his tongue in mock-anger. "Like you could do better."

"Yeah, I can actually," Lali said, giving a mock-sneer back. Then to Alaka'i. "Watch captain, permission to tie down the rudder so I can show that guy how to shoot?"

Alaka'i laughed as he gave his approval, crossing the deck to take his place. Lali grabbed a rope for the rudder, he and his cousin stink-talking each other all the way up until he was ready to start shooting. He braced the frame against his shoulder and gestured at me with his free hand.

"Go ahead, Toa," he said. "Throw a plate for me. Let's go."

I tossed out a plate far enough for it to land away from the rudder. Lali yanked on the trigger cord, piercing it in the middle. He lifted his chin at Loli as he reeled it back in.

"You see?" he said. "That's how you shoot."

Loli waved the comment away. "Small bubbles, this guy. Toa, throw one up in the air. Throw it high."

I glanced at Alaka'i, wondering if that was a good idea. He shrugged at me in a way that said, *Do you wanna tell him?*

"Toa," Loli insisted.

Praying that I wouldn't regret it, I hurled the next plate at an angle that sent it flying up and away from our canoe. Loli picked up the speargun—wooden frame, six-foot spear, and all—and aimed at the plate spiraling overhead. He pulled the cord, the loud crack of it echoing as his spear shot clean through, arcing in a rainbow before landing in the water. The plate spun around the cord attached to the end of the spear.

We passed the next half hour like that, with me throwing a plate however Lali or Loli asked me to, and watching them criticize each other after making one perfect shot after another. I would never say this out loud, but Lali was the better shot, setting the standard by shooting through two flying plates with a single spear. But even if Loli couldn't do that, I didn't doubt that we had the right men on the spearguns.

"Alright, men, playtime's over," Alaka'i said after Loli reeled in a spear that had somehow pierced an unsuspecting kahala fish. "I need all hands on deck. Toa, untie the rudder and help me hold her in place."

We obeyed. I undid the bowline Lali had used to secure the rudder. Behind me, Lali and Loli reloaded their guns, exchanging colorful remarks as they went to their stations. Lali stood behind me at the rudder, and Loli helped Pule and Temanu untie the sheet while the forerunner stood watching by the safety nets.

The *Inati* pulled up beside us. Tāwhiri had his patu and his quarterstaff out. Alani wore her shark-tooth rings on both hands. Worn like a knuckle duster in reverse, the shark-tooth rings were eight bands with teeth that jutted out where they rested on the middle and lower sections of her fingers, making Alani's hands more like claws. The rings were all connected to each other, and if Alani wanted to, she could slide them into her hair like a comb. She ran her thumb along the teeth lining her hands, her shoulders tense.

Ori looked over at Alaka'i. "Remember the signals?"

"Yes, captain," Alaka'i said with a half-smile. "It's hard to forget them when they're just numbers."

"How much further?" Pule asked.

"Roughly fifteen minutes, but the attack could start any moment now," Marama answered.

His words put everyone on edge. Three nights ago we had been in this exact same spot, and it had been a disaster. Could we end things differently this time?

Alani bit her lip, looking at the forerunner. "Will you still be able to do the...." She started gesturing with her clawed hands, unsure how to finish.

Marama nodded. "I'll be ready. However, we might find it wiser to wait."

He pointed at the water. Temanu and Tāwhiri looked over the edges of their canoes. Temanu jumped back, and Alani had to cover Tāwhiri's mouth to keep him from crying out. Ori swallowed hard, lifting his oar out of the water and pulling the sheet, relying on the wind to keep him on course.

"What's everyone gawking at?" I asked Loli in a whisper. I looked over the hull behind me, but saw nothing.

Loli twisted the rope in his hands, looking unsettled. "Trust me, Light child," he said. "You are not missing anything."

Moments later I saw what he meant. Floating under the surface were more demons, these ones undoubtedly alive. Water passed through their gilled necks and their eyes stared sightless at the sky above them. And unlike the carcasses that marked a trail for us, these were scattered all over—a legion of monsters just waiting for the call.

"Toa, Lali, don't move." Alaka'i said. He wasn't looking at me, but I nodded anyway, my chest tight with anxiety.

We glided along, neither the *Inati* nor the *Ta'ifetū* daring to use the rudder out of fear we might wake them. Some two hundred feet away I saw a green light dancing under the water. My knees went weak. We were here again.

I felt something bump into the rudder and my heart stopped. Cringing, I looked back at Lali, who in turn was looking down at the water. He bared his teeth in a silent wince.

A monster had crashed into the rudder; it shook its head as its bulbous eyes darted about. Then it looked up, locking eyes with me.

I abandoned all hope of silence. "They're coming!"

Ori stabbed his oar into the water and the *Inati* took off.

All around us the sea spat and hissed as hundreds of demons stirred, waking up to our presence. Their garbled cries sent chills down my spine. Fear gripped my heart, and it was all I could do not to curl up on the deck.

Lali snapped me out of it, calling for me to take over as he went for his speargun. I grunted under the extra weight, struggling to keep up with Alaka'i's commands.

"Turn her right, Toa!" he yelled. I threw my weight against the rudder, pushing and lifting with my legs to pump in big circular motions. I felt the canoe shift under me as Loli and Marama helped Pule and Temanu adjust the sheet, compensating for the sudden change in direction. The boom spun outward, catching the cross breeze and sucking us forward at an angle. We sailed away from the *Inati*, our canoes making a V in the water. The splash and spray marked where the monsters divided as they separated into two swarms, one that went after the *Inati*, and the other coming after us.

"So far so good," Alaka'i muttered.

I clamped the rudder to my side, feeling winded. Behind me I felt something grab onto the rudder. I looked back to see a demon holding on to it. Gods, those things were fast. I opened my mouth to tell Alaka'i, when a spear shot out, stabbing the creature through the tail. It shrieked and let go.

"That's one for me," Loli said cheerfully.

Lali scoffed. "Dug luck."

A faint green glow pulsed off to the left side of our canoe. I thought Alaka'i would call for us to switch directions, to start pushing to the right to make the canoe turn left, but he waited. He was watching for Ori's signal on the *Inati*.

The little skiff darted about, turning circles, figure eights, and cutting diagonals in the water. Monsters leapt aboard, but Alani and Tāwhiri cut them down. Finally, Ori looked in our direction, wrapping the sheet around his wrist and holding up two fingers.

"Take her left!" Alaka'i called.

I pulled, pushing with my legs and squatting low. Temanu slackened the sheet as Marama pulled, keeping the pressure just right so that our speed wasn't hindered. We raced toward the *Inati*, the hulls pointed towards an invisible spot in the water as though we were two sides of a triangle racing to meet at the summit. The demons followed in the water. Closer and closer the *Inati* came, and when they were close enough for me to see the teeth on Alani's rings Ori yelled something to Tāwhiri. He looked straight at Alaka'i and pointed his index finger to the sky.

"Go right!" Alaka'i yelled.

I took a step back before throwing my weight against the rudder. Across from us Ori ran and jumped onto the left hull of the *Inati*, pulling on the forward stay. The canoe spiraled, its back end tipping up as it made a sharp left turn. It landed with a splash, and Ori was back at the sheet again.

The two demon hordes converged in the water. Splashes went up as they rammed into each other. We took advantage of their disorientation to run our canoes around the edges, both of us heading closer towards the pale green light. I bared my teeth as I pushed and pulled with Alaka'i's, amazed at how agile our bulky canoe could really be.

"Lali," Alaka'i called, "bring your speargun by the left hull, in between Loli and Pule's."

"Yes, watch captain," Lali said, hefting the speargun with both hands as he went.

"On my mark, Toa," Alaka'i said. I nodded, heart fluttering from the adrenaline rush. I looked back at the demons chattering as they reoriented themselves. Then, they divided themselves in half and pursued us with renewed vigor. I thought Alaka'i would order us to go south by southwest again, but he kept us steady. My stomach churned as the demons raced closer, the outliers now visible from where I was.

"Hold her there, Toa," Alaka'i grunted. "Just a little longer."

Dark shadows surged towards the left hull of the canoe, and the cracking of the spearguns rang through the air. For men who had just picked them up hours ago, I was amazed at the agility Pule, Lali, and Loli showed. By the time Loli had launched his spear, Pule was aiming his gun, and Lali wasn't far behind him.

Over on the *Inati,* I saw Ori and Tāwhiri use their body weight to tip the canoe onto its side. They braced themselves against the right hull sticking up in the air, each of them gripping unbound stays for balance.

Alani was across the deck from them. The crook of her elbow wrapped around a rope and she held her right hand out, claws raking through demons as though she were cutting long grass.

Up ahead I saw another flash of green. My heart leapt to my throat; I hadn't realized how close we were. The entrance couldn't be more than seventy-five feet from us now.

The *Inati* didn't alter its course. Neither did we. Closer and closer they came. Behind me I felt another demon snag onto the rudder. It was almost immediately answered by the crack of Loli's gun and a squelch as it hit its mark. But then seconds later I felt more clawed hands grabbing onto it. The all-too-familiar sound of demons scraping the hulls grated against my ears, and I knew we were close to getting swarmed again.

"Alaka'i..." I started, well aware that the sound of Loli's spear finding its prey was getting closer than I would've liked.

"Not...yet...." Alaka'i grunted. His eyes were on the *Inati*. They were so close to us now that I could make out the patterns dyed into Alani's apron. Ori and Tāwhiri hopped back onto the deck, and the right hull came down with a splash. "When you see Alani's signal," he said, "Help me make a hard left."

Ori maneuvered the *Inati* parallel to us; the demons below swirled around us like a current of dirty water. Ori looked at Alaka'i and shook his head. Alaka'i nodded; that wasn't the signal. Wait a little longer.

Our canoes continued to jostle as more clawed hands scraped against them. Both canoes started to slow down. Panic swelled in my chest and I bit back a scream. There was a plan for this, right? Ori wouldn't put us through this unless he had a plan.

Right?

The green light pulsed again, and this time we were close enough to see it wasn't just a mass of floating lights in the ocean. The lights swirled and coalesced around a black hole in the middle. And it wasn't like a cyclone, or a whirlpool, either. Water flowed straight into it as though it were a mouth, or a bottomless hole that could never fill up. I swallowed hard, trying to feel good about the fact that we were this close, rather than panic at the thought of having to go in there.

Alani held up a hand and started counting down on her fingers. Our canoes continued to be battered and scraped. I winced at the sounds, not sure how much more we could take.

When Alani got to one, she pointed at Marama. "Now!" she yelled.

I cried out as I heaved with Alaka'i, forcing our canoe into a hard left. At the same time, Marama slapped both hands to the deck. Light bled off of him, seeping into the wood and wrapping around the hulls, bathing the entire canoe in light and forcing me to squint. The demons hissed, overwhelmed by the sudden brightness.

Ori whipped the *Inati* around the front end of our canoe, using us as a shield as he pulled up next to the right hull. Marama grabbed one of the loose ropes hanging from the mast and used it to swing onto the *Inati*. The moment his foot touched the deck the smaller canoe, too, became engulfed in the soft glow that radiated from his skin.

Ori looked up at the gaping hole in the ocean, then back at us. "I've got a clear shot!" he yelled. "Toa, get over here! Now's our chance!"

Lali dropped his gun and stood behind me at the rudder. "We've got this," he said. "Go save your sister."

I nodded, fingers trembling as grabbed one of the ropes. I needed to do this. I needed to run, and jump, and pray that I pushed off with enough momentum to land on that little canoe. I didn't need to worry about looking like an idiot if I missed, or if one of those

demons got to me. I just needed to make it in there. I could do this.
I could do this....

"Oh my goodness, Light child, you are taking too long."

I jumped, startled at Loli's voice. I looked up at him, trying to
find the right words. Did he know I was scared? Was he mad at me
for it?

Loli smirked. "Remember that one time I said it was a good thing
you skinny?" he asked.

I blinked at him. "Huh?"

Before I could even process what he said, Loli grabbed my right
arm and leg, throwing me over his shoulders and stepping up to
the splashguard.

"Loli!" I cried out, struggling against his grip. "Put me down!"

But Loli didn't listen. He didn't even flinch when I hit him with
my free hand.

"Relax, Light child," he said. "We can take care of this. But over
there is something only you can do."

I froze, surprised at the calmness in his voice.

Loli cupped one hand to his mouth. "Oi, captain!" he called.
"Catch!"

The four-man crew of the *Inati* whipped around and tipped the
deck up to face us. Loli un-shrugged me and spun around in two
circles before he sent me flying. I screamed, arms and legs flailing
before I smacked into the deck of the *Inati*. I started to slip, but
Ori caught me.

The canoe came back down with a splash and Ori let go. He
pulled hard on the sheet and the *Inati* sped forward. I looked back
at the *Ta'ifetū*, at Loli standing with one foot on the splashguard,
his fist raised to me before turning to help the others.

Would they be okay? I thought. A crew of four men wasn't much to work with; we had barely managed with eight when Ori was sick.

I didn't have long to think about it, though, because seconds later Ori sailed straight through the green light and into the blackness. My stomach lurched as we went over the edge. Behind us, the hole in the ocean closed up, and our entire world went black.

Chapter 26

Even with Marama's light, there wasn't much to see. All five of us clung to different parts of the canoe as the front end pointed straight down. Darkness surrounded us. At first, I dreaded the moment we would ram into the ground, but the longer we fell, the more I wondered if that would happen. You could only fall for so long before the nerves of it wore off.

"I thought the deadlands would be more terrifying than this," Tāwhiri murmured.

"It's coming," Marama promised. "Just wait."

I couldn't tell how long we waited. It felt like we were falling forever. But at the same time, it was like no time had passed at all. Like we either had been falling for a million years, or for less than a second. I would blink, and suddenly our canoe was falling up instead of down. But then I blinked again, and suddenly we were upright, suspended in the middle of the nothingness.

Finally, I heard the faint kiss of water beneath us and our canoe started to move forward. By Marama's light, I saw that we were on water again. Stalactites clung to the cavern ceiling overhead, and in front of us was nothing but blackness. Ori defaulted to what he knew best, guiding our canoe through the darkness. There was no wind in here, and he grunted as he started to paddle.

"Is this it?" Tāwhiri asked, his voice echoing in the darkness. "Are we in the deadlands?"

White objects bobbed in the water ahead of us. As Ori sailed by, a wave of nausea hit me as I realized they were bones. Human bones. All of them slick and slimy from saltwater decay. My last meal crawled up my throat, and I had to cover my mouth.

"That answer your question?" Ori asked.

A single torch marked the place where water met dry land. Tāwhiri jumped off first. When his feet sank into the gravelly sand, more torches ignited, making us jump. They marked a path that stretched around the bend and out of view.

I hopped off after him, feet sinking into the damp sand as I tread forward. Behind me I heard a rustling sound as Ori got off. He rested his oar against his shoulders, frowning as he looked back.

"Marama," he said, "aren't you coming?"

I turned. Alani was digging for something in a storage compartment, but Marama still stood by the mast, his face stony.

I frowned at him. "Is something wrong?"

"I..." he hesitated. "I shouldn't be here."

Tāwhiri shrugged his shoulders. "Should any of us? I mean, look around mate. We're not exactly well-seasoned, if you know what I mean."

The forerunner grimaced. "It's not that. I—"

"Found it!" Alani popped up from the storage compartment, cupping something in her right hand. Then she noticed Marama, and her brow furrowed.

"Out of all of us, you should be the least scared," she said, jumping off. She dusted her apron and held Masina's kaulima out to me. My eyebrows went up as I took it.

"Thanks, Alani," I said in relief.

"Don't thank me until we find her." She looked down the torchlit trail, her lips pressed into a tight line.

I looked at the wooden bracelet in my hand, not sure what I was supposed to do with it. Hina said it would lead me to Masina, but she never told me how. I stepped forward uncertainly. The lights shifted behind me followed by another splash as Marama decided to join us.

As I walked past the first pair of torches, the kaulima started to glow. The white light reminded me of Hina. We followed the torchlit path around the bend, where the road forked. One side went down to the left, the other snaked up to the right.

Tāwhiri frowned. "Which way do we go?"

I walked towards the path on the left, craning my neck to see what was up ahead. The moment I stepped away from where the two roads met, the light from Masina's kaulima went out. Surprised, I backtracked and took a few steps up the path on the right. The light returned.

"Right it is, then," Ori said, nodding. "Lead the way, Toa."

We made our way through the endless tunnels of the deadlands, relying on the kaulima to keep us on the right path. We made so many twists and turns, that I wondered if even Ori would be able to get us back out without the kaulima acting as our guide.

We turned down a path that didn't have torches and had to rely on Marama to give us light. The path went deeper into the earth, making the air dank and the silence almost palpable. We ducked into another passageway. I heard someone whispering.

"Who's that?" I asked, my free hand shooting out to the side.

The forerunner stepped past me, his expression sour. "The name of the place is the deadlands," he said. "Did you really expect them to be uninhabited?"

A few moments later, I saw what he meant. We rounded a corner and nearly collided with a woman. Tāwhiri screamed, and Ori jerked back, but she only stared at us. Her visage was pale and transparent, her eyes wide and unfocused. She had the same milky white appearance Masina had when I saw her. Locks of disheveled hair fell into her face, and her pale lips were chapped.

"Have you seen my son?" she asked.

Alani's knife faltered in her hand. "You're...who?"

The woman didn't reply. Her bug-like eyes tilted up to look at Marama. I didn't think it possible, but her eyes grew even wider.

"You!" she said, raising a ghostly hand. "You've seen my son, haven't you?"

Marama ignored her, waving for us to follow as he stalked past the specter. Mouth dry, I followed, checking the kaulima to confirm we were still going in the right direction.

The woman drifted alongside us, her gaze fixed on Marama.

"You have seen him," she insisted. "You've seen my son, haven't you? Is he safe? Can you bring me to him?"

The light around Marama flashed brighter, and he whirled around, irritated. "I cannot take you to your son because you are dead, and he is not," he spat. "Do not waste your time searching for him. You are better served at the judgment seat."

His tone was so harsh that even Alani winced. I felt like someone had dumped cold water over me. Marama had always been aloof, and distracted; this was the first time I had ever heard him be outright mean to someone.

The woman, however, wasn't offended. She blinked at Marama, then turned and walked straight through the wall.

"I know my son is here somewhere," she murmured.

Her conviction made me shiver. How long had she been down here? Were those her bones we saw in the water?

"Marama..." Tāwhiri asked. "What was that?"

"Just a wayward spirit," Marama said. "They either can't or won't accept that they are dead. Rather than meet the gods at the judgment seat, they choose to wander the caverns in search of a better option."

As the echo in his voice faded, I heard more whispers and repressed another shudder. Just how many wayward spirits were there? Was my mother one of them?

I shook my head, forcing myself to concentrate. We ran into more spirits, but thankfully none of them spoke to us. All of them instead called out the names of loved ones as they glided to and fro in the tunnels.

We squeezed through a passageway that opened up to a large cavern. Torches ignited as we entered, showing a stone altar on the far right and two tunnels on the side opposite of us. Both were dark. The one on the left had music coming from it, while cries of anguish rang out from the other. I had heard of this place before in stories; it was where the god of the underworld or his daughter judged men's souls. If they were good, they could take the left entrance into the heavens. If not, their souls were sent to eternal torment.

I took all of this in and quickly discarded it. Because once I saw what was floating in between the two tunnels, I lost sight of everything else. I shoved past the others and broke into a run.

"Toa!" Alani cried out.

I wasn't listening. I sprinted ahead, feet slapping the earth and my arms pumping, unable to look away from her. I didn't dare let myself feel any kind of relief. I had to touch her, had to hold her in my arms before I allowed myself to believe things would be okay.

Yet even still, I couldn't deny the growing excitement inside of me. And as I skidded to a halt beneath her, a part of me wanted to turn back out of fear that this was too good to be true. Her features were veiled by a shroud of darkness that covered her body and kept her suspended in the air, but I could still see the design on the tapa cloth around her waist and the kaulima on her arm. Her hair swayed up and down, and her eyes were closed. She looked so peaceful.

I reached for her with trembling hands. The moment my fingertips passed through the mist, the black cloud dissolved. I grunted as Masina landed hard in my arms. I had forgotten how heavy she was. I staggered, trying to right myself but ended up falling to one knee before sitting down hard. I hugged her head, careful to make sure she didn't get hurt.

"Masina!" I said, my voice little more than a strangled yelp. Tears came unbidden to my eyes, and I felt a surge of euphoria rush through my veins. This was it! We had done it!

I shook her shoulders gently, trying to wake her. "Masina," I said. "Hey, Masina, wake up. It's time to go."

I could hardly wait for her to open her eyes. I wanted to tell her everything, how much I had learned, and how sorry I was for making her come here. She would brush it all off, of course. She was just too good like that. But that didn't mean I didn't want to say them to her.

Masina's hair spilled over my arm, and a few stray locks landed over her face. I swept them aside, surprised at how cold she was. Her body was limp. And despite my efforts, she hadn't stirred.

"Masina, hurry," I said, annoyed that she could sleep so soundly. Didn't she have any idea what was waiting for us outside of the deadlands?

The forerunner's light drew closer behind me, making my shadow over Masina's face darker. I was only half-listening to the others, but I thought I heard Alani gasp.

"Toa—" she tried to say, but I ignored her. I started shaking Masina more insistently.

"Masina, we don't have time for this," I said to her. "Our friends are waiting for us, and there's a whole ocean we still need to go through and—"

A hand rested on my shoulder. I recognized it as Ori's.

"Toa," he said. "Don't."

Tāwhiri knelt across from me. He reached for Masina's hand, hesitating. I wanted to pull her away from him, not sure why I hated the thought of having him touch her. But as Tāwhiri lifted her wrist, I didn't object. He pressed his thumb to her veins, and his next breath hitched in his throat. When he set her hand down, his face was grave.

"What is it?" I asked, but Tāwhiri only shook his head. Irritated, I grabbed Masina's wrist, pressing my thumb where Tāwhiri's had been. I felt...nothing. Startled, I tried again, but still nothing. I checked her other hand, then rested two fingers on the side of her neck. When neither of those worked, I pressed a hand to her heart.

Nothing. No warmth, no heartbeat, no rising and falling of the chest to mark her breath.

Like a trapped fly slowly taking in the spider's web around it, everything started to make sense. Masina didn't have a pulse. Masina wasn't breathing. And Masina felt so, so cold. She wasn't reacting to my touch or my voice because she...she was already....

A wretched scream ripped out of my lungs. The sound bounced around the cavern, amplifying my voice as the raw emotions tore at my insides. Here I was, holding her cold and limp body, yet somehow I was the lifeless one. Something had broken inside of me, and I was filled with a pain I hadn't felt in ten years. I didn't even try to stop the tears as I cradled her head to my chest, resting my cheek against her hair.

Everything in me wanted to reject it, to say it couldn't be true, yet here we were. After everything that happened, everything we had been through, it had all been in vain.

We were too late.

Chapter 27

Grief overwhelmed me. My chest exploded in pain as one sob after another racked my body, tumbling from my lips in an incoherent mess. I clutched at her hair and rocked back and forth, unable to believe she was really gone.

How was it possible? How was it possible for her to be in my arms, yet she had never felt further away? How could she die on me when I had come so far to save her? Did she really think I wouldn't come?

I thought back to my vision of her on the boat, that night when she showed me the scars from our fight and cried her moonlight tears. Had she been dead then? Did she die thinking I still hated her?

Guilt mixed in with grief, grinding into my soul. I would never get a chance to tell my sister I was sorry. I would never get to do anything with her. All the good times, the bad times, it was all gone now. And it was all my fault. I had squandered the time I had with her out of jealousy.

I could never forgive myself for that. If someone were to gouge my heart out of my chest, it couldn't have hurt more than this.

A hand pressed in between my shoulders. I wrenched away from it, not wanting to see the others right now. How stupid I must've looked to them, tasting the regret they knew I should've felt all along.

But when Alani knelt in front of me, she wasn't angry. Her eyes were red as she looked down at Masina. She caressed her cheek, rubbing her thumb against her forehead. Then she looked up at me, her expression of sorrow reflecting my own.

"Alani," I gasped. "I—"

Alani threw her arms around my neck, pulling me into a tight hug, and I broke down again. Tears streaming, nose running, I must've been crying a mess onto her clothes, but she didn't seem to care. More hands wrapped around us, Ori and Tāwhiri's. I didn't feel any of the blame or hate I had been expecting, but found only sympathy and love. None of them were interested in playing judge and executioner. Instead, we were equals: four friends mourning the loss of a loved one.

Marama's light went out as a new voice echoed in the cavern. "Well, who would've thought?" it said. "Havaiki's boy came through, after all. Looks like Tahi wasn't lying."

I looked up. Sitting on the steps of the altar was a man with a thick chest and hands larger than my face. His tall frame was relaxed, eyes watching us with mild amusement. He dressed like a high chief, but I heard enough stories about him to know he was Iva, the god of the underworld.

Kneeling on the altar behind him was his daughter, Hala. She was strikingly beautiful for the daughter of death. Hala was known as a temptress in the old tales. Legend had it she used her beauty to lure abusive men to an untimely death. With her curvy build and sultry eyes, it wasn't hard to imagine her doing just that.

"Father, you know Tahi never lies," she said, her voice a rich alto. "It was only a matter of time before they got here."

Lord Iva rubbed his chin. "Even still, I had my doubts about this lot."

Marama fell to his knees, bowing low to the god of death. Ori, Alani, and Tāwhiri followed. I stayed where I was, hugging Masina's body tighter as I bowed my head. My mind was racing. All this time I thought we were fighting against Mā, but was the god Iva involved, as well?

"Speak, nephew," Lord Iva rumbled. "Tell us what brings you to the deadlands this time."

Marama bowed lower. "Yes, uncle."

He told him of our mission and how far we had come. Lord Iva listened with a hand under his chin. He gave the occasional nod to show he was listening.

In the old tales, Iva was Havaiki's older brother. After men began to populate the earth, the gods quickly realized that not all of them were worthy of returning to the heavens. Iva sacrificed his place in the ninth heaven, giving it to Havaiki so that he could act as judge for men on earth. He had always been described as just and benevolent, but if he was involved in this, I didn't know what to think of him.

"All of this I already knew," he said when Marama finished. "Tahi told me as much after you visited her island. However, I've yet to hear you explain to your travelers why you are with them."

Marama's hands tensed, his face still pointed to the ground. In front of me, I saw Alani exchange a curious look with Tāwhiri.

"I'm here to see to the will of my Lord Havaiki," he said stiffly. "He desires that I return Alai's daughter to him."

"That's partly true," Hala said, tilting her head to the side. "But your emotions betray you, Rama. Don't tell me you have nothing to gain from this, as well."

"I..." Marama looked uncertain. The light about him dimmed even more, growing timid with his nervousness.

Lord Iva made a shooing motion with his hands, "You waste our time, nephew," he grunted. "I thought you cared for these mortals. Yet your fumbling words are eating the little time they have left. Would you have Alai's daughter die for real?"

I inhaled sharply. Die for real? I hugged Masina's body, not daring to believe it.

"Child, your sister is not yet dead," Lord Iva said, lifting his chin at me. "You may recall Marama saying that Hana has no claim to her spirit. As the lord of these lands, that decision rests with me, and I have sent her up there." He looked skyward, indicating the heavens.

I stared up at the stony ceiling, my heart racing. "So she's...she's still okay?" That felt so bizarre to say, when I was holding her lifeless body. But if her spirit was up there...if we could still get to her....

"She was too innocent for eternal torment, and I'll not have her wandering these dark halls," Lord Iva confirmed. "I've been preserving her body here, keeping it ready for her spirit should she return. But time is of the essence. In a matter of hours her body will truly perish."

"How do we get to her?" Alani blurted. Lord Iva raised an eyebrow, and Alani dropped her head to the ground. "Forgive me," she murmured, "I misspoke."

Lord Iva gave a throaty laugh. "Your ancestor would be proud," he said. "She's got quite the attitude, that one. As for you," —he turned back to me— "I can send you to the heavens right now. We could have this done in a matter of seconds."

I bowed low to him, gratitude overwhelming my heart. "Thank you, my lord."

But Hala held up a hand. "Not so fast," she said. "Marama still hasn't answered our question."

From where I was sitting I could only see the back of his head, but the forerunner looked like he was sweating. His hands clenched in front of him. I frowned; out of all of us, he was the last person I would expect to be nervous in front of gods.

"Hurry, nephew," Lord Iva chided. "Your new friends are still fighting the great demon at my doorstep, and I've gone to great lengths to keep her powers in check. I haven't broken any rules, mind you." He held up a finger, as though defending himself. "But if she is going to draw power from my realm, I have a right to put a spending limit on it."

"Go on, Marama," Hala insisted. "Tell them. Tell them what your relationship is to the great demon Mā."

Marama's head flicked up in disgust. "Her name isn't Mā," he spat.

Hala folded her arms. She cocked an eyebrow. "So, what is it, then?"

Marama sighed in defeat as he spun on his knees to face us. The light was all but gone from him now, and when he looked at me there was shame in his eyes. "Her name is Mahana," he said. "But we always called her Hana. And she's...she's my sister."

My mouth fell open. Questions flooded my mind but before I could say anything, Lord Iva snapped at me and flicked his hand upward.

I vanished.

At first, I thought I had been sent back to Faletahi Island. The dank caves of the deadlands were replaced with white shores and lush foliage that bloomed up the mountainside. It looked greener and richer than anything we grew in our village. The sun was warm overhead, and grains of sand rubbed against my skin as the whitewash tickled my feet.

I sat up, staring out at the water. It was a curious sight. There were no clouds in the sky; they were all hovering along the horizon. If this was one of the heavens, did those clouds mark the edge of it?

Sand shifted behind me, and I heard someone, a woman, speak.

"My, how you've grown, little Lā," she said. "Although I guess you're not so little, anymore."

Chills erupted all over me and tears sprang to my eyes. I hadn't heard that voice in years, yet how could I not recognize it? I leapt to my feet, kicking up sand as I whirled around, trembling as my eyes confirmed what I already knew. It was her.

I started running. So did she. Her arms outstretched, I threw myself forward and she hugged me. We landed on our knees in the sand, laughing and crying. She was just how I remembered her. No, she was better than that because now she wasn't sick. Her body wasn't frail from months of battling disease, nor was she weak from a child labor full of complications. She stroked my hair as I sobbed into her chest.

"Hi, my boy," she said, squeezing me. She sounded like she wanted to say more, but her voice cracked. Despite how overwhelmed I felt, I smiled. She had always been a crier.

"Mother!" I cried, amazed at how foreign the word felt my mouth. "Mother...."

INTERLUDE

Masina's body started to fall. Alani jumped, but Hala got there first. She scooped up Masina in her arms, making a shushing noise as though she were a fussing infant. Alani's hand twitched, and she fought the urge to pull a knife out.

"She is so sweet," Hala said. "I can see why he wouldn't like her, though. She's far too docile. A little aggression can be a good thing. Although I suppose she can use that when she wants to."

She tossed Masina into the air. Alani cried out, but Masina didn't fall. A cloud shrouded her in darkness, and she floated. She looked exactly the way she had when they arrived.

"You'll have to forgive my niece for her dramatics," Lord Iva said. "I've been trying to evict her for centuries, yet she won't leave my house." He sat tall, his hands resting against his knees, looking completely calm.

Tāwhiri cleared his throat. "I hope this doesn't get me struck by lightning, or anything," he said, "but could someone please explain what just happened?"

Alani groaned inwardly, wishing she could hit him over the head. Someone really needed to teach that boy about *timing*.

Hala stopped beside the forerunner. "Ask him," she said, swatting the back of his head. "Seeing as it's his fault for stalling. You should've known all about this before you left Faletahi."

Marama rubbed his head, scowling at her. She scowled back. "Don't make that face," she snarled. "You know I'm right."

Marama grumbled but didn't argue. Alani eyed him warily, a part of her still shaken from the news he'd given them. That demon—that half-eel, half-woman that abducted Masina—was his sister? Why hadn't he told them?

He locked eyes with her and turned up his palms. "I'm not here to betray you," he said. "So if you would kindly lower your weapons?"

Alani didn't realize she had pulled out a knife. The flaxen-wrapped handle was so smooth against her skin that it felt like an extension of her hand. Out of the corner of her eye, she saw she wasn't the only one who had armed herself. Tāwhiri held his patu, and Ori had grabbed his oar. All of them were tense, ready to fight their navigator if they needed to. Tāwhiri glanced at Ori. Alani did, too. Their captain's face was unreadable, but when he set his oar back down, Alani and Tāwhiri followed suit.

Alani tossed her knife out to the side as a sign of good faith. But anyone who knew her would've realized how empty the gesture was. Alani still had another knife in her dress, her patu and two throwing clubs tucked into her apron, plus a third knife strapped to her thigh. Not to mention the shark-tooth rings she had combed in her hair.

It was always better to be prepared.

One thing Alani hadn't done, though, was come up with a contingency should the forerunner turn out to be evil. She had mentally rehearsed different tactics and strategies for every possible scenario, but she hadn't thought of this. She never expected a member of their crew to turn on them. But wasn't it a general's job to plan for the unexpected?

And we all called Toa the inexperienced one, she thought.

Marama studied each of their faces in turn before he spoke. "The demon you know as Mā wasn't always like that," he said. "Long before she had wings or a tail, she wasn't that different from me. Her magic was strong, and she loved to laugh. We all thought she would be the first to obtain godhood."

Tāwhiri tilted his head to the side. "Are you two the last of the celestial siblings?" he asked. "Hina said there were more of you."

Marama nodded. "Hana is the oldest. Then it's me, Hina, Tane, and so on."

Ori excused himself before sliding from his knees to a cross-legged position. "What happened to her?" he asked.

Marama winced. He glanced at Lord Iva, who waved for him to keep talking. He sighed.

"It started during our earthly trials. Like how Toa and Masina went through chief trials, demigods go through trials to prove they are ready to become gods. I came down with Hana. Our mission was to kill the demon Olu, who had been terrorizing the Light Village."

Alani nodded; she had heard stories about that. Olu was the first demon to bite a man, showing all nine villages how deadly their venom could be. But the stories had never mentioned a hero named Marama before.

"I always heard that Tane killed Olu," she said, frowning. "How come no one ever mentioned you?"

"Because I didn't want them to," Marama said. He looked pained. "A lot of the stories that credit Hina, Tane, or Kina were actually Mahana and I. But after what happened with Olu, I thought it best for our names to be forgotten."

"So you didn't kill the demon?" Ori asked.

"We did." Marama grabbed the back of his neck. "Or rather, I did. But not before Hana fell in love with it."

Tāwhiri gasped. Ori looked disgusted.

Alani shuddered. In her mind, she tried to picture someone like Marama falling in love with one of the barbaric demons she had spent the last hour fighting. Looks weren't everything, she knew, but still. There was a big difference between dating a homely man and one who tended to eat people.

"Is that why you killed him?" she asked. "Because he wanted your sister?"

Marama wrinkled his nose, but shook his head. "I should've. When I found out about the relationship, I certainly wanted to. Hana had been leading me in circles for months. But she advocated for him, said that he promised to stop killing. And for a while, he did."

He paused. Alani could tell this was painful for him, but she needed him to keep talking. She needed to know what had happened. What had made a former goddess turn evil?

Hala came down the steps and knelt next to him, rubbing the small of his back. He turned away, but she pulled him in, resting her chin on top of his head in an unexpected sign of affection. She winked at Alani.

"It doesn't matter how many centuries you've been alive," she said, "little cousins will always be little cousins."

She let go and he shrugged away, still looking sour. Alani was surprised at the interaction; it reminded her so much of something she would do with her brothers.

Hala clasped her hands in her lap, her back perfectly straight. "Please don't think Hana dim-witted for falling in love with a demon. Olu was very handsome and quite charming when he wanted to be.

"Marama didn't kill the demon out of jealousy, or spite. He did it to protect the Light Village. While Olu did stop biting the villagers, there was evidence he was planning to sever the line between my uncle Havaiki and his earthly descendants."

Alani frowned, remembering where she had heard that plan. "I thought that was why Mā"—she paused, catching herself—"why Hana wanted Masina. Wasn't this whole thing part of a revenge story?"

"There's more to it than that," Lord Iva said. "It's possible Olu wanted to get to Havaiki. My brother and I are speakers for the dead. I send the wicked straight to hell, and he determines who can enter the heavens.

"If Olu killed Havaiki that judgment seat would be left open. The title would fall to his firstborn, Hana and she would have the final say in who was allowed to enter the heavens. Theoretically, this would also mean she could cast people out of there if she wanted to."

Tāwhiri frowned. "I didn't know people could be kicked out of heaven. I always thought it was one of those 'once you're there, you're there,' kind of things."

"It's never been tried before." Lord Iva said. "But the lore has been around for centuries. Olu wouldn't have been the first to try killing a god in order to play god.'"

Alani covered her mouth, stunned by such blasphemy.

Hala nodded grimly. "Contrary to popular belief, gods are not necessarily immortal. We have enhanced powers, and we are not subject to mortal sickness and injury. If left to ourselves, we could live forever, but there are ways for us to die. Foolish men in the past have tried to exploit this."

Ori frowned. "How did you know this was Olu's plan?" he asked Marama.

Marama's eyes flashed with hatred and his lips peeled back in a snarl. "Because he told me!" he seethed. "That slithering beast told me to my face that he planned to kill my father and use my sister to expel his former enemies from the heavens. He never cared for her; he was just using her to get what he wanted."

"But then you told her, right?" Tāwhiri asked, his eyes wide. "You told your sister everything, and his plan fell apart."

"No..." Alani murmured. That was far too optimistic. Olu wouldn't have told Marama anything if he thought Hana would believe her brother over him. Alani didn't have any personal experience with it, but she knew love was one of the easiest ways to manipulate someone. Feuds started over it, countries battled to defend it, and loyalties were often discarded because of it.

Marama ground his teeth, and Hala rested her hand over his, finishing the story. "This all happened while Hana was asleep. Marama said he would kill the demon before letting him touch her again, and a battle ensued. Hana awoke to find her lover slain by her brother's hand."

Alani tried to picture that in her mind. She'd never been much of a romantic, but what would she think if she woke up to the sight of her crew mates killed by an uncle, or a brother? Family loyalties were supposed to come before everything, but she would trust the crew with her life, even though she hadn't known them nearly as long. What would she do if those two sides ever conflicted with one another?

"I'm sure you can guess the rest," Hala continued. "Hana claimed Marama was jealous and overprotective, that her beloved was becoming a better man. And for all we know, maybe he was. Maybe it was wrong for Marama to kill him so quickly. But it's impossible to say now."

From the way his palms sweated and how he kept clutching at his hair, Alani could tell Marama felt the weight of that. The guilt must've been eating at him for years now. For decades or possibly even centuries, the forerunner of the light god had struggled to know if he made the right choice.

"Is this why you never told us who you really were?" Tāwhiri asked. He leaned forward on his knees, brow knit with concern. Sometimes Alani wished she could be like that; people thought she was strong for her skill with a club, but there was a strength that came from compassion—the ability to connect with people in the ways they needed most.

Marama nodded. "She ran away from me that night; I spent weeks trying to find her. Sometimes I would find her, only to have her tell me how much she hated me and then she'd run again. I kept at it for months, but—" He shook his head, unable to finish.

"My uncle finally called him home," Hala said. "He knew Hana had made her choice, and he couldn't stand to lose Marama as well. For his bravery, Marama was offered the rank of godhood but he refused, electing to step down and become a forerunner."

That wasn't surprising. If Marama was too ashamed to claim his family name now, there was no way he would've been able to do it then. Alani thought about how Marama always insisted there was nothing special about him, that he was just an errands boy. She thought he was being humble. Now she saw it was really self-loathing. He didn't think he deserved the title his father had for him.

"And Hana?" Ori asked, shaking her from her thoughts. "She came here after becoming a demon?"

"Neither my father nor I encouraged it, but yes," Hala said. "She swore to bring Olu back after getting revenge on the family who took him from her."

"So she is out for revenge, then," Alani said, nodding.

Tāwhiri shot her a dirty look, but she ignored him. She was used to getting looks like that. Alani didn't mean to, but she knew she was intimidating—downright scary, even. It wasn't that she couldn't be nice, she just knew that the world would not show mercy simply because you were a good person. Those were the times when Alani would dull her empathy and allow her analytical side to take over. Her father warned her that too much time in that mindset could be harmful, and Alani tried to be deliberate about when she needed to be a warrior and when she could be a normal girl.

When they found Masina's body, Alani knew it was okay to be a normal girl. That had been the time to weep, mourn, and fall apart in the wretched experience of being human. Now they had a clear enemy to fight and a battle to prepare for, one which Alani had no intention of losing.

"Hana wasted her days learning every unnatural curse under the sun," Lord Iva said. "She says she's from the deadlands, but she's really more of a squatter."

"Can you tell me how her powers work?" Alani asked. "You said you've been keeping her in check, could you take them away if you wanted to?" She looked at the god of death as she spoke, then respectfully averted her eyes while waiting for his reply.

"I can...bend her powers in certain ways," he said after a while. "But not to the extent that you're hoping for. Gods cannot directly interfere with the lives of mortals. Claiming godhood means stepping up to be a guardian of this world, not an active participant in it. It's why no one from the heavens has confronted her outright; she's out of our jurisdiction. I can slow her down, but even I can't stop her on my own."

Alani cursed inwardly, struggling to come up with a plan. The gods couldn't help them, and they still had men out at sea. Alani worried about them. Every minute they spent away from them was another minute they left the Navigator men exposed to a sea of monsters.

She turned to Hala. "If you can see our friends at the entrance, does that mean you can take us to them?"

She nodded. "The living do not belong in this place, so it's fairly simple to send them back."

That was good. If nothing else, at least they had a way out. Now they only had two problems to deal with. She turned to the forerunner. "And what's your plan? Are you here to help your sister, or to stop her?"

Marama looked shocked. Alani made a mental note to dial it back if she ever had to ask that question again.

"I don't want her to hurt anyone," he said. "And I know it might be too much to hope for, but I still want her to come home with me."

Alani's eyebrows went up. She knew Marama felt guilty, but she hadn't expected him to sound so hopeful. Now that she thought about it, though, it made sense. Before Alani thought Marama wasn't a god because he had somehow failed the test. But Marama was much more altruistic than that; the gods couldn't bring Hana to the heavens, but a demigod could.

Lord Iva chuckled. "I know that look," he said, his playful tone reminding her of her father. "You're scheming up something, aren't you?"

"Just trying to keep everybody alive," Alani admitted.

The god of death spread his hands. "Allow me to help you, then," he said. "This is purely hypothetical, and you are in no way bound to accept my direction, but I would recommend you all go with Hala. She can take you to your little boat and you can help your friends at the entrance. Marama will wait here. When the time is right, I will summon my niece to face him."

Marama paled. Alani, however, felt relieved. That wasn't a bad plan. Now she only had one thing to worry about.

"And what about them?" she asked, pointing with her chin at Masina's body. "Will they be able to find their way back?"

Hala smirked. "They should be the least of your problems. Especially the girl; she can handle herself here."

Alani nodded, reminding herself who they were talking about. She had seen Masina do remarkable things, things no ten-year-old should've been able to do. Toa was a walking banana leaf, but he would be fine with his sister looking out for him.

Ori bowed low to the gods, thanking them for their generosity. Alani and Tāwhiri followed suit. When Alani came up, she promised that songs would be written of their deeds this day; children in the War Village would praise the goodness of the god Iva for generations to come.

The lord of the deadlands laughed it off. "You fight with wisdom, and you fight for love. May your lives be full of triumph, that you will have many stories to tell me when it is your time to stand at the judgment seat." He paused, then added. "One of the reasons why I wanted Marama to tell you his story was to help you see what kind of enemy you're up against. You see that now, yes?"

Alani nodded. Knowing your enemy was the best way to overcome them, and she had indeed learned much about the demon Mā. Alani had wondered why she hadn't been more devious, more cunning in her plans to stop them. A big part of that had been because the god Iva was impeding her, but Alani was willing to bet it was also because Mā still carried herself like a broken-hearted lover, one who hadn't learned to let go and move on.

Lord Iva gave them leave to go. Hala led the way, and Alani retrieved her knife before following behind Ori and Tāwhiri.

The forerunner stayed where he was. Alani turned back and saluted him with a raised fist. He saluted her back, his face more melancholy than Alani would've liked. Lord Iva had confidence in him, but Alani didn't know if he could do what needed to be done when it was time to face his sister.

You better not die on us, she thought, letting a chink of empathy penetrate her armor. Her heart fluttered as she allowed herself to worry about him. *I already found one of my friends dead today. I don't know if I could handle losing another.*

Chapter 28

Father might've said my tears were unmanly, but I couldn't stop crying. I clung to my mother, holding her tight as though she might fade away. With my face buried in her chest, I inhaled that comforting smell of ti leaves and pikake flowers, a scent I had almost forgotten.

It was perfect. Just being with her. Holding her, having her hold me. The last time she'd wrapped her arms around me had been on her deathbed. I had been crying then, too. Not out of relief but terror that I would never see her again. That this—this sheer bliss—would never happen again.

I cried my eyes dry, wishing I could say something helpful, something intelligent to the most important woman in my life. But she didn't mind. Like the angel she was, she just held me, not needing to speak for me to know how much she loved me.

"You haven't had one of those for a long time, have you?" she asked when we finally broke apart.

I shook my head, turning away as I tried to find something to wipe my nose on. She handed me a cloth and I blew my nose into it, embarrassed at how loud it sounded.

She laughed. "I see the past ten years have done nothing for those allergies," she teased.

"Yeah." I said, drying my eyes with the back of my hand. "That's what they are. It's all because of those allergies."

She hugged me again, kissing my forehead. My mind went back to the days when she had been with me, and everything had been so simple.

"I've missed you," she said, her voice growing soft.

"I missed you too, Mom," I said, my own voice little more than a squeak.

I felt her chest swell as she inhaled deeply. Then, straightening up, I could tell her practical side was about to kick in.

"I wish I could have you to myself for the whole day," she said, "but we have other things to attend to."

I nodded, drying my eyes as she pulled me to my feet. That was one of the many things I loved about my mother; she was one of the most caring, affectionate people I knew, yet she could get things done. She wasn't like my father, who was all business all the time.

Mother draped an arm over my shoulders, holding me in a side hug as we walked. I wrapped an arm around her waist, slightly disappointed that she was still taller than me. It was a vain thought, but somehow all those years apart made it easy for me to think I had passed her.

"I've been talking to your sister for days now," she said, leading me into a place with buildings set up like our village. "But no matter what I tell her, she's determined to believe this is all her fault. I love that girl, but I blame your father for her stubbornness."

"How is she?" I asked, partly distracted by the strange village around us. Heaven really didn't look all that different from earth, as far as this village was concerned. People still farmed, others wove in their huts, and children were running in the fields. Yet something was different. Everyone here was so happy. Nobody was sick, hungry, or arguing with anyone else. There was a relaxed air about the place that was usually reserved for the closest of friends and family relatives. This could've been the Light Village on a really, really good day.

Mother followed my eyes, nodding in agreement as she waved to the villagers we passed. "It's beautiful, isn't it?" she said. "The true difference between heaven and earth isn't necessarily the location; it always comes down to the people."

She led me up a hill to where the high chief's encampment would've been in our village. Along the way, she introduced me to some of my ancestors. I met my great-great-grandfather, who helped to rid the village of the first demon raids. Then there was my maternal grandmother, who challenged her brother for the title after he had poisoned their father in an act of treason. All the heroes from our family stories were here, and none were the least bit bothered that their skeleton of a descendant had walked into their camp. Many stopped what they were doing to greet us.

"Ta'i, is this your boy?" asked my great-uncle Misi.

"He looks just like you!" said Aunty Tala before giving me an affectionate pat on the cheek. "Of course, he could use a little more meat on his bones. Look at these hollow cheeks he's got." She smiled, and I could tell she was only teasing.

"Eh, leave him be," laughed Uncle Koru. "You know how many of us ended up here from having too much meat on our bones?"

I was surprised and a little overwhelmed at how welcoming they were. I was used to being dismissed and hated for not being the ideal man, but nobody here cared about that. To them, I was just another member of the family. Maybe that was something else that made the heavens so much better than earth; nobody judged.

"Thank you, Uncle," my mother said, wrapping her arms around me to cut off the others. "As you can see, my son is not dead. But, if we don't act quickly, my daughter will be. Has anyone seen her?"

My great-great-aunty Salote pointed to one of the huts that dotted the hill of the encampment. "She's in there," she said. "Apologies, my niece, but when she heard he was coming, she ran."

Mother sighed, and I felt her arm sag around my shoulders. "Oh, my daughter..." she murmured. She shook her head, thanking our ancestors before leading me to the designated hut. The coconut-frond curtains around the open walls had all been drawn, meaning I would have to pull one of them up to go inside.

I glanced at my mother. She nodded, and I knocked on one of the wooden masts. "Masina?" I asked. "Are you in there?"

No answer. I knocked again.

"Masina," I said. "I clawed my way through the deadlands to get here. You'd better answer me."

It sounded harsher than I had intended, and I worried I might have overdone it. But I had always been irritated before when Masina came to me; maybe an annoyed older brother was what she was used to.

Sure enough, someone stirred inside the hut. "Okay," a small voice squeaked. "I'm in here."

I nodded at my mother before pulling up the curtain in front of me, flooding that section of the hut with light. I stepped inside, feeling a strange sense of reverse déjà vu; usually it was Masina coming to get me like this.

Her spirit huddled against the opposite side from me. She was so transparent that looking at her was trying to get a good look at a passing wind. If I focused hard, I could make out the outline of her body, along with her facial features, but it terrified me at how far gone she was. How much longer before she faded away entirely?

I crouched low, trying to look as non-threatening as I could. Her head shrank into her shoulders, and I held up my hands, trying to reassure her.

"It's okay," I said. "I'm not gonna hurt you. I just want to help."

Masina's lower lip trembled. When she spoke, her voice was little more than a whisper. "You don't have to pretend, brother," she said. "I know the truth now. I...I know why you hate me."

I froze. My heart jumped up to my throat. I thought about the retrials at Faletahi. Had Masina somehow heard that?

"No, Masina," I said quickly. "I don't hate you. That was a long time ago, and it wasn't your fault, I just—"

"No!" Masina covered her ears, shaking her head. "You do hate me! You do, and you should!" Her voice broke, and she stared at her fading hands with disgust. "I'm a monster," she whispered. "I'm the reason our mother is dead." She jerked her head up to face me, and I stumbled backward. Again, she had pinpricks of light trickling down her face, those tears of moonlight that stabbed at my heart.

"You were going to save her, Lā," she whimpered. "You were going to save her, but then you tried to help me. I really am the devil child who killed our mother!"

She fled, her spirit rushing past me like a strong wind on a stormy night. She was gone before I could blink.

I stumbled out of the hut, my heart thumping in shock. I stared wide-eyed at my mother, who smiled sadly.

"How did she—" I started.

Mother cut me off. "She knows, son," she said. The implication of her words made me want to evaporate on the spot.

I swallowed. "How much did you tell her?"

"Everything."

Oh, gods. I stared down the hillside, watching the flurry of wind that was my sister running away. *Oh, gods, help her.* I thought. *She was never supposed to know.*

Chapter 27

Long before he ever had a daughter, High Chief Alai was blessed with an heir of great and unusual powers. Ever pious, Alai hadn't doubted the prophecy would come true. And when the medicine women told him of his wife's first pregnancy, his heart fluttered with anticipation. She was never nauseous, nor did she have any of the mood swings or fatigue most women had when they were expecting.

Although—and Alai found this particularly amusing—there were times when she would get the most incurable cravings for salted pork. Ta'ifetū was normally the more frugal and practical one, yet now she was randomly waking him in the middle of the night.

"Lai, wake up," she'd say. "Your son is hungry."

To which Alai would yawn and brush her arm away. "Tell him to wait until morning like the rest of us."

That usually earned him a slap. Not a hard one, just enough to let him know his wife was irritated. Then she would snuggle as close as her belly would allow and kiss him on the cheek.

"Please," she'd say, "I'm fat and pregnant, and there's a little human inside of me. You know he always sleeps better after I eat pork."

Alai sighed. That was the trump card all pregnant women had. It wasn't their fault; it was the baby. And if the baby didn't get the salted pork he wanted, it was the husband's fault. At this rate, Alai wouldn't be surprised if their son was born with gout or if he got sick every time he smelled a pig roasting in the 'umu.

Don't blame me son. That was your mother. I told her to wait until we ate with the council, but noooo. Some people needed a fourth meal between dinner and breakfast.

Of course, every time his wife woke him up like this Alai knew he had already lost the battle. He massaged his eyes with one hand, moaning as he stretched out on his mat. "Okay, fine," he said. "I'll cook a pig."

She kissed him. Alai couldn't see her face in the darkness, but he could tell she was smiling. "What would I do without you?"

Alai lit a torch outside of their hut. He rubbed the back of his neck as he stared down the hill, thinking of all the work ahead of him.

"You'd probably eat pork in the afternoon like a normal person," he muttered, scurrying away before his wife could find something to throw at him.

When she came to term, Ta'ifetū gave birth to a healthy baby boy. He had his mother's attached earlobes and her round nose.

Alai thought that was good; he hoped he would look just like her someday.

However, there was something peculiar about the high chief's son. Most babies were born crying, and quite a few kicked or flailed their arms as they entered the world, their faces red from the screaming. High Chief Alai's son, however, came out of the womb *glowing.* Light radiated from his skin, like the sun peeking over the horizon at dawn. Even after they washed him off, the light didn't go away.

Startled, Alai called for a healer. "Is this some kind of ailment?"

"No, High Chief," the old woman said, bowing her head. "It is a gift from the gods. Our ancestor has fulfilled his promise. You should take him to the sacred pool and offer gratitude."

The moment his wife was up for it, they did just that. Alai guided her along the rocky path as she held their son. Once at the banks of the god pool, Alai summoned the forerunner of Havaiki, who at that time was a woman with koa brown skin and flowing hair. She confirmed what the healer had said.

"The heavens smile upon your family, my chiefs," she said. "Raise him well, and your son will indeed become a great man. One who can lead with both wisdom and compassion."

Alai was thrilled. A good, strong, chief—that was what his people needed.

"But why is he glowing?" asked Ta'ifetū. She looked worried. The light coming off of him wasn't so different from the one radiating off of the forerunner. Alai understood her fear; their own son looked like he really belonged with this woman instead of them.

The woman gave a reassuring smile. "Fear not, good chiefess," she said. "It is a gift from my father. Your son has been endowed with power that will manifest in due time. When that day comes, make sure that he doesn't overexert himself. His powers are great, but there are limits."

Alai frowned. "What are the limits? Will he be in danger if he goes over them?"

She tilted her head, uncertain. "It is...difficult to say. He wouldn't die, I think. However a continual strained effort would certainly wear on his body. But do not trouble yourselves with this. For now, rejoice in the birth of your child and know we will be watching over him. So long as his actions are fueled by love and guided by wisdom, he will be okay." She paused, then added, "As for the light, it should go away in a day or two."

The light did fade by the next morning, and it wasn't long before their son was drooling and babbling like every other infant. Six months later he still didn't understand that humans weren't supposed to sleep for only twenty minutes at night, but other than that, he was an easy baby. He didn't cry when other people wanted to hold him, and when his wife was tired, Alai could feed him with a wet cloth dipped in milk.

"What do you think his power is?" Ta'ifetū asked one night after bathing him.

"Power?" Alai had almost forgotten about that. The two of them already had enough to think about as high chiefs, but add the stress of being new parents to it? Alai was beginning to miss the days when all it took to keep the peace was a cooked pig in the middle of the night.

"Yes," his wife insisted, staring down at their son as she rocked him to sleep. "He used to glow, Lai. I half-expected him to be floating out of bed by now."

"Thank Havaiki that hasn't happened," Alai muttered. He could barely keep up with a baby that crawled nonstop and liked to put everything in his mouth. Did Ta'i really want to see what would happen if he *flew*?

"I'm serious," she insisted. "How are we supposed to help him if we don't even know what he can do?"

Alai rose to his feet, kissing her gently as he took the baby from her arms. "This is my first time being a father," he said, "but I think those are the kinds of things all parents worry about. It's not like their kids can tell them their likes or dislikes when they're born, nor do they know what they'll grow up to be. I don't think our son will be any different from them."

"I know," Ta'ifetū rested her head against his arm, watching their son sleep. "I just worry about him, that's all."

"Welcome to parenting," Alai said. He knew he couldn't exactly talk, but all of the other fathers in the village had been saying that to him for six months straight. It felt good to say it to someone else, for once.

Over time Toa's power did begin to manifest itself, even though his parents were slow to recognize it at first. It took several oddities for them to finally piece together what was happening. When he was two, Toa had wandered off and started playing with a centipede near the bush. Ta'ifetū screamed, beating the insect away before rushing her son to the healers. But, to everyone's surprise, Toa hadn't been bitten. He was fine.

Several months after that Toa, then age three, ate raw crab some of the other children had fed to him. None of them, however, realized that the crab was infected, and they all started throwing up. When the other parents warned Ta'ifetū of what had happened, she waited with dread for her son to vomit, but he never did.

"That's my boy!" Alai said, laughing with relief. "He's got a strong stomach, that one."

The worst, though, had been when Toa snuck out of the hut one night while his parents were sleeping and found one of his father's hunting knives. Alai stirred when he heard the faint slashing of a blade against skin. When Toa screamed, his eyes flew open in panic. Alai tore out of the hut. His son was bawling next to the bloodstained knife, his red fingers telling his father exactly what had happened. Alai scooped him up, trembling as he tried to comfort his child while scolding himself for being so careless. Ta'ifetū ran out to them with a candle, the dancing firelight making her terrified face all the more frightening.

"It's okay, son. It's okay," Alai shushed, bouncing Toa in his arms. "Did you get hurt? Here, show Daddy."

Toa sniffled, holding his bloody fingertips out to him. Ta'ifetū raised her candle, giving them a perfect view of the angry cuts sliced through their son's infant hands.

Alai's heart wrenched in agony. *I'm a horrible father.*

But then something happened. The open wounds on Toa's hands started to seal themselves. The torn skin knit itself back together, and the blood evaporated. Within seconds, Toa's hands were completely normal. Were it not for the stained knife at his feet, Alai might've thought the whole thing had been a dream.

Toa smiled at his clean hands, then waved them both at his parents. "Uma!" he said, trying to use the word for *all gone* as he wiggled his fingers. "I uma!"

Alai gaped at him. Ta'ifetū looked like she might drop her candle.

"Ta'i," he whispered, "did you just see that?"

"I did," she said, leaning on him as though she were about to fall over. "Lai, our boy can *heal* himself!"

For a moment they just stood there, watching their son clap his hands and point at the knife, probably wanting to play with it again. Alai lifted the blade with his foot and kicked it away. He looked down at his wife, breaking into a smile of relief

"It's a lot better than flying if you ask me."

Alai and his wife never openly talked to their son about his powers, but that didn't stop him from using them. Much like how children naturally learned how to walk and smile, Toa naturally seemed to know when his healing powers were needed. If someone was sad, Toa would sit with them and before long they'd be laughing. If someone was sick, Toa would give them something to eat, and their recovery time was cut in half.

Not wanting their four-year-old son to get overwhelmed, Ta'ifetū made him promise not to tell anyone about the healing. She said that would make him a "secret helper," and those were the best kind. All too eager to obey, Toa promised to do as she said.

Still, neither Alai nor Ta'ifetū could stop the villagers that suddenly wanted to make a trip to the healer's hut whenever Toa was playing nearby. And since his wife normally spent a lot of time there, anyway, she took him into the hut. Alai watched with amusement as she described the different medicinal plants to him. He doubted Toa would remember any of it by the time he was grown, but he didn't care.

But when his wife became pregnant again, Alai started to see what a blessing his son's gift truly was. The first time Ta'ifetū woke up with a fever and chills, he didn't know what to do. She was so delirious she could hardly speak, and as Alai tried to get her to tell him what was wrong her whole body started shaking. Alai had never felt so powerless in his life. He jumped up to fetch one of the healers, when Toa woke up.

He stared up at his father blearily. "Daddy, what's wrong?"

"It's okay, son," Alai lied. "Mommy's not feeling well. I'm going to find someone to help her."

"Mommy?"

He looked over at his mother, her brow slick with sweat as she slept fitfully. Alai thought he would cry, and almost decided to take the boy with him, when Toa stood up and walked over to her. He sat beside her, swiping her limp hair out of her face. Then he laid down across her chest, his arms holding her head, as though he were trying to hug her.

"Son!" Alai protested. He ran to pull him off, but then Toa started *glowing*. It was faint, the same soft shade of white he'd had when he was born. As he held his mother, the light started to dim again, transferring from him into her. Alai watched, dumbstruck.

Slowly, his wife stopped twitching, and when Toa rolled off of her, she slept peacefully again. Alai checked her temperature. Her fever was gone. He stared from his wife to his son, utterly bewildered.

Toa smiled at him before he broke into a yawn. "All better," he said. "Mommy's all better now, Daddy." Then he closed his eyes, and fell asleep.

That wouldn't be the last time Toa used his powers to heal his mother. For the next three months Ta'ifetū battled the fever and chills that seemed to come out of nowhere. She drank all kinds of tonics, and did everything the healers told her to do, but she couldn't stop the illness. Desperate, Alai even tried applying red-heart leaves in case it was a demon, but bite marks never appeared. Not on her arms, her legs, her abdomen—as unnatural as it seemed, Alai couldn't find an unnatural cause for it.

The only thing that helped was Toa's magic. Every night his mother was sick, Toa would unfailingly come to her side and heal her. She slept easy after that and would be refreshed in the morning, only to fall ill again the following night. Toa never complained, but Alai could see that the effort it took to heal his mother was starting to get to him. At first, Toa would simply fall asleep after using his magic. But several weeks into it he started to be sluggish in the morning. After a month, Alai could've sworn he saw Toa shrink a little when he pushed his magic into his mother, like a lemon being squeezed dry. He would be back to normal a few hours later, but the sight was unsettling.

"I don't like it, Lai," Ta'ifetū said when her husband told her what had been happening. "He's pushing himself too hard, and he's getting so skinny."

"So are you," Alai pointed out. Even with Toa's healings, his wife was losing an unhealthy amount of weight. Her curvy hips were narrowing and her cheeks were hollow. And even though she was seven months pregnant, she was hardly showing. If he didn't know his wife so well, Alai would've wondered if she was even pregnant, at all.

He would never say it out loud, but Alai feared their second child might not make it. As his wife's health continued to deteriorate, he felt paralyzed at the thought that she might not make it, either.

He ground his teeth, forcing himself to push the thought back. *Don't...*he warned himself, *Don't go there.*

"But look at him," Ta'ifetū frowned as she watched their son play with the other children. Toa had thinned out, Alai admitted. He had brushed it off as his son merely growing out of his baby fat. But that didn't explain the way he lagged behind the other boys when he used to be faster and stronger than them all.

Alai laid a comforting hand on her arm, even though he felt like he was holding on to her to reassure himself. "He'll be alright, love," he said. "Once the baby's here and you're all recovered, things will go back to normal. You'll see. I'm excited for our boy to be a big brother."

Ta'ifetū rested a hand on her stomach, her lips pressed in a closed smile. "He'd be a good one, wouldn't he?" she said. "I can see him fussing over her all the time."

Alai raised an eyebrow. "You think it's a girl?"

"I think..." Ta'ifetū looked uncertain, her hands shifting on her abdomen as though she were trying to find the baby. "It's hard to say. She's so still. Lai, she doesn't kick, or wiggle the way that our son did. I'm worried about her."

"She'll be alright," Alai said, squeezing her hand. "Have faith, Ta'i. Things will work out in the end."

I hope.

One month later, High Chiefess Ta'ifetū fell into premature labor. Ironically, giving birth had been the easiest part, although the midwives agreed there was no hope for the child. Alai didn't want to admit it, but they were right. The baby was so small, she hardly looked like a baby, at all. Alai didn't touch her. She was no bigger than his right hand. Amazingly, she breathed, but it was only a matter of time before she passed. She was just too fragile.

Alai's heart hung heavy at the loss of his second child, but even more terrifying still was his wife's condition. Another month of battling her illness had not gone well for Ta'ifetū. Her fevered hand clung to her husband, teeth bared in pain as the midwives rushed about her, all of them trying to stop the bleeding. Alai had fought in wars; he had seen death and bloodshed in ways most men would never believe, yet all of that paled compared the terror he felt now. And all the while, his wife kept asking about the child.

"Where's my baby?" she croaked, her eyelids fluttering. "Alai, where did they take our daughter?"

A lump pinched his throat as Alai brought her hand to his lips, not sure what to say.

She looked at him, her eyes now more lucid than they had been in days. Tears welled in them as she started to understand. "She didn't make it, did she?"

He took her hand in both of his, closed his eyes, and shook his head. He had been trying so hard to shove that grief aside, to save it until after his wife was in recovery. But seeing the heartache in her face, Alai felt the despair crashing down on him. They had lost their child, the baby girl they had been praying for. Alai had wanted a daughter badly, a little girl he could love and spoil, and—when she was old enough—train with a spear to keep her brother on his toes. But that...that was all gone now.

Ta'ifetū's hand laced through his own and her grip tightened like a claw. Alai could feel her trembling. "Oh, Lai," she said, "I'm so sorry."

"What?"

Had she really just said that? Here he was, praying to every god he knew that her life would be spared, and she was sorry? After everything she had been through, the months of illness and now the pains of early childbirth, all she could think about was him. Never mind her present condition, she was sorry that she couldn't give her husband his baby girl.

Fool woman, he thought, loving her even more.

"Mommy?"

Alai's head jerked up. None of the midwives or nurses had noticed Toa standing inside of the hut, his eyes wide in terror as he held open the curtain.

"Son!" Alai yelled. "Get out of here!"

Toa didn't listen. He ran inside. One of the nurses tried to grab him, and he pushed her away. A midwife grabbed him around the waist, and Toa kicked in her arms, prying himself free.

"No!" he screamed. "That's my mommy! Don't hurt my mommy!"

His young, broken voice halted the nurses. They turned to the high chiefess.

"It's alright," she said. "Let him come to me."

Alai wished he would leave. He was only five; this was not something he wanted his son to see. But as Toa nestled beside his mother, he knew he wasn't going anywhere.

"Hi, my boy," she said, kissing the top of her head.

Toa was a blubbering mess. He brought his hands up to her face. "It's okay, Mommy," he said. "I got you. Everything's gonna be okay, now."

He started to glow. Alai was torn between stopping his son and letting him use his magic. Of course he wanted his wife to heal, but if healing a fever and chills had pushed Toa this far, he didn't want to see what would happen to him now. Surely this was beyond his abilities.

Oh, gods, what do I do? he thought. *I've already lost a daughter. I can't lose them all.*

His wife, ever practical, took Toa's hand and brought it to her lips. "I know, my boy," she said, soothing him. "I know you're strong and you always help whenever you can, don't you?"

Toa nodded, still sobbing uncontrollably as he tried to touch her face. But his mother stopped him.

"Why don't you go help your sister, then?" she asked.

Toa's next sob came up short. "My...sister?"

"Yes." His mother smiled. "You have a new baby sister. But she's very sick, Lā. She needs your help more than I do. Why don't you help her first? Help your sister, and then you can come back to Mommy, okay?"

Toa looked from his mother to his father, torn about what he should do. Alai held his wife's hand and rubbed her head reassuringly.

"It's alright, son," he said. "Go. I'll stay with Mommy."

His confirmation was all the boy needed. "I'll be right back," he promised, running off to find where the nurses had left the baby.

Ta'ifetū let out a ragged sigh once he was gone. "Thank you, Lai," she said, leaning back and closing her eyes. She looked so tired.

"Of course, love," Alai's own voice was growing hoarse. He understood what his wife had done. She didn't want their son overexerting himself, either, and sent him away so that he wouldn't be here when...when it happened. Alai wasn't ready to feel everything that came with that finality, but he knew he needed to be here with his wife. To stay by her side until the very end.

They had been at this for hours now. Dawn had broken when Ta'ifetū first went into labor, and here they were nearing nightfall. The medical staff worked diligently, but Alai could see the grim looks of acceptance on their faces. The high chiefess, they knew, would not last the night. And Alai, for all his power and all his strength, could do nothing to stop that.

Suddenly, the most unusual noise pierced the hut. Alai and his wife jerked upright, startled. The nurses stopped working. Alai couldn't believe it. Was that...was that a *baby* crying?

Seconds after he heard it, Toa staggered into view, the wailing child in his arms confirming what they had all heard. Against all odds, Toa had saved his sister. What used to be a fist-sized lump of tissue was now a healthy baby girl with a shock of dark hair. She kicked and screamed, her face beet red.

Alai had never heard anything more beautiful in his life.

He wished he could say the same thing for his son. Toa had been thin before, but he looked like death personified now. His skin stretched tight over his bones, his face like a skull and all of his ribs poking out of his chest. His arms wobbled as he struggled to carry the infant. One of the nurses quickly relieved him of her.

"High Chiefess, look!" she said in wonder. "Here is your baby!"

She laid the child on Ta'ifetū's chest. Alai was still in shock from the sight of her. Ta'ifetū shushed the infant as she hugged her.

"There, now," she said. "It's okay. It's okay, Mommy's here."

The baby's head perked up. She couldn't open her eyes, but Alai could tell she was searching, searching for the voice she'd been hearing for the past eight months.

Toa stumbled beside them, resting his head on his mother's shoulder. "Sister," he rasped, breathing heavily. Gods help him, he was so thin.

Ta'ifetū leaned over and kissed the top of his head. "You did so well, my boy," she said. "I am so proud of you."

"Mommy..." Toa raised a hand, his fingers showing all of the bones on his knuckles, and tried to grab her arm. His eyes screwed shut in effort, and he grunted. Alai felt his heart break. His son—his brave, stupid, selfless son—was still trying to save his mother.

Ta'ifetū kissed him again. "I love you, my boy," she said. "And I know you're going to be a great brother." She looked down at the little girl, now resting peacefully on her chest. She squeezed her husband's hand.

"Oh, she's beautiful, Lai," she said. "Absolutely beautiful. Can we name her Masina? Let's call her Masina, after your mother. I think she'd like that."

"She would," Alai said, his vision going blurry. "She'd like that, love. Masina it is, then."

Ta'ifetū smiled. She let out a deep breath, leaning back as her eyes fell closed. Her hand went limp in Alai's grasp. Seconds later Masina started to bawl, probably confused now that the steady thump of her mother's heartbeat was gone. Alai didn't blame her; he felt confused, too. His wife...his best friend...everything he loved most about the world had slipped through his fingers.

Masina screamed louder, and Toa picked her up, straining to hold her with what little strength he had left. Masina fell quiet, turning into his bony chest in a sign of complete trust.

Alai lifted his wife, gathered her up in his arms, and wept.

Chapter 30

Masina was never supposed to know. My father had ingrained that into me after the burial: Do not tell anyone how my mother had died, *especially* Masina. The last thing he wanted was for his daughter to feel responsible for her own mother's death. All of the midwives and the nurses who had been there were sworn to secrecy. Most of them were so old that they died not long after that, anyway. Aside from my father and I, there were maybe two nurses left who knew the true nature of Masina's powers, and they never uttered a word.

Everyone in the village quietly forgot that I had ever had powers. All the miracles I performed as a child were reassigned to Masina. It wasn't that my father tried to cover anything up; people were just so used to seeing Masina outperform me they figured it must've been her, all along. As the whole village praised and adored her, I stayed silent in her shadow, watching her live the life that had been meant for me.

"Why would you tell her?" I breathed, feeling my knees buckle. I leaned against the wooden mast behind me for support.

"She needed to know," my mother said. "Just like how you were incomplete until you understood your hate, she was not whole without a knowledge of her past."

I thought back to Faletahi, and how easy it had been to love Masina once I realized I had never really hated her at all. It had been easy to pretend that I did because she stole my strength and took the life I might have had, but there was more to it than that. Festering under a thick layer of jealousy was my worry that I had made the wrong choice. I thought I loved my mother more than anyone, but in the end I didn't saved her. I picked Masina, instead.

Mother gave me one of her knowing smiles. "None of this was your fault," she said. "You did more than any of us thought possible, and it wasn't fair of me to put so much pressure on you at such a young age."

I felt a lump well in my throat. "So, you're not mad then?"

She smiled. "Oh my boy, look at how far you've come! How could I be mad? Any mother who can't be proud of that doesn't deserve a son like you."

I hugged her, my mouth breaking into a crooked grin. "Thanks, Mom."

We left the encampment in search of Masina. Mother suspected she had gone to the ocean again. As we walked, my mother said there were things about Masina that I needed to know, things she had struggled with growing up.

"How hard can it be to be perfect?" I said.

Mother glanced at me reprovingly. "She looked perfect to you, but she's been through a lot. A little girl with the strength of ten men? That's enough to get her branded as a freak."

I only ever noticed the people who drooled when Masina came by, but she'd had her fair share of opposition. Mother told me how Masina had often been tricked into doing tests that supposedly proved whether she was a demon or not. Then there were people who befriended her so that they could take advantage of her. "Don't mess with me, or I'll send the devil child after you," they'd say. Or, "The devil girl might get hungry if you don't pay extra tonight..." And Masina, pure as she was, couldn't see through their lies until it was too late.

No wonder she learned how to sail to the War Village; Alani was one of the few people she could actually trust.

"But if she wanted to get away from those kinds of people," I started, "why did she come to me? I was awful to her."

We were up on a cliff that overlooked the ocean. Sitting on one of the rocks towards the edge of it was the ghostly visage of my sister, her arms wrapped around herself as her hair blew in the wind. I thought about all those mornings she had come knocking on my hut day after day. If she was tired of people who didn't appreciate her, why did she waste her time on me?

Mother squeezed me gently, her eyes also on Masina. "Your sister lived with so much uncertainty, and she's dealt with a lot of two-faced people. I think she wanted something consistent she could rely on. I guess she figured she'd always have you."

My heart ached, and I saw my sister in a way I never had before. I smiled at my mom and walked towards her, hoping I wouldn't mess it up this time.

"Hey..." I said, sitting down on the rock next to her.

She hunched her shoulders. "Hey."

I tried to think of what to say, something that would make her realize why she needed to come with me. I opened my mouth, then hesitated. Was it possible that talking was the wrong thing to do? Every time I had seen her, whether in real life or in my dreams, I tried to explain myself, tried to tell her why I was sorry or why she needed to do things my way. That had gotten me nowhere. So rather than talk, I just sat with her and waited.

And waited.

Finally, she started fiddling with her hair. "Why did you come here?" she blurted.

My eyebrows shot up in surprise. That wasn't what I had been expecting. I thought she would've gone with "I hate you," or maybe "I don't want to go home with you." Why had I come? Wasn't that obvious?

I rested a finger on my lips, trying to think. "Well, you remember all those mornings when you would come knocking at my hut?"

She nodded.

"You did that for years, even though I kept sending you away. And yet, you still came. Why did you do that?"

Masina cocked her head at me, searching my face as though she were afraid it was a trick. I gave a small smile, turning my palms up to emphasize I honestly had no idea.

"Because...you're my brother," she said. "We're family. I want to be with you."

"But why, Masina?" I pressed. "I mean, look at me. I'm not strong. War tactics confuse me, and everyone jokes that I'm one bad sneeze away from launching myself to the Navigator Village."

Masina laughed, and I couldn't help but smile, too. I slipped an arm around her shoulders, relieved that my hand didn't pass straight through her. "Why would you want to be with me?"

"Because you're my brother," she said again, more confidently this time. "And I love you."

I felt something inside of me melt at the words, and I squeezed her affectionately. The last time she said that to me, I tried to club her into submission. But this time, I would get it right.

"I love you too, Masina," I said. "I love you so much."

Masina let out a small squeak. She threw her arms around me. Even as a spirit, it was amazing how strong she was. I felt air rush out of my lungs, but I hugged her back, my heart full.

Then something strange happened. The warm feeling in my heart continued to bubble; it swelled until it filled my whole chest, then spread to my legs and arms.

Masina gaped at me. "Lā?"

"I..." I stared down at my hands, at the rest of me that was now glowing. "I don't know what's happening."

The light seeped into my skin, and I felt my arms grow taut. The hollow spaces in my ribcage filled out, and toned muscles evened out the areas in between my bony joints. The sulu around my waist felt tight, and as I stood up I noticed it now only went down to my knee. Before it had been mid-calf.

Masina's eyes went wide. "Woah."

She walked over to me, standing up as straight as she could. Even then, I was still a head taller than her. She frowned.

"Not like my quiet strength," she said, "but do you like it?"

I pulled her to my side and messed up her hair, smiling. "It'll do for now."

The truth was, I was thrilled. I felt good, better than I had in years. I wasn't the hulking monster Hana had made me, but that was okay. Somehow this felt better; this felt right.

Mother walked over to us, our ancestors trailing behind her. They stood proud like an army awaiting the call to arms. She smiled at me.

"Actions that are fueled by love and guided by wisdom," she said. "That was all you needed."

"You knew?" I asked.

She raised an eyebrow. "Am I not your mother?"

She held her arms out, and we ran to her. Masina snuggled into her left side, and I clung to her on the right. Our ancestors gathered around us in a circle.

"Would you look at that?" Uncle Mote said, his hands on his hips. "Instant abs, this boy, I tell you. You know how different my earth life would've been if I got a six-pack like that?"

"Well, you did gain weight in mortality, love," his wife teased. "Just not in those same places."

Mother kissed Masina on the top of her head. "Are you ready to go home, my darling?"

Masina nodded, burying her face into her. "I'm really gonna miss you, Mom."

"Oh, darling, I'm never far away," she said, rubbing her shoulder. "I'll always be watching out for you. And if you ever miss me, you can always come visit the garden. I'd love to see what other lei you can come up with."

"I'll make one for you every day," Masina promised.

Mother laughed. "Maybe not every day, love. That might get wasteful." She turned to me, her face growing somber. "There is one more thing I need to tell you before you go."

I frowned. "What is it?"

"How I died."

I stared at her, confused. Why was she telling me this? I already knew how she died.

Mother let go of us and pulled back the hair over her right ear. She felt for something in her scalp, then parted her hair and told us to look. Puzzled, Masina and I squinted at the open space she had made through her thick locks. At first I didn't see anything. Then I noticed dark lines that perforated her head in a circle. It wasn't much bigger than a kukui nut.

"Mom," I said, revulsion rising inside of me. "Is that—"

"A demon bite?" she finished. "Yes."

My blood ran hot as I realized what that meant. For months, *months,* my mother fought for her life and Masina's just to have Mā try to take it night after night. If it wasn't for that stupid demon, my mother would still be alive. It was her fault that—

"Son," she said sharply.

I looked up, not realizing I had gotten distracted. She gestured at me and I looked down, startled to see I had thinned out a little. I wasn't the skeleton I used to be, but a part of my new strength had washed out of me.

"The gods gave you a gift to help you protect your people," she said. "Sometimes that will require aggression. But if you kill for the sake of getting even, that gift will leave you. Do you understand?"

I closed my eyes, willing myself to swallow my anger, and nodded.

She relaxed. "Good. I told you this in case the demon tries to use it against you. And because of how it affected you." She paused, looking down at Masina, who swallowed.

"That's not gonna go away?" she asked.

Mother shook her head. "But you needn't be afraid, my darling. What you have is also a gift." She turned to me. "There's more to your sister's strength than what you put into her," she said. "You're about to find out what it is. I wish I had more time to explain, but know that there is a reason why she is stronger, and why she could never heal the way you could."

"I...okay." I said.

"Do not avenge me, children. Judgment is for the gods." She hugged us one at a time before throwing her arms around us. "I love you both very much. Give my love to your father, and try to take it easy on him. He never expected to be a single parent."

The ancestors closed tighter around us, all of them holding hands and singing. Standing in the midst of them was the goddess Hina. She smiled when I recognized her.

"Until next time, little chiefs," she said. She snapped her fingers at us and pointed down.

We vanished.

Chapter 31

I was back in the deadlands. The sudden darkness blinded me, and I held my hands out my eyes adjusted. Slowly, I saw Marama sitting at the stone altar. He sprang up when he saw me. And beyond him were the portals to heaven and hell. In between them Masina's body hovered, shrouded in darkness.

I ran to her, the cloud dissolving again as my hands pierced through it. This time I caught her, holding her steady in my arms as I knelt down. At first she felt cold, but as I held her she started to warm up. She inhaled and opened her eyes, smiling at me.

"Hi, Lā," she said.

"Hi, Masina," I said, smiling back as I helped her to sit up. "I hope you're ready for a long trip back with some of the—"

Masina doubled over, crying out as she hugged herself in pain. I wrapped my arms around her protectively.

"Masina?" I asked. "Masina! Talk to me. What's wrong?"

She whimpered, holding up her hands to show me her palms. Something...something was *growing* out of them. Pointed teeth jutted out of Masina's hands, lining her fingers like Alani's shark-tooth rings. Only these weren't rings, they were growing out of her *skin!*

"Masina..." I started, at a complete loss for words. I looked at her face and had to fight the urge to push her away. Her pupils had contracted into vertical lines, like a tiger shark. When she spoke, her mouth was full of rows and rows of jagged teeth.

"I'm sorry, brother," she said. "I didn't want anyone to know."

The tremble in her voice, the sheer vulnerability of it made it easy for me to look past the monster and see my sister. Even now when she was more demon than human, Masina still looked so small, so frightened. I realized now why our mother had told us the true nature of her death.

Masina had been exposed to demon venom long before she was born; of course it had some kind of effect on her. And even though I filled her with light, a part of that darkness remained. She must've been suppressing this side of herself all these years, afraid of what would happen if anyone found out. But now that she was in a place made of dark magic, she couldn't fight it anymore.

I shook my head. Light *and* dark magic; Masina had them both. And she had no idea how to use either.

I took her face in my hands, ignoring the sandpaper rub of her skin. "Hey, look at me," I said. "Look at me, Masina."

She did. As our eyes met I felt something transfer between us, a kind of energy that flowed out of me and into her. Masina's breathing started to steady. Her eyes dilated back to normal, and the teeth in her hands retracted as she relaxed.

"There, see?" I said. "No harm done."

She still looked troubled. She stared down at her hands, "I wanted to be good," she said quietly, "I didn't want to be like this."

"You are good," I said. She tensed, and I could tell she didn't believe me. I rested a hand on her cheek, prompting her to look at me again. "Masina," I told her, "you're one of the best people I know."

She gave a small smile. "Thank you, Lā."

As I helped her to her feet, I understood what Tahi had meant. Masina didn't need a warrior for a brother. She didn't need more killing, or brute force; she was already terrified of her own ability to kill and slaughter. No, what she needed was a comforter. Someone to remind her of her innate goodness whenever she felt like giving in to the darkness. I could be that for her.

"I see the heavens were good to you," Marama said, sizing me up. He was taller than me before, but we were eye-to-eye now.

"They would be good to you, too," I said. "Everyone tells me you're better suited for that realm, anyway."

Marama cringed. "We still have unfinished business here."

He told us how Mā came to be and why he wanted to take her back to the heavens. His story didn't surprise me much; I had been able to piece together most of it with my mother. Still, his ambition was bold.

"You do realize it's not your fault, right?" I asked him once he was done. "Hina told me to tell you as much."

Marama looked uncertain. "Does it make a difference?" he said, meeting my gaze.

I thought about all the times Marama said he understood me. Now that we were here, I could see how right he was. We were two foolish brothers bending over backward to make things right with our sisters. Foolhardy as he was, I couldn't fault him for that.

"How much longer until she gets here?" I asked, pulling out the knife from Alani and unwrapping the blade.

"Could be any minute," Marama said. "My uncle never gave a set time."

Moments later a sound cracked in the air above us, like someone with a giant hand snapping their fingers. The demon Mā appeared.

I raised the knife. Marama took his stance Masina glanced at me, brow furrowed, and I nodded at her.

"It's okay," I said. "We're fighting to protect our friends and our village. This isn't revenge."

Masina nodded. I stepped back as she crouched down, allowing the transformation to happen. When she rose, her eyes were slits and she had shark teeth lining the insides of her hands. She bared her fangs at Mā.

The demon snarled. "And what is this?" she sneered. "A trio of lost children seeking to challenge me?"

Her tail thrashed behind her. I exhaled slowly, fighting to stay calm.

"This isn't a challenge," I said. "We just want to make things right. Don't let this end in violence."

Mā hissed, and I couldn't tell if she was sneering or laughing. "How odd of you to say it shouldn't end in violence," she said, slithering closer, "when that is exactly how it began."

Marama hesitated, then shook his head. "I've told you a thousand times, Hana," he said. "I never wanted to hurt you. I was only looking out for you."

"Shut up!" she snapped. She beat her tail against the stone walls, The entire cave rattled.

"I've told you never to call me that," she seethed. "That name is dead, just like how your sister is dead. You killed her when you stole her only love."

Marama bristled. He stepped forward, but I threw a hand to the side, halting him. I recognized the tone in Mā's voice, the blind rage that kept her from seeing things as they really were.

"Is your hatred so fixed that you would kill your own brother?" I asked.

She bared her teeth. "If my brother cared for me, he wouldn't have killed me in the first place!"

Mā lunged and the three of us scattered. Masina got to her first. She jumped into the air and landed a backfist alongside the demon's head. Mā shrieked, and Masina kicked her chest. She sprawled backward, swinging her body around as she recovered. By that point I was behind her, and I drove the tip of my knife into her tail.

Mā howled in rage. She rounded on me, but before she could attack Masina was on her again. She dug her claws into her skin as she scaled up her back, kicking away the demon's arms as she tried to grab her. Masina stuffed her neck into the crook of her right arm, slicing with her left against the back of her neck, choking her. Amazingly, Masina held her in place using the backs of her hands. She could've killed her right there, but she held back.

A cord of light shot through the air, wrapping itself around Mā's left hand. She screamed, pulling at the restraint, but Marama held tight on the other end. Masina inched up the demon's back, sinking her choke hold deeper around her.

Remembering the way energy had passed from me to Masina, I tried to recreate that feeling, pushing out to Mā with that same energy. Another cord of light appeared, this one coming from my hands instead of Marama's. I looped it around the demon's right arm, stopping her from swinging at Masina.

Masina turned to me, serpentine eyes wide in surprise. She let go of Mā and rushed over to me.

"I'm alright," I grunted, staggering to my feet. Masina stroked my head with the back of her leathery hand. She still looked scary as ever, but I appreciated the sign of affection.

Across from us, Marama was trying to talk to his sister. Mā writhed and twisted against her restraints, her cries becoming more desperate as she pulled. As her frustration grew, the fear she had struck into me fell away, like an old shell.

Her demonic form started to shrink. At first she had been bigger than Ori; then she was slightly bigger than Loli. Now, now she wasn't much bigger than I was. Gone was the terrifying demon Mā; here now was only Hana. The girl who ran away from home out of hate.

Marama's voice trembled as he talked to her. "It's been years," he said. "Years that I've been trying to get to you, years of me trying to make things right." He stepped closer, the rope of light twisted firmly in his hand. "I don't know how many times I've tried to tell you, but I'm sorry. I'm really sorry that I hurt you. I'm not sorry for killing the demon, but I am sorry for taking something you loved. But please." His voice cracked. "Please, Hana, just come home."

Hana stopped struggling. Her arms went slack against the ropes, but I held on, not trusting her. Masina stood next to me, her shoulders tense. We watched as Marama lowered the rope in his hand, showing his palms to her as he took another step closer.

Hana's eyes flicked from the cord of light dissolving on the ground to her brother coming towards her. She hesitated, then her face twisted in rage and she lunged at him.

"No!" I screamed, pulling against my rope, but it was useless. She was too strong.

Masina shot forward, intervening before Mā could get to him. She wrapped her clawed hands around the demon, this time sparing her no pain as she took her to the ground.

It was over in a matter of seconds.

I landed on my back, breathing heavily. Then I scrambled to my feet, running to pull Masina away from the demon's motionless body. Masina's legs wobbled, and I sat down with her on the stone steps of the altar, pulling her into my arms as she started to whimper.

"I killed someone, Lā," she croaked, her rows of teeth garbling her voice. "I killed someone."

"Shh, it's okay," I said, cradling one hand against her head as I held her. "You didn't want to hurt anyone. You were just trying to protect him. If she wasn't gonna kill him, you never would've done it, right?"

Masina shook her head.

"There, see?" I squeezed her tighter. "You stopped her from hurting someone else, and that's a very good thing."

Masina nodded, but she looked unconvinced. "I still killed someone."

"I—I know," I said. Masina had killed wild boars and all kinds of creatures in the sea, but she had never killed anyone; until today, she'd never even hurt another person. This sort of thing was traumatic, the kind of thing that took years to get over. My heart ached to know that my ten-year-old sister was the one who had to go through it.

I rested my chin against her head, feeling some of the energy in me transfer to her. "It's gonna be okay."

I looked over to the middle of the cavern, where the forerunner was tending to his sister. She wasn't a demon anymore but instead looked very human as he held her body in his arms. He closed her eyes and kissed the top of her head, rocking her back and forth.

"Marama..." I started. He looked at me, and I wished I hadn't spoken. It seemed cruel, for me to be here with my sister when he had lost his.

Marama looked down at his sister, then back at me. "She made her own choices," he said. "This is not your fault."

I nodded. The words didn't comfort me as much as he probably wanted them to, but I was grateful, anyway.

"Wisely said, nephew." came a new voice.

Lord Iva had arrived. He stood on the altar, hands clasped behind his back. His daughter appeared at his side. She descended the steps, motioning for Marama to move aside as she took his sister in her arms. I was surprised at how easily she carried her; Hala was much stronger than she looked.

"Is there anything you can do for her?" I asked, glancing from Hala to her father.

Lord Iva's face was grim. "I can try," he said, "But it's like my nephew told you. She has made her choices. And now justice must prevail."

Chapter 32

The trip back home flew by much faster than the time it took for us to get there. Maybe it was the strong winds, or because we all felt lighter now that Masina was with us. I suspected it was a mixture of both, along with a friendly push in the water that might have come from a certain curly-haired forerunner.

Masina kept us energized with her constant hopping back and forth from the *Ta'ifetū* to the *Inati*. She gave all the Navigator men a run for their money with the way she could man the rudder by herself or adjust the sheetline with ease.

"I'm guessing she inherited all of the crazy in your family," Loli said, watching her buzz from one crew member to another, asking each of them what they were doing and how she could help. She hadn't slept at all in the past two days, yet she showed no signs of slowing down.

I smiled. "You could say that."

Masina was becoming more comfortable with her demon side, too. It took a little coaxing, but after she saw how accepting the Navigator men were, she transformed and dove into the deep, swimming at unnatural speeds.

Alaka'i whistled. "You know, I wouldn't mind growing a sharkskin if it meant I could swim like that."

Minutes later Masina returned, heaving a fat octopus onto the deck, and everyone loved her "sharkskin" trick even more. She dove several more times when one of us told her something we were 'ono for, or if she was getting restless.

We still only had ten crewmembers rotating between the two canoes. Marama opted to stay behind, saying that we were more than prepared to travel on our own. He was also needed more in the heavens, where his family was no doubt mourning Hana's death.

I looked away from the fish I was frying to the stars floating behind us. Counting down from Hina, I saw the two new stars at the end of the Celestial Sibling line. Unlike the five other stars that were spaced out, these two were right next to each other. One hovered above the other, as though it were trying to help the lower star to climb the heavens.

I sent a prayer of thanks to Marama, and hoped he would be alright.

On the morning of the fifth day, our island came into view. I rode with Masina, Ori, Alani, and Tāwhiri on the *Inati*. The Navigator men steered the *Ta'ifetū*. As we rounded the bend to the landing bay, I could see a man sitting on the shore. He was there alone, and was too far away for me to make out his face.

Masina gasped. "Lā, look! It's Dad!" she said. "It's our dad!"

"How could you—" I started, then reminded myself it was Masina I was talking to. There was nothing natural about her senses; I wouldn't be surprised if she could see from here to the Wind Village.

She cupped her hands to her mouth. "Dad!" she shouted.

The man on the shore started. He clambered to his feet, and when he saw us he raised a pū to his lips, sounding it. The song it made seemed to rattle the trees.

Masina beamed, her smile growing wider as she called to him again. "Dad!"

Again the pū sounded to answer her. The echo of it rang joyfully across the waves.

"Daddy!"

Unable to contain herself any longer, Masina ran the full length of the canoe and flung herself in the water, swimming the rest of the way to shore. I had a feeling that the strongest trade winds in the world couldn't have helped us beat her there.

Tāwhiri made a face at me. I just laughed and shrugged. Was he really that surprised?

Ori guided us into the bay, navigating past the shallow reefs and letting the canoe ground to a soft halt on the sand. By that point the villagers were trickling through the bush, all of them excited and curious at our arrival.

Leading the charge in front of them were High Chiefs Moe, Manaia, and Senidra. I barely got out of the way as they barreled into their kids, all of them laughing and sobbing with relief.

"Father, I'm fine!" Alani protested. But when High Chief Senidra kissed her forehead and threw his arms around her, she hugged him back.

High Chiefess Manaia looked completely undignified as she asked her son over and over how he was doing. All of her poise and class forgotten now that Tāwhiri was back. I laughed, the sight of it amusing.

As I passed him, Tāwhiri mouthed, *Save me!*

I pointed at his mom, who had her back faced to me. *From her? I mouthed back. Are you crazy?*

Ori had a rare smile on as he talked with his father, who stopped me as I walked by.

"My son tells me that you were valiant on your journey and relentless in your efforts," he said. He lowered his head a little, "I am...sorry if I ever mistreated you."

Woah. An apology? From a high chief? I thought I would be with the ancestors before I heard anything like that. But it really wasn't needed; I didn't blame anyone who had doubted me. I hadn't exactly been godlike before.

"There is nothing to forgive, my good high chief," I said. "If anything, I owe you my thanks. Ori has taught me so much. Not just about sailing, but about leadership, and how to be a better man."

High Chief Moe smiled, and I excused myself to find my family.

I found them at the center of the bay. My father still knee-deep in water, his arms firmly wrapped around Masina. Saltwater dripped down her hair and sand stuck to her skin, but she hugged him fiercely. Her shoulders bobbed up and down as she cried.

I stepped up behind my father, then hesitated. Masina, sensing me, opened her eyes. She tapped our father, and he turned around. When he saw me, he did a double take, and it took me a while to realize it was because I didn't look the way I had when I left. But even though I was taller now, he still towered over me. His broad shoulders and sharp features so severe I wanted to evaporate on the spot.

I swallowed hard and bowed my head. "Hello, Father," I said. "I—I did what you asked. I helped bring her back and—"

He cut me off. Before I could say another word my father embraced me. The force of it was so strong my legs buckled, and we landed on our knees in the water.

I was stunned. My father had never been affectionate with me before. With Masina, he had; there was a reserved softness he saved for his little girl. But for me....

"All the strength of a thousand suns," he said, "could never compare to the joy of being your father." He squeezed me tighter. "I love you, my son."

"I love you too, Dad," I said, not even trying to stop the tears. Why bother? It wasn't like the added emotions were my fault, anyway. Those had obviously come from my mother.

A ceremonial headdress worn only by chiefs, the tuiga is a symbol of status meant to humble leaders due to the fact that it's made from things that belonged to the ancestors.

EPILOGUE

"It's so heavy," Masina complained, her hands working as she tried not to touch the tuiga on her head.

I laughed. "You'll get used to it," I said, tapping the tuiga that rested on my own head.

A ceremonial headpiece worn only by high chiefs, the tuiga was a crown made mostly of red hair and vibrant feathers. Masina's hair had been rolled up in a bun so that it sat hidden in the tuiga. My hair was already short, which made it easier to slip the crown on. On both of us it looked like the bright hair coming out of the tuiga was actually ours.

Masina wore an ofu of painted tapa cloth. The sash around her waist was adorned with mother-of-pearl shells that matched the ones on her tuiga, and the feathers on her kiki were purple, like the colors of the setting sun. It was unconventional, but when it came to the two of us, hardly anything ever was.

I wore something more traditional. Like Masina, I had a tapa cloth around my waist, but the feathers on both my tuiga and my kiki were bright reds and yellows. I tied my ula nifo around my neck, then helped her fix her vesas.

"Are you ready?" I asked her.

She let out a quick breath. "I think so."

I held out my left hand, making sure it was up by my shoulder and out in front of me. Masina rested her right hand in my palm, and I closed my fingers around hers.

"Alright then," I said, tucking my right hand behind me. "Let's do this."

I walked her down our family encampment to where the procession was waiting for us. Villagers lined the walkway on both sides, drawing a straight line that led to the orator's hut. Music played, and many shouted their support as we passed.

As we walked, I thought about how much had changed in the past eight months. Sometimes I couldn't believe it had really been eight months since we went to the deadlands; everything felt so different that I could've sworn it had happened years ago. Yet at the same time, it felt like we only got back yesterday.

After the initial excitement of having Masina back had worn off, the villagers started to wonder who would be their next high chief. Ori, Alani, and everyone else in our crew vouched for me, saying that I would make a great chief. I wasn't sure which surprised me more; the fact that all of them could support me, or that nobody dared to argue about it. Nobody balked at the idea of having "skinny Toa" as their chief. But, then again, that could've been because I wasn't skinny anymore. Given my new strength and experience, the village felt like I was someone they could rally behind.

The only problem was I didn't want to be high chief. Or at least, not by myself. I could handle agriculture and politics, no problem. But there was more to being High Chief than knowing when it was the right time to plant crops. It would be a disservice to my people if I couldn't protect them in times of war, or find other ways to fish and hunt for them. I couldn't do any of those things, but I knew someone who could.

She had been hesitant the first time I presented the idea to her, but after I explained why it was necessary Masina came around. Our people needed her strength just like how they needed my knowledge. We really were two halves of a whole. Day and night, sun and moon, light, and darkness—we needed each other. The two of us provided a balance that the Light Village never had access to before.

And so, after I shocked the entire council to get their approval, Masina began her own protocol training. She met with Orator Ra'i every day, cramming in all the information it had taken me eight years to accumulate. But her studies had paid off. She was still a little rocky on some things, but knowing that I would be with her Orator Ra'i gave his blessing.

Father was waiting for us in the meetinghouse. Standing outside of Orator Ra'i's hut across from him were the rest of the high chiefs with their heirs, each dressed in their best ceremonial attire. I tried to look stoic as we passed Ori and Tāwhiri. Masina forgot her poise and waved at Alani. I laughed inwardly. Some things never changed.

We took our places next to our father. He took our hands in his, and the village fell silent.

"I present to you my son Toaolelā and my daughter Masina," he said, his voice booming out over the masses. "The next high chiefs of the Light Village!"

Everybody cheered.

Acknowledgements

It takes a village to make a good book. Anyone who tells you otherwise is either fooling themselves, or they're about to go insane. Because dang—publishing is haaaard. If it weren't for all the help I've had along the way, I know for a fact this book wouldn't exist right now.

But of all the people to thank in my "publishing village," first props have to go to my parents. Thank you for always encouraging me to pursue my dreams and for being there throughout all the highs and lows. I love you.

Second, I'd like to acknowledge my grandparents, as much of this story comes from their influence in my life. I miss having them around and am so grateful for everything they taught me. In everything I do, I hope I can always live up to their legacy and make them proud.

Thank you so much to Tawsh Lav, XaTi Draws, and Folo Tafua for the incredible artwork. Uncle Folo created the logo for my publishing brand, and XaTi did all of the interior illustrations. I absolutely love the logo and am blown away at the reference pics and character profiles XaTi created.

Tawsh designed the beautiful cover art along with the chapter headings and the custom font used throughout Shadowed By Moonlight. She's also been an incredible hype woman—coaching me through the highs and lows of putting my work out into the world. Thanks so much for everything, sis, you're the real one.

Special thanks to Ana Joldes and Lenore Madden for being my editors. Thank you for catching all the fluff words and for working with me to understand the cultural nuances that needed to be here.

Also a special shoutout to my "first editor," Mari! To this day you're still the only person that's read all of my books, and I seriously can't thank you enough for that.

Another shoutout goes to my sensitivity reader, Popo. Thanks so much for helping me to bring out those aspects that highlight the beauty of our Pacific Island cultures. Love you longtime, sis!

Thank you to the cultural specialists at the Polynesian Cultural Center for allowing me to conduct my research there. I started writing Shadowed By Moonlight after four years of dancing at the center, and was humbled at just how little I had learned in that time. Special thanks to the crew of the *Iosepa* who helped me to fine-tune the voyaging aspects of the story.

Also gotta thank my big sisters, Tilo and To'a. Tilo pushed me to attend my first writing conference. If it weren't for her, I don't think I would be publishing this book.

And To'a was the one I would go to whenever I got frustrated with writing Shadowed By Moonlight. Thanks, sis, for putting up with me every time I came over and declared, "I'm stuck!!" Grateful for you and seriously miss all our late night talks.

Special thanks also to Aunty Jolene, the Miller family, my ride-or-die Ti, Te Fano St. George, Jay's Legacy Foundation, and my Mo Street Tapusoa fam. I love you guys.

And all the props in the world to everyone that supported me on Kickstarter! Thank you all so, SOOO much for believing in this book long before it even existed. Seriously beyond grateful for all of you.

• Ah Fook – Cruz Family • Amy Fredlund • Ashiya Rose • Author Candace Osmond • Autry Hansell • Bethany Tomerlin Prince • C. Empey • C. Evans • C. Nautu • Carla Q. DeMille • Christiana Laudie • Clara Luca • Collin Shoemaker • Conte 'Ohana • Deborah Clark • Dominique Vasquez • Elizabeth Corpus • Hardy family • Harvey Homer • Jacqui Knighton • Jasmin Will • Jay's Legacy Foundation • K. Hancock • Kamaehu & Santiago Ohana • Kamila Komisarek • Kathleen M Hadd • Kathryn Craig • Katie Wasley • Kayelee Blake • Keishamarie Lavatai • Kelsey Gonzales • Kinsey & Kevin Brown • Kiyomi Hattori • Kyle G Wilkinson • Leila & Mosaea Stevenson • Maho Hattori • Matthea W. Ross • McArthur Family • Michelle • Milton Timoteo • Odyssey Tinitali • Patrice Heaton • pjk • Rebecca L. Rodri • Rina • Robert Zangari • Rosa. Alo. • Salote Aoelua-Fanene •Shadel Jipp • Shaik - Stephenson Family • Shirley & Tufi Stevenson • Sister Jones • Solstad family • Steve & Sara Santana •-Stevenson Family • Stevenson family •Suva T. • Sydney

& Namu Stevenson • The Wintch Family • Tiare Brede • Torsha J. Baker • Tracy Sahleen •

And of course, thanks to you—the reader. Thank you so much for reading Shadowed By Moonlight. As an author, it's always been my dream to write and publish books, but even greater than that was the hope that those reading it would actually enjoy them. If you liked what you read here, please be sure to leave a review that others can find Shadowed By Moonlight.

See you in the next book,
Kryssa

Born on the north shore of Oahu and raised in Southern Utah, Kryssa Stevenson has always had a passion for storytelling. She wrote her first book when she was nine-years-old, which was an embarrassing tale about a green-haired girl who turned into a snail at a basketball game.

Hopefully the stories you read from her now are much better than that.

When she's not writing, Kryssa enjoys Polynesian dancing, Olympic weightlifting, and vying for the role of favorite aunty among her nieces and nephews.

To learn more about Kryssa and to keep up with her writing adventures, be sure to follow her on social media and subscribe to her newsletter at kryssastevenson.com.